"You ever s

"Yes."

"Not like this you hav

Proctor saw the sheet

"Gladman?"

She nodded.

"The Ripper?"

She nodded again.

"So what's so different about this that I have to see it?"

She nodded, and the sergeant yanked off the sheet.

Proctor swallowed hard.

"That's not all," she said quietly. She touched her forehead, and Proctor squinted through the dim light. The blood was smeared across Gladman's face, soaked into his shirt and the top of his trousers. "Closer," she said.

"I don't think so."

She touched her forehead again. "Above his eyes."

He looked again, and shrugged. "I don't get it."

"Neither do I. He carved a *P* in there, Proctor. Right into the bone."

BLACK OAK

HUNTING GROUND

by

Charles Grant

A ROC BOOK

ROC
Published by New American Library, a division of
Penguin Putnam Inc., 375 Hudson Street,
New York, New York 10014, U.S.A.
Penguin Books Ltd, 27 Wrights Lane,
London W8 5TZ, England
Penguin Books Australia Ltd, Ringwood,
Victoria, Australia
Penguin Books Canada Ltd, 10 Alcorn Avenue,
Toronto, Ontario, Canada M4V 3B2
Penguin Books (N.Z.) Ltd, 182–190 Wairau Road,
Auckland 10, New Zealand

Penguin Books Ltd, Registered Offices:
Harmondsworth, Middlesex, England

First published by Roc, an imprint of New American Library,
a division of Penguin Putnam Inc.

First Printing, June 2000
1   3   5   7   9   10   8   6   4   2

Cover art by Rick Leider

 REGISTERED TRADEMARK—MARCA REGISTRADA

Printed in the United States of America

PUBLISHER'S NOTE
This is a work of fiction. Names, characters, places, and incidents either are the
product of the author's imagination or are used fictitiously, and any resemblance
to actual persons, living or dead, business establishments, events, or locales is entirely coincidental.

For Huck, Lovejoy, and Tinker, the Heroic Trio of Newton, all three of whom ought to be bald for all the hair they leave on my chair.

Previously, in *Black Oak*

To all those who apply for a position at Black Oak Investigations, Ethan Proctor eventually asks:

"Do you believe in ghosts?"

Taylor Blaine, a wealthy businessman living in Connecticut, has hired Black Oak to find his daughter, Celeste.

She has been missing for thirteen years.

Blaine promises Proctor all the money he needs to find even one small hint that she's still alive. However, his other children, the twins Frederick and Alicia, are opposed to the idea.

"He doesn't like you," Lana Kelaleha tells her boss. "I think he thinks you're just in it for the money."

"He's a snob," Proctor answers. "I can handle it. Don't worry."

"You'd better handle it soon. Frederick has just taken over the company and fired us."

Proctor has a dream:

A vast obsidian plain under a huge faceless moon. Obsidian trees whose stiff sharp leaves clack and clatter in the wake of a swift dark wind. The ground's surface smooth and even, reflected moonlight giving the surface a depth that makes crossing it seem like crossing clear ice over still black water. Winged creatures in the sky, silent, gliding, leaving faint trails of gray smoke that twisted and tore and soon vanished.

Proctor knows it's a dream.

He has been here before.

*   *   *

Ellen Proctor hasn't said a word in almost seven years.

While in England, Proctor receives a telephone call from his mother's physician:

"Proctor? It's Paul Browning."

Proctor can't speak, can barely breathe.

"Proctor, you there?"

"Tell me quick," he says, tries to swallow, and can't.

A pause before Browning laughs. "No, Proctor, it's all right. Honest to God, it's all right. Your mom's okay."

He doesn't know whether to be angry or relieved. "Then what's—"

"She spoke, Proctor. Last night, she spoke. I heard her, man, I actually heard her."

On the Boardwalk in Atlantic City, a two-bit gambler named Shake Waldman talks to a female colleague:

"You're leaving?"

"Gotta move on," she says, her accent not quite true. "You know how it is."

"Gonna miss you."

"Thanks."

"Do something for me?"

"If I can."

He gives her a folded piece of paper. "Take care of this, okay? If something happens to me, read it, you'll know what to do."

"Shake, what's going on?"

"Don't worry about it, Petra. Just do an old friend a favor. That's all I ask."

do you believe in ghosts?

EPISODE 4

HUNTING GROUND

PROLOGUE

Hushed voices in a large room. A handful of candles in soot-black twisted candelabra throw more shadows than light, and in the background the sound of a slow steady wind.

In the darkness above, where candlelight cannot reach, the muted flutter of wings.

There are scents and odors collected in pockets where the air does not move, where drafts do not reach them—candle wax and burnt logs, sweet fruit and rotting fruit, rodent droppings winged or not, flowers of all kinds, meat cooled and raw, perfume, cologne, new clothes and old clothes, dust, flesh.

There is no telling how large the room actually is. But by its echoes and its silences a visitor knows it is vast.

And old.

The barely seen walls of dark wood made darker by the twisting smoke from the candles, from torches now unlit, and the natural aging process; the stone floor made darker by the shoes that have trod across it, the furniture dragged across it, and the natural aging process; the long table in the center, most of it dull, some of it polished by arms and hands drawn across it, has legs thick as trees and chairs with high backs carved in patterns with no discernible meaning, all of it darkened by age beyond measure.

The sharp tap of a sharp fingernail against wood, a call for attention.

When the voices finally quiet, there is only the wind, and the wings.

A full minute later a series of soft chimes sound, a chair

scrapes back, and a voice clears its throat and says, "All goes as it should. We are well."

Another voice disagrees, with deference but not subservient: "Maybe it does, and maybe we are, but *he's* still alive."

The first voice sounds amused: "You actually expected him to die?"

A soft chuckle from the complainer. "All right, maybe not, but one can dream, right?"

Laughter fills the cavernous room. When it fades, when silence returns, the first voice says, "A lost battle is not a lost war." A pause for more laughter, and not a few groans. "He will do what he will, and believe what he believes, but in the end, just like all the rest, he will die."

A third voice, a woman's: "I don't care. He frightens me."

"And me," admits a fourth, this one a man who sounds very young to be in a place like this.

No one else speaks, just the wings and the wind, until: "Fear is neither a sin nor a crime. It will keep you alert. It will keep us all alive."

"Maybe so," the woman answers, "but I still want Proctor dead."

ONE

They say the beach is haunted.

When midnight slips into the dead hours of morning, the Boardwalk is deserted more often than not, the Atlantic City streets empty and cold. A patrol car cruising the side streets, trailing faint static; a desperate hooker in fake fur clinging to the shadows; a corner bar with sputtering neon; a vacant lot strewn with rubble and garbage; a dead rat in a gutter, matted fur slick with oil.

The glow of casino lights reaches over the sand, doesn't quite reach the ocean. Streetlamps along the boardwalk aren't bright enough to reach each other. And a flurry of headlights from automobiles leaving a multitiered parking garage aim west, not east. This isn't Las Vegas; night and day do not blend.

It's winter, and the wind off the Atlantic is dull and cold and damp. Flapping pennants sound like crackling ice, and footsteps sound as if they tread on hollow wood. An icicle hangs from a back corner at Caesar's, another from one of the garish turrets at the Taj. It hasn't snowed yet, but it feels as if it has. Many of the tourists, day-trippers and weekenders, wish it would, if only to cover the rest of the city so it would be easier to pretend they're someplace special when their wallets finally empty.

Once in a while a gambler leaves one casino to hustle up to another, shoulders up and head down, hands in pockets, paying no attention to the sand that stretches into the dark. Once in a while lovers, bundled for the season, stand arm in arm at the boardwalk railing and watch the flashes of white out there in the dark, early cresting waves pushed toward them by the wind. Once in a while a lone man or woman will take the stairs down to the sand, peek under the boardwalk, look over at the waves, and climb up again, quickly, with a shivering that has nothing to do with winter winds.

They say the beach is haunted, and they're right.
But not quite.

"Listen, Murray, I don't want to be the wet blanket," said Fred Dailey, "but in case you hadn't noticed, it's goddamn cold out here." To prove his point, he stamped a foot hard on the boardwalk as he walked beside his friend. "Frozen, see? Damn foot is frozen solid. I'll have to thaw my shoes just to get them off."

Murray, twice his normal size in a Russian greatcoat almost as long as he was tall, adjusted his Russian lamb's wool hat with one gloved hand, and walked on without responding. His cheeks and pointed chin were red, the condensation of his breath had frozen on his mustache, and his eyes were half closed against the wind that nudged and poked him.

Fred, taller, thinner, his bloodhound face just as red, glared over Murray's head at the sand off to his right, then out to the ocean. It's too cold, fifty bucks gone, only one hundred left, what the hell kind of a way to celebrate a birthday was this?

"Murray."

"Fred, we're going, we're almost there, why complain all the time? You don't like it, go back. Or sit on one of these benches, they look very nice."

"I don't like it, it's too far to go back, it's too cold to sit, we've already passed four very respectable hotels . . . I don't get it."

Murray lifted a hand, pointing at the sky. "They didn't feel right."

"What, they were too warm?"

"They didn't have the feel, Fred, you know? They gotta have the feel."

"Well, I feel like ice, what do you think about that?"

"I think you should've gotten a better coat," Murray said, and laughed so hard he veered into the steel railing at the boardwalk's eastern edge, ricocheted off, and bumped into his friend. Laughed again, a series of wheezes that ended in a violent coughing.

Fred, resigned, patted the other man's back gently until the spasm passed. More gently now: "Murray, this is crazy."

But it wasn't just this that was crazy. The whole idea was crazy: Two old men drive all the way down here in a car that should have been junked when Moses was pulled out of the reeds, get a room too expensive by half, eat enough fatty food to kill an elephant, and proceed immediately to start giving the casino all their money. And for what? So former New York City police detective Murray Cobb can celebrate his sixtieth birthday in the vain and futile hope of turning one whole pension check into a fortune.

"A onetime thing," Murray had argued when Fred protested. "A onetime thing. You're my friend, you going with me or you staying in Queens and watch the sidewalks rot?"

The sidewalks rotting, Fred thought now, was a better bet than anything Murray had bet on tonight.

Still, it was his pal's birthday, and what was a little frostbite between men who'd been friends for almost half a century.

Murray, the coughing finally done, scrubbed a hand under his nose and spat over the railing. Then he grabbed the top rail and leaned against it, lifted his chin to point at the surf. "You ever go out there, Fred? Cruise ship, I mean. You ever go on a cruise?"

"Nope." He looked around nervously. They were in one of the dead spots along the Boardwalk, a place where the casinos' light didn't fully reach because the distance between them was too great. It wouldn't have been that bad if all the Boardwalk streetlamps were lit, but they weren't—burned out or shot out, only one working dimly a few yards up ahead, it didn't do him much good at all, here in the dead spot.

Behind him were a dozen or so summer shops boarded and chained until spring, the two-story building they were in so run-down, it was a wonder it hadn't been condemned already.

It was too dark here, and too cold. He adjusted his scarf, checked to make sure all his coat buttons were fastened, and looked north and south, positive there were gangs of muggers out there, just waiting for a chance to knock guys like him and Murray off.

Then Murray asked a question, and he said, "What?"

"You hear one word I say?"

"I'm making sure we don't get murdered."

Murray laughed, wheezed, coughed but controlled it. "What I said was, cruises aren't what they're cracked up to be. And if you hate it, you can't walk away, go home, have a better time."

Fred closed one eye. "The point being?"

"The point being," Murray said, a finger raised to the sky, "that I forget what the damn point was, you got me off track by not listening." He leaned over and spat again. "Son of a bitch."

"Hey," Fred said. "No call for that. My mind was wandering, that's all. To, I might add, someplace warm."

"No, that's not what I meant." Murray began to sidle along the railing, looking over every few feet, then checking to his right to judge the distance left to the next set of stairs. "I wasn't talking about you."

"I'm blessed."

"Think there's a body down there." He began to move more quickly, leaning over the rail almost all the time now. "I think there's a body down there."

Fred followed slowly, putting a shoulder to a gust that tried to knock him into a shop. "Murray, there's no body down there."

"You a cop?"

"You?"

Murray stopped and straightened, and Fred realized he'd just made a huge mistake. Murray had not taken well to retirement, still thought of himself as the same cop he always was, except without as much work.

Fred put a hand to his forehead. "Sorry. I didn't mean that."

"You owe me one."

"Yes. Yes, I do."

"Good." Murray sagged against the railing. "Then, you go down there, see if I'm right."

"I am not going down there to touch a dead body."

"You don't have to touch it, for God's sake. Who said anything about touching? Just go down there, see if I'm right, okay? If there's someone lying there, maybe he's hurt, we'll go get a cop. If there isn't, you can buy me a drink at the next bar."

Fred opened his mouth to make a suggestion, shook his head, and walked over to the stairs. As he passed his friend he could hear faint wheezing, but when he looked, Murray just waved him on impatiently.

"I'll be right up here," he said. "Got you covered the whole way."

"With what? That hat?"

"I got a gun."

Fred stopped before he'd taken the first step down. "You've got a what?"

Murray shrugged. "A gun."

"Jesus, Murray, we're gonna end up in jail, for God's sake."

Murray pointed. "Go. It's freezing up here."

Oh, great, Fred thought; *now* you're cold.

The steps were wide, wood, and worn, a little slippery, and Fred held tightly to the railing as he climbed down to the sand. When he looked up, he found himself staring right at Murray's shoes, which, even in this dim light, looked as old as their owner.

"See anything?" Murray whispered.

Yeah, Fred thought sourly, and what he saw he didn't like.

The streetlamp's faint glow slipped between cracks in the boards, pale slants and hazy cones that barely reached the sand. He could faintly see empty liquor bottles, crushed beer cans, clumps of dried seaweed, broken shells, bits of glass.

He could hear the surf magnified under there.

He could hear his own breathing.

What he couldn't see was anything that looked even vaguely like a body, or somebody that had been hurt.

Just the dark, and the sound of the surf.

He gave himself another fifty feet, just to be sure. Murray hadn't said anything, but Fred could hear those shoes shuffling along the boards, keeping impatient pace, could hear the rail groan a little whenever his friend leaned against it.

This is stupid.

He had to bend a little to see under each time, and his back had begun to complain.

This is stupid.

At the end of his fifty feet, he shook his head and looked up. "Nothing. Just junk."

Murray scowled. "Could've sworn."

"Shadows, Mur. You saw shadows, that's all."

His old friend shrugged acceptance so quickly, Fred had to blink. Then snarl. Then grin.

"Don't be so smug, Dailey. I'm sitting down. Come on up."

Fred checked under the boards one more time, just in case, and wondered if that piece of fallen piling over there was what Murray saw. Had to be. From the right angle, with the right lighting, he supposed it could pass for someone lying on his back. Except it would have had to have been out here more, not back there, or Murray wouldn't have seen it at all.

He bent lower and eased under, one hand gripping a piling as he leaned closer. Just in case.

Not enough light; there wasn't enough light, but it sure as hell looked like someone's stiff leg. An illusion of some kind, he'd have to ask Murray.

Keeping the edge of the boardwalk directly above his right shoulder, he took a few steps up and in, grabbed another piling for balance, and squinted.

It moved.

He straightened in surprise, caught himself just before he cracked his head against the underside of the boards.

"Fred," Murray whispered.

Fred waved a hang-on-a-minute hand before he realized Murray couldn't see it, and took another step, another, until he faced the length of piling and, with a gasp, saw the shoe on the end of it. Realized that he wasn't looking at one leg, there were two.

Son of a bitch, he thought; the old fart was right.

Visibility was too shallow here; he could only see as far as the fallen man's waist, and when the legs trembled again, he said anxiously, "Mister? Hey, mister, you all right? You need some help?"

A weak voice: "Help."

Fred looked behind him, up at the boards, was about to call out to Murray when the voice spoke again, low and husky: "Help. Help me up."

A drunk, he decided; damn, it's just a drunk. But he reached out anyway.

And a hand drifted out of the dark, as pale as the pale light that barely reached the sand.

Fred automatically gripped it and pulled gently, frowned, and pulled again; frowned and inhaled sharply when those fingers squeezed until he thought his knuckles would shatter. He went instantly to his knees, feeling the cold sand through his trousers and the cold wind turning the back of his neck to ice.

He opened his mouth to cry out, but the only sound he could make was a desperate quiet choking.

Movement, then, back there in the dark as he was pulled forward, and he had to snap out his other hand to keep from falling on his face.

Another face, barely seen, as though it were covered in a thin black veil.

"Please," Fred said, no louder than a whisper.

A death's head smile, eyes made of fire.

The hand yanked, and he was pulled off the ground, landed on his back, all the breath gone from his lungs in an explosive gasp. He couldn't speak, couldn't breathe, and when he saw what had taken him, he couldn't even scream.

TWO

9 February

The January thaw was a month late.

Although the situation was much worse in the high hills of the northwestern part of the state, there was still enough snow on the ground in the rest of North Jersey to cause major problems when the overnight temperature charged out of the teens and into the high forties by noon without half taking a breath. Over the next three days cellars flooded, streams and creeks ran faster and higher, low roads slipped under small instant lakes, storm drains overflowed. Icicles melted, a skin of water rippled over the ice on ponds and lakes, and half the population prematurely shucked their topcoats and heavy sweaters.

Paul Tazaretti's mother called it pneumonia weather, and if she could see him now, she'd probably die. Or worse— drag him into the house by the ear and stand at the foot of the steps, her arms folded across her chest, waiting until he was dressed warmly enough to suit her.

At the moment he stood, in white T-shirt and jeans, in front of an open empty garage, trying to decide if it was worth going on, this emergency operation on his old Jeep. He'd been able to keep ahead of the rust, but the engine was something else, and he was pretty sure he was losing that race hands down.

The problem was, he had gotten the old junker for graduation, it was his first car, and it thereby had great sentimental value; he couldn't bring himself to get rid of it, replace it with something else.

A loud, self-pitying sigh, and he peered into the empty garage, looking for something that might perform the miracle he needed. But it was preternaturally clean in there. No spiderwebs, no grease or oil stains on the concrete floor, the few garden and lawn tools all hanging neatly from nails pounded into the walls and . . . nothing else.

It was as if the man who owned the house not only didn't own a car, he didn't even live here full-time.

Taz leaned back against a fender and shook his head. It wasn't natural. It just wasn't natural.

Still, Taz was lucky he was back here at all, lucky that his boss had no problems with him working on the Jeep during company time, as long as he made sure his other work was done.

It was.

In fact, the last report had been filed over a week ago, and with no new cases either assigned or pending, the inactivity was getting on his nerves. His, and everybody else's at Black Oak Investigations. Proctor, for whatever reasons, hadn't been attending each day's routine mail check. Which meant any possible new clients had so far gone unnoticed or unexplored. Which meant he was about ready to go out of his mind from boredom.

The most exciting thing he'd done over the past couple of days was pick out goofy valentines for the women who worked here. He'd managed to kill most of an afternoon with that one. Aside from that, it was curse at and mourn for the Jeep, flirt a little with Eri, the new girl hired to fill in for RJ when RJ was at class, and throw snowballs off the redwood deck to see how far he could get them across the Hudson.

He was about ready to see if he could climb down the face of the Palisades without a rope, but he figured Proctor would skin him for that stunt.

Still, it was better than doing nothing, which was what trying to fix this damn Jeep pretty much was.

A breeze coasted over his arms, and he shivered, rolled his shoulders, considered going into the house to grab a sweater, and changed his mind. Lana, Black Oak's office manager and computer wizard, was still talking to that guy who'd arrived a few minutes ago. She stood in front of the kitchen door, a coat thrown over her shoulders, and from the set of her head and the way she kept snapping a finger at her squared bangs, she definitely wasn't happy. Still, it was weird that she hadn't invited him in; that wasn't like her. And since the guy clearly wasn't a bill collector or something, he figured it was better if he just stuck around, just in case.

The man was on the bottom of three steps, which put him and Lana almost eye to eye. Taz didn't know who he was, but he didn't like him anyway. Didn't like the way he stood with his gloved hands crossed in front of him, his head cocked in that way that told Taz he was only pretending to listen to whatever she had to tell him. Doc had often told him he was too quick to judge, but Taz didn't care—in his gut he knew this guy was trouble, or about to be.

He watched a moment longer, then turned back to the Jeep, stared at the engine and blew out an exasperated breath. Hopeless; it was hopeless. He didn't say so aloud, of course; it would hurt the vehicle's feelings and make her run worse than ever.

A grin, and he checked back to the porch, just as Lana looked over the stranger's head and raised a hand.

The grin snapped off.

If she wanted him to meet this guy on a possible case or friendly basis, she would have beckoned with a cheerful wave. What she had done, however, was crook a finger—*Taz, get over here, I need your help.* So he grabbed his black leather jacket from the front seat and put it on, picked up a greasy rag and hurried down the drive.

When he was closer, he heard them:

"I believe you're making a terrible mistake."

"I'm sorry, Mr. Blaine, but I am still not going to let you in. Not while Proctor isn't here. I have my instructions."

"And I pay the bills."

Lana's smile was coldly polite. "Not all of them."

"Enough, my dear lady, enough."

"Well, I think your father would have something to say about that, don't you?"

"My father," said Frederick Blaine, "is no longer in daily charge of operations. And it is therefore my right to see exactly what my sister and I are paying for."

Taz slowed, his dislike for the younger Blaine intensifying, again for no other reason than he had what his old man called an "Eastern snob" accent. Not quite British, not quite North American, but an irritating combination of both, making just about anything he said sound condescending.

"Oh, Taz, there you are," she said cheerfully, her smile widening. "Do come here and meet Frederick Blaine, Taylor Blaine's son."

Oh, boy, Taz thought; this guy is in deep trouble, and he doesn't even know it. Because Lana was short, Polynesian, and seemingly delicate, everyone who didn't know her tended to misjudge her. By the time they figured out how wrong they were, it was much too late.

Blaine turned to face him, a tall man whose face was rough and lightly pocked, thin lips, eyes that seemed to be in a perpetual squint at the corners, a slight widow's peak. His hair was dark brown—dirt-brown, his old man would've called it; the kind weeds grow in, not crops.

Quickly Taz wiped his clean hands on the rag, then held one out. "Pleased to meet you, sir."

Blaine automatically accepted the offered hand, and said, "The feeling is—" before he realized something was wrong.

With a shocked expression, Taz snatched his hand away. "Oh, gosh, Mr. Blaine, I'm sorry. I'm really—I was working—see, I was—" He pointed back to the Jeep's upraised hood, took a step up to the porch as if to run inside, stepped down again. "Gosh, I'm really sorry. Gosh, I'm—"

"It's all right," Blaine said, staring at his greasy palm and fingers with distaste. "It was an accident."

Taz nodded quickly. "Yes, sir, it was, sir. An accident. You want me to go in and—"

"No." Blaine glanced at the house, at Lana, and said, "No, I'll take care of it myself." A slight bow to them both, and he walked down the driveway to the street, where Taz saw a dark green limousine big as an ocean liner waiting at the curb. A liveried chauffeur was at the back door long before Blaine arrived, and Blaine looked back only once before he climbed in and the door slammed shut.

Taz waited until the limousine was gone before he said, "Okay?"

Lana laughed. "Excellent, Taz, excellent." She wiped a hand over her mouth and chin. "That son of a bitch is about to cause big trouble around here. I sure hope Proctor knows what he's doing."

The room was small and pleasant. A comfortable bed, a chest of drawers, two armchairs, a table between them with a vase of fresh flowers. In the back wall was a sliding glass door that led onto a small patio, beyond which was a lawn that sloped gently away from the building. Summer and spring, there was nothing but flowers out there, and full-crowned trees; now it was dead grass and patches of snow and empty gardens. The winter sunlight kept it bright, kept it from appearing as lifeless as it was.

A woman sat in one of the chairs, facing the doors, a distant smile on her face. Her greying hair was cut short, utilitarian, not stylish; she wore a simple brown dress, and slippers on her feet. Her hands lay loosely clasped in her lap.

She didn't move.

She hadn't moved since Proctor arrived two hours before.

He was in the other chair, watching her, watching what the thaw had left behind. Every once in a while he would say, "Mom?"

She didn't move, and she didn't answer.

Until nearly four weeks ago, she hadn't spoken in nearly seven years. And then, all she had said was, "Tiger's eye."

"Mom, I'm going to have to go soon."

Ellen Proctor didn't move; the smile didn't change; she didn't speak.

He rose stiffly, defeated, and stood in front of her, leaned over and kissed her on the forehead. "I'll be back soon, Mom," he whispered. "I love you."

When he left, he closed the door quietly and leaned heavily against the wall, head down, eyes briefly closed. The tiled corridor was wide and bright, sunny even though there were no windows. Ahead and behind he could hear soft voices, other visiting family members, nurses, doctors, therapists, a television, a radio.

tiger's eye.

He had been in England on a case when the news came; he had returned as fast as he could, but nothing had changed. All was the same as it had been, before "tiger's eye."

Neither he nor Paul Browning, her doctor, had the faintest idea what it meant. A marble? The actual eye of a tiger? Some symbolic piece of the internal world she had lived in all these years? Almost every day since his return from England, he had visited her, talked to her, asked her, once nearly yelled at her when his patience reached an end, and his weariness grew too strong.

And nothing.

Just that smile, and . . . nothing.

He blew out a breath and headed for the exit. Paul wasn't in today, and for that he was relieved. Dr. Browning had not lost his excitement, and the enthusiasm, the optimism, was wearing. Better he return to the office; at least there he had some measure of control.

A wave to a couple of nurses, and he was outside, taking in the too warm air, trudging to the car, sitting. Just sitting.

I don't know, he thought when he finally pulled out of the parking lot; *I don't know how much more of this I can take.*

It was a familiar feeling, one he had virtually every time he left his mother behind. But he always took it; he had given himself no choice. Something had happened to her to drive her into that mysterious world of hers, and he wasn't about to rest until he found out what it was.

tiger's eye.

Had it been anything else, he might not now be so frustrated, but the phrase had echoes. He couldn't remember where, and he couldn't remember when, but he was positive he had heard it recently. Within the last several months. He doubted there was a connection—hell, there couldn't be a connection—

but the coincidence of memory and his mother's words sparked him, and tired him at the same time.

By the time he reached home, his momentary despair had lifted somewhat, and he was ready for something else. Something new. The Celeste Blaine case, something in the mail, something referred to him alone . . . it didn't matter. What he wanted was something else to occupy his time. Occupy his mind.

He walked into the small kitchen, grabbed a can of soda from the refrigerator, passed into the dining room, and hollered, "I'm back, what's new?"

Lana came immediately out of the hallway to his left, where the offices were, a concerned eyebrow raised.

"No," she said. "Nothing."

"I'm sorry."

A shrug. "Don't be. It'll change. I know it will."

"Changes here, too."

He walked into the high-ceiling living room, pushed his shoulders back to drive out the tension, and said, "Taz drove through the garage wall."

"I heard that," Taz yelled from down the hall.

"No," Lana said. "It's Frederick Blaine. He paid us a visit an hour ago."

Proctor sagged into an ugly wing chair that was his favorite, more so because everyone else had, at one time or another, tried to get rid of it. "What?" he said flatly.

"He wanted to see the files; I told him no. He as much as told me he'd be back." She waited until he looked at her. "It wasn't a promise, Proctor. You can ask Taz; it definitely was not a promise."

Proctor rolled his eyes. The Blaine twins had been thorns in his side since he'd first begun the search. As far as he was concerned, they were pests, not much more. "I'll talk to the old man, don't worry."

"Talk all you want," she told him.

He looked at her sharply.

"It won't do a bit of good. Apparently Frederick's in charge of everything now, including the family's private affairs. It looks like he and Alicia have pulled off a coup."

THREE

The Lighthouse was not the most elegant of the city's casinos, nor was it as elaborately furnished and appointed as those farther down the Boardwalk. It's only claim to Atlantic City fame was its ocean-side facade—a twenty-three story lighthouse replica complete with a sweeping beam of intense light directed out over the water; the beam moved in a 60-degree north-south arc, changing colors every thirty minutes. A guest didn't need to know the address; all he had to do was aim for the light.

Inside, save for the nautical themes and low-key atmosphere, there wasn't a lot to distinguish it from its seaside competitors. The noise was the same; the gamblers looked the same; the showgirls in the small theater looked the same as any other.

The difference was in the way the owners and management treated its employees. It wasn't only the higher wages and decent on-site treatment; it was, as manager Reno Baron put it, the benefits.

Long before the murders began, he had convinced the owners to allow him to set aside a half-dozen rooms on the fourth floor, to be allocated at his discretion. He used them for his employees—those who needed a quick nap between double shifts, those who didn't want to walk home on particularly nasty weather days, those whose transportation plans didn't pan out. It wasn't a big thing, but it was appreciated, especially since he didn't charge his people a dime.

Once the third body was discovered, however, he reserved a half-dozen more rooms, took out the guests beds, added roll aways and cots to produce a dormitory effect, and assigned an extra guard to the floor to foster the impression of security. He also ordered an armed guard to accompany those who lived nearby. Just in case. Just to show he cared.

Charleen Caje thought it was dumb. A publicity ploy so blatant she couldn't believe any of her friends actually believed the self-important manager really gave a damn. Not that she cared. Normally she wouldn't walk home in the middle of the night while some creep roamed the city, tearing people's throats out and not even bothering to hide the bodies. The papers said he was taunting the police; the newscasters on TV said the police were helpless because there was no clues, no witnesses, and no pattern to the murders.

She didn't care about that, either.

What she wanted tonight was her own bed to crawl into. Her feet hurt. Her back hurt. The underside of her right breast was killing her because that damn wire in her costume had come loose and had stabbed her throughout the show. It even drew blood. And she was cold—the neon blue scarf she'd bought in Philly last week was too thin, her coat was too thin, and too many drafts slithered up her legs.

What she did care about was the distance between the hotel and her apartment building, only two blocks away.

Not far now; not far.

The hotel behind the facade was nothing special. Eighteen stories of red-trimmed windows in white brick. A handful had balconies with potted plants on them, but those were in front, where the high rollers, when they weren't rolling high, could see the ocean. Aside from the oversize lifeboat-shape portico above the crescent drive, the lighting was poor, and on the other side of Pacific Avenue was a fenced-in, long and narrow empty lot, which may or may not eventually become a parking garage. On the north side of the street that ran past the lot were empty houses jammed so closely together there was no room between them—they looked as if they were part of the same building.

Charleen didn't mind walking by them. Until now she'd

always pretended people still lived there, that they were sleeping, dreaming, maybe making love. It kept the street from feeling empty.

Nothing could do that tonight.

Two days ago someone had shot out all the streetlamps along the block, and the city hadn't yet gotten around to replacing them.

Beside her, Dacey Logetta grumbled to herself, a cigarette in her mouth, a large red beret jammed onto her red hair. They had been hired at the same cattle call, had found themselves next to each other in the dressing room that first night, and had decided without a word that it would probably be a good thing to look after each other.

"Goddamn cold," Dacey complained, blowing smoke toward the street. Her coat didn't reach her knees. Her skirt was even shorter. She wore no gloves.

Charleen grinned. "Next time, think winter, not summer, you dope."

The block was long. The empty lot swam with shadows, and the dark windows of the houses stared at them as they walked by.

The guard wasn't with them.

Dacey, whose apartment was one floor above Charleen's, hadn't felt like waiting an hour just so some guy could do the swagger macho thing, not to mention hit on her at the same time.

Besides, the killer never attacked anyone who was with someone else.

It hadn't taken much argument to convince Charleen it was all right.

She checked behind her, the lights were brighter because of the darkness they'd gotten used to. The night wind danced a candy wrapper between her feet and into the gutter, made her adjust her fringed scarf to keep the cold out.

She wished she hadn't worn her tennis shoes tonight. She thought she'd feel better if she could hear her footsteps. A solid pair of heels made an awful lot of noise. As it was, except for their breathing, there wasn't a sound. She adjusted the scarf again, and kept her hand at her throat, to hold her coat closed.

"I think," Dacey said, pulling her head as low into her hunched shoulders as she could, "I'm gonna quit, y'know?"

"What? What for?"

Dacey laughed. "What for? Christ, I got legs that half the time don't work like they're supposed to because they're dancing all the time. I got a bank account that needs serious financing, and I could do better in . . . well, hell, in a bank. And I'm getting sick of those guys staring at me all the time."

Charleen shook her head. "Dace, that's what they do. I mean, we're practically naked up there, right? In Vegas we would be naked. So they stare, so what?"

"So they think I'm a hooker, Char."

"Yeah, so?"

"So I'm not."

"Well, I know it, and you know it, and you aren't ever going to see those guys again, so why do you give a damn what they think?"

Dacey waved a disgusted hand. "I don't know. I . . . I don't know."

Charleen took a sidestep and bumped her friend with a hip. "You need sleep, that's all."

"No, I need to get outta this place."

She laughed silently, bumped Dacey again, and took a deep breath. Ahead she saw cars drift silently through the distant intersection, the neon beer ads of a corner bar, a couple crossing the street, heading the other way. Because of the cold, everything in the light had an edge, sharp as if cut out by a razor blade. A moment later the intersection was empty, and she concentrated on the spotlighted stone stairs that fronted their apartment building.

Dacey tossed her cigarette into the gutter and picked up the pace.

Charleen said, "If we had a fog, this would be just like London, right?"

Dacey gave her a look. "Oh, please."

"Just talking. It's too quiet tonight."

"Then, let's run for it," Dacey said, grinning. "I'll race you."

"I thought your legs were too tired."

Dacey slapped a thigh. "These are Logetta legs, girl. They do what I tell them."

"Do they really?" a voice answered.

Charleen yelped and jumped sideways, nearly falling; Dacey uttered a short scream and nearly fell against her.

He stood in the middle of the street, in a spot where everything seemed to stop—light, sound, movement.

At least Charleen assumed it was a he. The voice was husky, quiet, and she could not see a face. He was a shadow broken away from the shadows, black from top to bottom, arms blending into a long coat that rippled in the wind.

"Jesus!" Dacey yelled, patting her chest with a palm. "Jesus, you freak, you damn near scared us to death." She grabbed Charleen's arm, pulled her close as she began walking again, almost sideways this time. "What the hell you want?"

The man didn't answer.

He stood there in the street, and he didn't say a word.

"C'mon, Char," Dacey muttered disgustedly. "Guys like this are the reason I want to get outta this place." She tugged, and frowned. "Char?"

Charleen couldn't move, couldn't speak. She pointed instead.

"What?" Dacey said impatiently. "Damnit, Char, come on. We got—"

Fog.

At the man's feet fog billowed as if it were spilling from under his coat. It swirled around his shoes and slid across the blacktop and rose in small puffs the wind could not move. It reached the gutters on either side and began to climb onto the sidewalks, low and thin, growing higher and thicker.

And the man did not move.

Her nose wrinkled; under the salt air and the city she thought she smelled something familiar, but couldn't put a name to it.

Dacey tugged at her again, desperately now. "Come on, Char, we gotta run." When her hand lost its grip, Dacey stared at her friend, looked at the fog that was chest-high now and filling the street from empty lot to houses . . . and she ran. Calling over her shoulder. Calling. Then screaming for help.

Charleen refused to believe what she saw, but the sight of it had immobilized her, kept her virtually paralyzed until Dacey's fading screams finally jerked her awake, an electric shock up her spine that momentarily confused her as to which way she should run.

It didn't make any difference.

Forward or back, it was all the same distance.

The fog rose and fell, an ocean of its own.

She couldn't see the man, and at last she began to move. But there were too many places to look—ahead, behind, this side, that side—and she tripped over her own ankle, stumbled a few steps, and fell. She caught herself before her knees hit the pavement, an awkward hands-and-feet crawl before she was able to stand again.

Surrounded by the fog.

The distant lights blurred and indistinct.

No sound but her own breathing.

This way, she thought as she walked faster, not daring to run in case she fell again; this way, it's this way.

Cold, damp, the fog slipped under her scarf, between the buttons of her coat, under its hem and up her legs.

"Dace?" she called. "Dacey?"

"Too late," a quiet voice whispered in her ear.

Dacey's screams turned to shrieks as she broke out of the fog, her hands still sweeping the air in front of her. She raced to the corner and fell against a telephone pole, hugging it with one arm while she tried to find a breath, sweat in her eyes while she tried to find someone for help. Saw a uniformed cop leaving the bar across the way, and heedless of the traffic ran into the street, calling him, begging him not to stand there, but help her.

He met her halfway, grabbed her around the waist, and tried to calm her down.

"The killer," she gasped.

"Where?"

"There, in the fog." And she pointed.

The fog was gone.

The block was empty, and dark, while a candy wrapper danced ahead of the wind.

"Oh, God, there," she whispered. "He was there. And my friend."

The cop, still holding her up, moved cautiously across the intersection, stopped when they reached the other side. "Where?" he asked.

Dacey could barely stand, could barely breathe, her hand shaking as she tried to point before it fell weakly to her side. "It was there," she said. Swallowed. "He was there."

The cop shook his head, clearly not sure if she was truly terrified, or if she was just another drunk escaped from a casino. He almost told her to wait, he would have a look himself, when a car turned the far corner into the street, its headlamps bright, and he saw it:

The dark bundle sprawled in the gutter.

Dacey moaned, and crumpled slowly to her knees.

The driver must have seen the body, too, because the car abruptly sped up, fishtailing a few feet before it charged the intersection, where the cop drew his weapon and held up his hand. When the vehicle stopped, angled toward the corner storm drain, he hurried over to the driver, pointed to Dacey, and said, "Watch her. You got a cell phone? Call 911."

Using the tiny radio pinned to his shoulder, he contacted his precinct as he ran up the middle of the street, half turning when he heard footsteps, snapping out a hand and missing when Dacey raced past him.

"Hey!" he called. "Hey, lady, come on, you can't—"

Dacey ignored him. She didn't want to see, and she had to see, because maybe it wasn't Charleen at all, maybe it was just some dumbass drunk taking a post-midnight nap.

Closer, and she slowed when she saw the neon blue scarf.

Closer, and she stopped, turned, and dropped, and vomited into the street.

"Jesus Lord," the cop whispered. "Jesus, where the hell's her throat?"

FOUR

16–17 February

Two days after Valentine's Day; no clouds, and the temperature couldn't make up its mind whether it was spring or still winter.

Everyone had left, and Proctor wandered.

He poked into the offices, the storerooms, walked around the dining room table a couple of times, stood behind the couch that served as a divider between dining room and living room, and snapped his fingers unconsciously as he stared at the long window opposite him. Distant lights, lightly hazed, from buildings on the other side of the Hudson River; blinking lights from an airliner on its way into LaGuardia; and the pane itself, like black ice.

If he walked over to it, he might be able to see the Hudson itself at the base of the Palisades, but he didn't; if he turned right and went into the kitchen, he might be able to make himself a quick supper, but he didn't. Restless, too many conflicting thoughts demanding his attention, he could only move around the office area of his home, a lost ghost who hadn't decided if this was where he should do his haunting.

Finally, annoyed with the sound of his own footsteps and his chronic indecision, he dropped onto the couch and stared at the telephone that sat on the coffee table. No messages. No one he felt like calling. No one, he thought suddenly, he wanted to call.

"Damn, Proctor," he whispered, "this is getting a little much, don't you think?"

Shortly after his return from England, he had met with Paul Browning, a young man with a goatee that didn't make him look any older, a serious demeanor severely undercut by the constant laughter in large pale blue eyes. For hours they discussed the possible meaning of Ellen Proctor's brief outburst until they'd drifted from the solemn to the ridiculous and ended up sounding like a comic's routine.

"What it boils down to is," Browning had finally said in admitted, frustrated defeat, "I don't think we'll get any further until you find out what the hell happened to her that night."

"We've been over that before, Paul. No one knows but Mom . . . and Dad."

"Well, damnit, go over it again until you do find out."

Proctor had sighed as he rubbed his eyes, nodding as Browning explained the tape and audio setup he'd ordered installed in Ellen's room.

"Maybe," the doctor said, "we'll at least find out what the hell 'tiger's eye' means."

Since then, nothing.

But the phrase was persistent; it ran through his mind on an endless loop because he knew, he just knew he had heard it before.

"Shit," he muttered and fell back, propped his heel on the table and stared at the ceiling. "Damn."

And after Lana had told him about the Blaines, he'd attempted to contact Taylor. No one had answered. Every half an hour, then every ten minutes, but no one had answered the old man's phone.

Three days, and nothing.

He was worried. On the trip back, Blaine had tried to remain cheerful, upbeat, but the closer they grew to New York, the more withdrawn he became—thinking about the photograph of his daughter he had been so sure he had seen, but had only seen once, because the next time he'd looked in the album, the photograph was gone. The same album he held on his lap all the way back; the album he tucked under his arm as he said his good-byes and climbed into a waiting limousine. Leaving Proctor to make his way back to Jersey alone.

Aside from what had initially looked to him like a wild-goose chase, it had been a curious trip in other ways. One that had nearly gotten him killed, a situation that had become all too familiar over the past few months.

He had suspected it before; he was positive of it now—someone wanted him driven off; failing that—dead.

And the maddening part about it was, he didn't know why.

If he were a card-carrying member of the Everything Is A Conspiracy Gang, he could easily believe that all this had to do with the missing Celeste Blaine. That there was a vast network of people across the country, and now maybe the world, which was determined to prevent him from finding the woman.

But for God's sake, he was only an investigator. A man who took cases that were . . . different. Exposure was his primary aim—cast a harsh light on the con men and scam artists who fed on their victims' gullibility and fears, vampires who sucked the life out of dreams. Phony ghosts and man-made monsters. Self-proclaimed psychics whose only abilities were those of a finely tuned magician's. Alien visitations that were anything but literally out of this world.

Yet once in a while . . . once in a very great while . . .

He shifted, grunted, told his stomach to stop complaining, and with an effort pushed off the couch and went into the kitchen. Made a sandwich that he ate while standing at the back door, looking at the moonlight that lay like thin snow on the lawn.

Blaine; his mother; and someone wanted him dead.

And yesterday he had a call from Frederick.

"We've spoken before about this matter, Mr. Proctor," he had said without bothering with a greeting. "And your staff's refusal to permit me access to my own sister's investigation files has proved to be the last straw. Alicia and I have agreed—Black Oak's services are no longer required. We will messenger you a severance check by the end of the week."

There had been no opportunity for Proctor to either lose his temper or attempt a compromise. As soon as the man was done, he hung up, and Proctor hadn't been able to reach him again, or get in touch with Taylor.

One more nail in the—

"Oh, Jesus," he whispered in disgust, and threw the rest of the sandwich away.

Sleep. He needed sleep. A chance to let his subconscious do some of the work. Then tomorrow he would put everything in order. Set the priorities. Concentrate.

A promise he'd been making himself for almost a month.

For the first time since his return, the dream reappeared:

an obsidian plain, an obsidian castle, guards in black, black pennants, black fire;

at the castle gate a solid black dragon whose gold breast scales were in the shape of a woman's face;

winged creatures as black as the starless sky above, pacing him overhead;

a voice neither man's nor woman's, whispering behind him, but he can't understand the words, and then he looks back, there's nothing there but the plain;

the last time he'd dreamt this he'd known something had changed; this time he thought he knew what it was—the guards are moving, the dragon has spread its massive wings and is ready to fly, and something large has appeared on the far horizon.

he doesn't know what it is, but it's moving.

Midmorning, and the thaw returned.

After being chased out of the offices, turned down when he offered to help Taz with his Jeep, and finding himself pacing again, unable to focus, he forced himself into the wingback, scooted it closer to the coffee table, and made another attempt to contact Taylor Blaine. When the man's bodyguard and confidante answered, he was so relieved he nearly laughed aloud.

"Vivian," he said, "you don't know how good it is to hear your voice."

"Proctor," she answered dryly, "you don't know how thrilled I am to hear that."

He did laugh then, and relaxed. Vivian Chambers was one of those who had learned that every once in a while monsters weren't entirely fairy-tale ogres. "Lana told me about Frederick's visit. I'm worried about Mr. Blaine."

"So am I."

"Can you fill me in?"

"Nothing to fill in. He took that English trip really hard. He mopes around here all day, doesn't eat right, won't tend to business—"

"I know about that part."

"—and whenever I try to get him going, he threatens to fire me." He heard the anger, and the distress. "I think the only reason he hasn't is because that little bastard's pushing for it, too."

He didn't have to ask. "He called yesterday. Told me he's fired the firm."

There was a silence, a faint static crackling on the line.

"He . . . what?"

"Fired me, Vivian. Frederick's fired me." He sat up, frowning. "Wait a minute, wait a minute. Are you telling me Taylor doesn't know?"

"He doesn't know much of anything these days. He's letting the twins run it all, and I think he's about ready to sign some power-of-attorney papers so he doesn't have to deal with any of it anymore."

"Damn." He looked around the room, needing something to focus on. He stared at the hanging brass lamp over the dining room table. As he watched, it swayed slightly, though he felt no draft. "Tell him, Vivian. Tell him, maybe that'll snap him out of it."

"Or it'll kill him."

He stood, he sat, he punched the air with his free hand. "Vivian, I need your help here."

A quiet laugh. "Take a vacation."

He blinked. "A . . . what?"

"I have seen you, you know, since you've been back. And Lana talks to me. You're acting just like Taylor, only you make a bigger production of it. Go away for a day or two, come back, save the world or something."

"Not funny."

She laughed. "Sorry. I know it isn't. But it's true anyway." She laughed again.

He made a face at the receiver. "Look—"

"Hey, you wanted my help, right? Look, I'm sorry about your mother, and I know what you're thinking about being a target, and you're worried about Taylor, but how the hell can you do anything about anything when you can't even think straight?"

He blinked again, and the ghost of a smile. For a moment there she sounded just like his mother. The way his mother used to be.

Her voice softened. "Proctor, you remember you once told me that dumb definition of confusion? So heal yourself first, or you're no use to anyone. I need your help, too, Proctor. I'm watching Taylor killing himself and losing everything he worked for bit by bit. And if Frederick and Alicia have their way, I won't be around long to protect him."

"But there's no time to take—"

"Oh, Proctor, for God's sake," and she hung up.

He dropped the receiver onto its cradle and pushed the chair back into its place. A hand brushed through dark sandy hair; the other tapped a rhythm on his leg. He stared at the lamp; he stared at the telephone; he knew people had entered and left the room, but he paid them no attention.

Tired, he thought suddenly; I'm so damn tired I can hardly breathe.

Maybe a visit to Mom, there might be a change, maybe a visit to Mom . . .

But he didn't move.

Out on the deck, Lana cupped her hands around her eyes and peered into the living room. Proctor was still in his chair; he'd barely moved for over an hour. She'd spoken to him once, but he'd only grunted, shrugged, and she knew he hadn't heard a word she'd said.

"I assume he's still alive?"

Doc Falcon leaned back against the railing, arms folded loosely over his chest.

"Barely," she answered, turning away from the window.

She stood beside him, listening to the last of the melting snow trickling through the rocks toward the river below. There were hazy clouds in the distance; sunlight glared off the Hudson and the windows in the buildings on the opposite bank.

"Doc, I'm worried about him."

Falcon lowered his arms, turned to face the river. "We all are, Lana."

She slapped the railing in frustration. "He's driving us all crazy. Even you."

He raised an eyebrow. "How can you tell?"

She grinned. "Your tie is crooked."

His hand was halfway to his throat before he caught himself and smiled. It didn't last long; she was lucky he had smiled at all.

"Doc?"

"I admit, he's not himself these days."

"Not himself? Hell, all you have to do is look at him to know he's not eating or getting any sleep. Half the time he's with his mother, the rest of the time he's prowling around here like some kind of ghost. He's not taking care of business, Doc. Now that we're off the Blaine thing, we've got to do something, or we'll be right back where we were before Blaine showed up."

She didn't have to explain; times had not been very good.

Unless something was done, she reminded him, times were going to get an awful lot worse. They had hired Eriko Nagai to help out with RJ; Proctor had promised RJ the firm would pay for her education; Lana had a line on a new man to replace Sloan Delany; and she'd just upgraded all the equipment the firm owned. Until the contacts Blaine had provided began to bear fruit, without the Blaine money . . .

"I don't want to be here when the roof falls in, Doc."

Her tone made him look at her suspiciously. "I believe I am about to regret this question, but . . . what do you suggest?"

Lana turned quickly and smiled. "Funny you should say that, Doc. Vivian and RJ and I have been talking."

"Without me? Without Paul?"

Lana patted his arm. "No offense, Doc, but you'd want to

take him to an opera or something, and Taz would want to take him out to get drunk." She laughed. "Well, maybe not, he's too scared of him. But that would be his plan."

"And you, of course, have a better one."

Her dark eyes nearly vanished, her smile was so broad. "I don't know if it's better, but it'll be a lot more fun."

FIVE

28 January

Mischa Acmarov did not consider himself an artistic genius, but he didn't think he was a hack, either. He didn't write jingles or ditties, he wrote tunes. Melodies. Lyrics. His goal was to write songs people would hum long after the music had ended. And he wanted to make enough money doing it so he didn't have to take jobs like this just to survive.

Although, he thought as he pushed a broom across the rehearsal room's worn hardwood floor, as temporary jobs go, this was probably the best he'd ever had. Up in New York he had washed dishes, waited tables, driven a cab, walked dogs, and had once hired himself out to birthday and anniversary parties, where guests would give him lines and he would turn them into songs.

He damn near starved.

Then his cousin, Suze, called from Atlantic City to tell him she had heard through the grapevine about this job at the hotel where she worked.

"We're not talking rocket science here, Mike. All you have to do is sweep up once in a while in the rehearsal hall, make sure nobody goes sneaking around the dressing rooms, keep the place warm, stuff like that."

It was, as he had discovered, a little more complicated than that, but all in all it wasn't bad.

The hall wasn't really a hall, just a large, low-ceiling, heavily soundproofed room one floor below the casino. Much of it was taken by a low bare-bones stage the same size as the one in the Sea Cruise Theater on the Gallery, no curtains, no sets. So he swept, kept the stage floor dry so the girls wouldn't slip, made sure there were folding chairs available for the director and his staff and whatever visitors there were, and kept the coffee urn full and coffee hot. A few other things, nothing terrible.

The pay sucked, but the musical director let him work on the piano that sat beside the stage when the hall wasn't in use; it gave him a great chance to meet showgirls—who admittedly didn't pay much attention to him; and it had allowed him to write. The revue's last director, in fact, had actually put one of his songs in the show. It wasn't a lot of money, and not a lot of people heard what he had written, but it was a start. It was definitely a start.

Best of all, it allowed him to keep an eye on Dacey Logetta.

He smiled at the image of her that seemed constantly with him as he pushed the floor's debris up to the wheeled trash can. He propped the broom against the wall beside the door that led to the showgirls' dressing room, took out a dustpan and brush, and knelt to sweep the dirt up.

He'd met her in just this position as she'd arrived for a matinee performance. She'd looked down at him, her face winter-flushed, her topcoat open, and said, "Hey, you're new, huh? Cute." He could only nod stupidly at those legs, that chest, that amazing tumble of red hair that disappeared when the doors slid shut.

He didn't even mind the "cute" remark.

His black hair was curly, eyebrows thick, eyes big and blue, lips a little full, and his face slightly pale and unlined. "Pretty" was what he'd been called since a child, and "pretty"—not to mention "cute," "cuddly," and "you remind me of my brother"—had followed him, and cursed him, all his life.

But on that day he hadn't minded.

On that day he decided Dacey Logetta would be his lady if it took him the rest of his natural born life.

"Mike, you're a jerk," Suze had told him.

"Mischa," he'd corrected sullenly.

"For crying out loud, Mike, we're in America, remember? And Dacey calls everybody cute."

"Mischa," he'd insisted.

"Whatever."

What Suze didn't understand was how he felt every time Dacey showed up, either for rehearsal or a performance. A kind of flutter in his stomach, an increase in his pulse, and what had to be a truly stupid grin slapped across his mouth. He had contrived a number of meetings since that first time— from a nod to a hello to talk about the weather and the show she was in; first names, a few jokes, a bashful nod when she'd said "You wrote that?" He certainly didn't have to fake concern when her friend Charleen had been murdered. In fact, it doubled his determination to get close to her, protect her. And she seemed to appreciate it, once even asking him to wait under the lifeboat portico with her until the security guy arrived to escort her home.

"Progress," he'd told his cousin.

"Yeah, right. She's scared, Mike. You could be a toad for all she cares. I don't trust her. She's the one who said they shouldn't wait for the guard that night, yet everyone's treating her like a victim, for God's sake. Even made her a floor waitress when she asked so the poor little thing wouldn't have to work nights all the time."

"Don't talk about her like that, Suze."

"Mike, you're sweet, but you don't see her all day, the way she acts. She's different than before." She'd touched his cheek sadly. "Find someone else, Mike, huh? Do me a favor, find someone else."

"Like you, right?"

She'd laughed. "Hell, no, I'm a bitch on wheels." She'd jabbed his shoulder playfully. "A bit too much for someone like you, cuz."

Mischa finished his cleaning, put his gear away, grabbed his windbreaker, and left the hall. The corridor outside was narrow and badly lit. Soft sounds. Faint echoes. He hurried to the service elevator down at the end and rode it up one floor. Break time, and he needed to breathe something other than old polish and dust. With a nod to the bellmen at the rear exit, he pushed through the glass door and walked along the curved drive's concrete apron until he reached the street. There he leaned against a high concrete obelisk atop of which sat a large bird on a gleaming gold globe. He wasn't sure if the bird was supposed to be a seagull or what, but the pigeons sure liked it. In fact, two of his bellmen buddies, Sal and Patrick, spent half their time chasing the winged rats away from this one and its twin on the other side.

The afternoon was clear and sharp, not very cold, and he could smell the sweet scent of the ocean in the deep breaths he took. After fighting with the constant breeze, he managed to light a cigarette, took a deep drag, and wondered what he should do next.

Suze had been right about one thing—Dacey had changed, and he was worried.

Far south of the Lighthouse, Murray Cobb stepped out of the Claridge, sniffed loudly and suddenly, grabbed a handkerchief from his pocket, and slapped it to his nose a split second before the sneeze erupted.

Pneumonia, he figured, would be about right just about now, a humbling illness in case he began to feel too good.

Murray believed, in a cautious distant fashion, in signs and portents, and since he had arrived yesterday afternoon, he'd been signed and portended half to death:

His one-night room had been accidentally booked to someone else, and the desk clerk, in compensation, had given him two extra nights, for free; his egg-and-bacon breakfast had had something disgusting in it, nobody even wanted to guess what it was, so his meals for his entire stay were now on the hotel; he walked into the casino—so much smaller than any of the others because the hotel was high and narrow rather than high and wide, had fussed and muttered for a couple of hours around the roulette table, and now there was twelve thousand dollars in the hotel safe, another one-and-a-half in his pockets.

What it all meant was, maybe today he would discover who had killed his best friend.

And if he didn't, he had enough money now to keep com-

ing back, to keep pestering that nice lieutenant to make sure
she didn't overlook anything. Pestering in the nicest way possible, he reminded himself as he headed for the boardwalk
half a block away. She was a nice lady, had a good head on
her shoulders, and knew as well as he that these murders—
five of them now—weren't going to be solved overnight.

Or without one hell of a stroke of luck.

It didn't bother him that she did her best not to cringe each
time he walked into the precinct house. He had felt the same
way any number of times in his career with well-meaning am-
ateurs, and had done his best over the past three weeks to
keep his questions and suggestions short and to the point. She
appreciated that, he was sure.

The trouble was, no one else would talk to him.

Two of the victims had been from out of state, so he
couldn't have a word with their families; two lived in miles-
apart sections of the metro city area and their kin wouldn't
even let him in the door; the last one was a homeless, name-
less woman. No good to him at all. Except he had grown convinced that this killer, this animal, made no conscious
connection among his prey—he stalked and attacked purely
at random, a suggestion the nice lieutenant hadn't taken with
much good grace.

Hard to pin down a murderer when he left no clues, and
there was no connection between his victims except their being
in Atlantic City.

Tough job.

He picked up a hot dog from a sandwich shop, took it to
the railing, and watched the tide slide back out to sea as he
ate.

Fred, he thought, I'm doing my best here, but you know
how it is. Old man, former cop, can't get it out of his blood,
they pat you on the head and show you the door. What I don't
get is, how that guy got away so fast. I'm getting old, but
I'm not getting deaf. I didn't hear him, didn't hear you—how
the hell did he do it?

The sun began to set. The hotels' shadows began to ripple
over the sand toward the water; as the waves broke, their
crests took on colors. The temperature began to skid, and the

breeze died abruptly. A flurry of pedestrians moved up and down the boards, their voices high and brittle, their footsteps cracking like whips.

"Bah," he muttered when no inspiration struck, and a curse when a series of sharp sneezes caught him unprepared. He decided it was better he stay inside tonight. Test the wheel again, maybe, or maybe make a few phone calls, see what was happening, see if anyone had learned anything new.

Or sit in his room, take off his shoes, pour himself a little rum, and try to figure out how that monster, that killer, that inhuman son of a bitch had done what he'd done to Fred without making a sound.

Several hours past sunset the breeze died again.

So did the city.

It was as if, without warning, all the clocks had jumped to a hour or more past midnight. Except for an infrequent patrol car, no vehicles moved on the streets, or on the expressway that brought tourists in from other parts of the state, from other states. No one walked. No animals prowled. Shades, blinds, curtains, drapes were drawn. The small airport was deserted. Bars and taverns were practically empty.

A moment when it seemed as if not even the waves moved.

Suze Acmarov concentrated on the Lighthouse beacon as she trotted northward along the boardwalk. She'd been down at the Showboat to have dinner with a guy who at the last minute decided he was going to stay where he was a while longer and told her it wasn't all that far, she didn't need a ride, and it was, for crying out loud, cold out there and he didn't have a coat.

She didn't think he understood when she tipped her water glass into his lap.

Still, he was right—it wasn't that far. And except for her breathing, her shoes on the boards, it was so quiet she'd be able to hear a feather sneaking up on her.

Mischa would kill her if he ever found out, though. And he would find out, she knew it. Although they were only cousins, they looked and thought enough alike that people often mistook them for twins. They might as well have been. One look at his face, and she knew what was going on inside; he could do the same. From each other they had very few secrets.

She ran easily, settling into a comfortable jog, glad that she hadn't worn a dress, that despite the season she hadn't worn a long coat. Just a couple of minutes and she'd be there, hardly even out of breath.

She smiled to herself.

She concentrated on the light.

She developed a mental script that would, with righteous indignation, explain to one of her fellow dancers why that dancer's brother was a swine, scum, disgusting, and not deserving to live one second longer, and why Suze had ever agreed to a blind date with him was beyond mortal comprehension. She had just gotten to the point of adding grand gestures to the monologue, when she saw what looked like smoke or steam rising between boardwalk cracks up ahead and to her right.

A fire? she wondered, and looked behind her as if hoping someone else had seen it as well.

Immediately she wished she hadn't.

There was no one there. As far as she could see, there wasn't a single person on the boardwalk but her. Nothing back there but empty boards and empty patches of pale light.

Suddenly the Lighthouse was too far away.

As she passed the spot where the smoke rose from below, she watched it, slowing, realized it wasn't smoke but thick mist, almost like spring fog. That didn't make any sense, but she wasn't about to investigate. A hundred yards or so and she'd be inside.

A few paces farther on, she checked it again—thicker now, twisting around itself slowly, tendrils curling along the boards like, she thought, the feelers of a plant seeking new places to root.

A shrug, a glance at her watch to tell her she'd make it to the dressing room with only a couple of minutes to spare, and she lengthened her stride, wincing at a stitch that grew in her side. She rubbed it absently, watched the Lighthouse's curved white facade resolve itself into windows and balconies high above her. Blinked and grinned when the white beam abruptly turned blue.

Looked back just for the heck of it . . . and saw him.

The mist was still there, sweeping across the boardwalk, spilling down into a side street on one side, to the sand on the other. *He* stood in the middle of it, a solid black form, only a hint of pale where his face should have been.

Watching her; she knew he was watching her.

Oh, my God, oh, my God, she thought, and almost tripped. The stumble sent her closer to the railing, and she nearly stumbled again when she swerved sharply back toward the hotel.

The night breeze returned, brought with it an amplified thunder of the surf; but it didn't touch the mist.

Oh, God; and she tried to sprint for the doors, the awning above them stretching out of the shadows. She could see dark figures in there, people walking around the lobby; she could see behind her that man coming after her. Swiftly, without running; the mist dragging behind him, sliding over his shoulders, billowing low and fast after her.

She heard his footsteps—hard heels walking, yet he moved faster than she did.

Oh, God, no; less than fifty yards when the first of the mist caught up to her. Less than thirty when she could hear him laughing softly. Less than twenty when a hand grabbed her shoulder.

She shrieked and spun wildly away from the grip, running backward, then forward and straight at the doors. Screaming for help. The mist rising along her legs, freezing them, stiffening them, and she flailed at it—freezing her hands, stiffening her fingers.

A low and husky voice whispered, "Too late," just as she reached the nearest glass door, pressed against it, pounding it with her fists, screaming while the people inside ignored her, couldn't see or hear her.

"Too late."

He laughed again.

And the door shattered inward, and she fell into the lobby, glass slicing through her hands as she scrambled across the marble floor. Screaming. Looking back to watch the mist fill the door without coming in.

Screaming until strong hands grabbed her, stopped her, and a rasping voice told her it was all right, there was no one out there, take it easy, miss, take it easy, you're all right.

But there was blood on her hands and the front of her coat, and when she held up a trembling palm, the man dipped into his coat pocket and pulled out a handkerchief, snapped it open, and wrapped the hand while he spoke—a rough voice but soft and calming, until she thought she could breathe without screaming again.

An arm around her shoulder, voices in the background.

"Quite a night," he said, staring at the boardwalk. He nodded. "They're getting a doctor, you'll be just fine, you're young, you'll live." He smiled. "Cobb. Murray Cobb. When you're feeling better, maybe we'll talk."

SIX

18 February

Proctor sat in his chair, legs crossed, hands gripping the carved wooden ends of the armrests. Although sunlight filled the room, colors bright, glass glittering, he couldn't help feeling as if he were in an old cop movie, the innocent suspect forced into a chair with a hooded light aimed at his eyes. He was feeling put-upon, ganged up on, hijacked, shanghaied, and generally the object of an unexpected mutiny.

"No," he said.

Lana sat in the middle of the couch. RJ, her long blond hair formed into a single, lethal-looking braid was on her right, and Eriko Nagai, the newest member of the firm, on her left—looking, Proctor noted with reluctant amusement, both excited and terrified, unsure how she was supposed to react when everyone seemed to be ganging up on the boss.

Taz and Doc stood behind the couch. Doc, as always, gave nothing away in his expression; Taz, as always, wanted to look stern and failed miserably. A valiant try, Proctor thought, and fought a smile away from his lips.

"You have no choice," Lana told him. She pointed at a folder on the coffee table. "Your reservations are right there and paid for. Taz and Doc will be with you. Taz was good enough to offer his Jeep as transportation, but I want you all back alive, so I've hired a car to take you down."

"No," he repeated.

"The car will be here tomorrow at ten. You will arrive at the Lighthouse Hotel sometime between one and two, depending on traffic on the Parkway. There are dinner reservations for Saturday night. There's some kind of package gift waiting for you at check-in. Twenty-five bucks worth of chips, coupons, things like that."

He shook his head. "We're not communicating, Lana. I said no. I meant no."

Lana shook her head right back at him. "No, Proctor, it's you who's not listening." She looked to the others. "You're not doing anyone here the least bit of good the way you are now." A hand up to prevent him from interrupting. "You look like hell, I can tell from the fridge that you haven't eaten anything decent in days, and Eri here probably thinks you're some kind of drug addict."

The young woman's already large black eyes widened abruptly, and she looked in mild panic from Lana to him before clasping her hands in her lap and lowering her head so she wouldn't have to look at anyone.

"It's called overload," Doc said, absently fussing the perfectly folded maroon handkerchief in his suit jacket's breast pocket. "Everything is important to you. You try to concentrate on them all simultaneously. As a result, you're overloading your circuits, and you undoubtedly don't even know it."

Lana nodded sharply.

Taz nodded solemnly.

RJ and Eriko showed no reaction at all.

Proctor scowled, but said nothing, because he knew they were right. Which angered him because he ought to know better. In fact, he *did* know better, but for some reason was helpless to do anything about it. Even worse, he had been too dense to realize how it had affected the others.

Doc seemed to read his mind. "Mrs. Proctor," he said matter-of-factly. "There is an emotional link there you cannot and should not break, and her apparent breakthrough has caught you completely unprepared. Dr. Browning hasn't figured it out yet, so you've taken it upon yourself to do his work for him. Plus, the unfortunate situation with Mr. Blaine." He lifted a hand as if to say the resolution is obvious. "You need a way to clear your head."

"And the answer," Proctor said skeptically, "is a weekend in Atlantic City?"

"Sure, Boss," said Taz eagerly. "We hang out, gamble, look at all the women—" He stopped and winced, as if waiting for Lana to chew him out. "Well, you know what I mean. Like, no work, you know? Who knows, you may even get l—" He cut himself off again, winced again, and waved a hand to tell him never mind, he was going to shut up now.

"I don't know," Proctor said, suddenly uncertain.

"Eri," Lana said.

Eriko reached around the end of the couch and dragged a cardboard box to her feet. After pushing a lock of black hair behind one ear, she lifted the box to the coffee table and opened it, reached in and pulled out a handful of envelopes, some of them open, most not.

"Your cases," Lana told him. "Since you've been back, you haven't paid attention to a single one. Not even that guy in Arizona with the alien cactus."

Eriko blinked. "The what?"

Lana patted her knee and smiled. "Later, dear. It's . . . difficult to explain." She dropped the envelopes back into the box, dusted her palms against each other. "Proctor, we're all aware of the problems. We can't really know how you're feeling about Mrs. Proctor, but we know that unless you shake yourself up, you're not doing her any good, either. So . . . you're going, whether you want to or not."

Again, there was a touch of mild irritation, a how-dare-you feeling that swiftly transformed itself into guilt. They wanted him back to normal; he wanted back to normal, and maybe they were right. Maybe this would be a good thing. He hadn't been at a gaming table in well over a year. Hadn't walked the boardwalk, hadn't visited his old pal, Lucy the Elephant, down in Margate, hadn't . . .

I'll be damned, he thought. He frowned, rubbed a cheek softly. I'll be damned.

He relaxed, and it must have shown because Lana smiled and sat back, pleased but not smug.

"All right," he agreed. "On one condition."

"Sure, Boss," Taz said before Lana could speak.

"Two conditions, actually. One, if you call me 'Boss' once more, I get to drop you headfirst off the Steel Pier. And two, RJ, I want you and Eri to go through all the phone tape transcriptions since Mr. Blaine hired us. Every one of them, you understand?"

"Sure," RJ said. She pursed her lips, closed one eye. "What are we looking for?"

"Tiger's eye," he told them.

Relieved and smiling, Lana hustled everyone out of the room, looked pointedly at the box Eriko had left behind, and suggested that Proctor make a dent in those letters before he left for Atlantic City.

"They deserve an answer," she told him, "no matter what it is."

He agreed, but didn't move. Taz popped out of the hall a few seconds later, pulling on a windbreaker and muttering something about taking care of the Jeep. When he wasn't asked to stay, he left, the kitchen door closing just hard enough to make Proctor lift a corner of his mouth.

Doc remained behind the couch, unmoving, elegant as usual. Proctor had never asked him where he found the money for his tailored suits and handmade shirts; he only knew it sure wasn't on the salary he made at Black Oak. When the room was quiet again, he shifted forward and clasped his hands between his knees, stared at the carpet for a moment before looking up.

"What's up?"

Doc turned to the dining room table behind him, opened a dark leather briefcase, and pulled out a folded newspaper. He tossed it over, and Proctor snagged it before it hit the carpet.

It was a copy of the *Atlantic City Press*.

"Lana," he said dryly, "tends to overlook some things you're going to find out anyway. I've marked the stories I think bear noticing."

There were two: the first warned the Absecon Island community to batten down, the winter storm forecast for the weekend was going to be a slammer. Larger than originally believed, picking up strength as it moved slowly toward the coast.

"Great," Proctor said. "All that way and I'll be stuck in the hotel."

Doc raised an eyebrow. "It's the middle of February. Were you planning on strolling along the beach, getting some tan, ogling girls in bikinis?"

Proctor gave him a look, and Doc cleared his throat, smoothed his perfectly smooth tie.

The second story, more a haranguing editorial than a reporting, wanted to know why the police hadn't yet caught the savage murderer who had been stalking the community since the beginning of the year. Seven deaths and not a single clue. Seven brutal, vicious deaths, and not even a suspect. Atlantic City cowered in fear. When were the police going to catch this seaside monster?

There were no pictures of the victims as they'd been found, and no follow-ups with witnesses, because there hadn't been any.

There was, in an accompanying article, only the usual "no comment on the investigation, we're pursuing all leads," from the police spokesman.

On the op-ed page he read the headline of the main editorial, read it again, and closed his eyes briefly.

"Yes," said Doc quietly.

Finally Proctor folded the newspaper and tossed it onto the coffee table. He sat back and crossed his legs. He looked at the ceiling while one finger tapped the armrest. He uncrossed his legs and said, "For God's sake, Doc . . . they think it's Jack the Ripper?"

SEVEN

18 February

The wind reached the city long before the storm.

It lifted the waves and shattered the crests and blew spray and foam nearly as far as the boardwalk. There were still stars, but they had begun to dim as the storm's thin outer edge moved up the coast; there was still cold, but the temperature, despite sunset, had begun to rise, creating pockets of mist around the island, pockets of mist in the alleys.

The rain would come later.

Reno Baron stepped out of his office and fell instantly into his role—the tall, tan, silver-haired, white-tooth smiling gentleman of extreme gambling leisure who never was too busy to talk to anyone who visited the hotel he ran.

And they did talk to him.

God Almighty, how they talked to him.

The slots are too loose, the slots are too tight; the dealers are too glib and unsympathetic, the croupiers aren't any fun and are unsympathetic; a pit boss was insulting, a waitress spit in my food, the bellhop made lewd suggestions, my registration has been lost so what are you going to do to make it right; I've won fifty dollars, aren't you going to comp me a room?; there's a little boy running wild in the casino, causing all kinds of trouble, the food's too cold, the food's too expensive, don't you know that in Las Vegas you can get a decent steak for a couple of bucks?

Reno Baron, who would rather die than tell anyone his real

name, had been hired because he was a genius at handling problems that would drive a lesser man insane. He genuinely liked most who stayed here, either for the day or a weekend, and there was no such thing as a frivolous or unsolvable problem.

He wasn't stupid. He knew full well that the Lighthouse wasn't the Boardwalk's prime attraction when it came to glitter and pizzazz, or big name performers, so he staked its reputation on the services it provided—the friendliness of the staff, and the constant availability and visibility of the management.

Which, in the long run, usually meant him.

It was his idea to take over the fourth floor for his employees; it was his idea to provide a professionally staffed day-care center for not only the guests, but for the employees as well; it was his idea never to wear a tuxedo like several of the other casino managers did, because that intimidated some guests and made him appear aloof; and it was his idea to provide two armed guards to walk his people home every night at various scheduled times, and because of his failure to implement this earlier, he had paid for Charleen Caje's funeral out of his own pocket.

He was also the one who closed down the Barnegat Light, perhaps his only professional setback.

The Barnegat was a large, glass-walled room just below the beacon, an expensive surf-'n'-turf restaurant with a great view of the city, the Boardwalk, and the sea. From late spring to early fall, diners could have cocktails on the wide balcony that ran the width of the rounded facade. But it didn't do very well. It didn't rotate, it was too vulnerable to the buffeting of storms barreling in from the Atlantic, and even Baron admitted the food wasn't worth either the price or the sights. It was finally closed down not long into its third year. Every so often, however, he would take someone influential up for the impressive panorama; every so often, a staff member brought a partner up not for the view at all; every so often, a pair of guests found their way up.

The Lighthouse wasn't Atlantic City's most famous casino, or even near the top in terms of profit. But pound for pound, guest by guest, it had been, since its opening, making a fortune.

The owners loved Reno, and Reno loved his job. Even when he had to kick a little ass once in a while.

He made his way to the lobby, an expansive sweep of marble and Spanish tile designed to evoke a calm, sea-like atmosphere without having to hang plaster fish and phony three-masters on the walls. The row of five glass double doors allowed an unobstructed view of the beach and the ocean; directly opposite them, companion doors framed in walnut and elaborately etched to make looking out, or in, something of a chore, opened onto the main casino floor one broad step down. Along the right-hand wall was the registration desk— long, mahogany, the clerks dressed in admiralty costume and looking, by contrast, a lot more important than he.

He stopped at the counter's end and leaned on it. The four clerks on duty knew he was there, and knew that before any of them dared recognize his presence, their current work had better be done first.

Reno was very patient.

Eventually one of the women closed a file and walked over, curly blonde hair, dark eye shadow, a touch of lipstick. Her figure was enough to give her outfit a challenge, another Reno idea—made the men reluctant to leave, dictate a lasting subconscious memo to get back here as soon as they can, who knows, they may get lucky.

"Good evening, Mr. Baron," she said.

He nodded. "Greta, how are things?" His voice, like his clothes, was carefully chosen to the greatest effect. Not too deep, not too imposing.

"Quiet, sir."

"What about him?"

In the center of the lobby was a replica of Copenhagen's *Little Mermaid*, the centerpiece of a wide marble fountain with a scalloped rim. Encircling it was a padded bench, the only seating the lobby offered. Tonight, an old man sat there, a black Russian hat beside him, salt-and-pepper topcoat unbuttoned. He came in two or three times a week. He bothered no one, spoke to no one; he just sat there and stared at the doors. As if waiting.

"The usual," Greta answered, keeping her voice low.

Reno didn't know what to make of him. The other casinos generally tossed him out after a couple of hours, or so the grapevine said. Yet the old guy didn't bother anyone, caused no trouble, and especially since it was so damn cold outside, Reno didn't see the point of throwing him out. Thanks to Greta, he also knew that the old guy was a friend of the Ripper's first victim. Not to mention the help he'd given that Acmarov woman two weeks ago.

Maybe, Reno thought, he was waiting for a ghost.

"Dacey Logetta in yet tonight?"

Greta tapped a keyboard, scanned a terminal. "I don't think so, no."

"Send her to me when she is. If she doesn't come in, cut her last check."

Then he nodded his thanks, patted her hand absently, and walked away. Wide, carpeted promenades ran down both sides of the casino, wood-framed glass doors here as well, and at least one was open all day. Spaced along the paneled right wall were two alcoves that each held three elevator banks. He glanced into each as he passed, nodding to the guard who stood against the back wall, his job to make sure only registered guests and their friends and families used the elevators.

Reno had been in the business a long time. He wasn't so stupid not to know that the occasional call girl visited his establishment. That he didn't mind. That was a prearrangement made by the guest, and the guards had been instructed to use a little discretion and make no fuss. What he didn't want were streetwalkers. No class, awful dressers, lousy manners; a disgrace to their profession.

At the end of the North Promenade he turned left toward the back entrance, which opened onto a circular drive that swept in from Pacific Avenue. A group of bellhops waited just inside the doors, two of them stamping their feet, blowing on their hands. One waved to him, and he waved back as he continued on his way, heading for the South Promenade, to more shops and three of the hotel's more expensive restau-

rants. It was time to have a look in, chat with the dining
guests, listen to their praises, note their complaints.

Once that was over, it would probably be around ten. Then
he would enter the casino, stroll, listen, chat, take one of two
escalators up to the Gallery and the other restaurants, the
shops, the snack shop and the lounges and the theater.

That would make it around midnight, and time to start all
over, one more turn around before he went to bed.

He thought of Greta and her jacket and that blouse, and
he smiled. When he'd patted her hand, she'd lifted a knuckle
to brush his palm. So at least, he thought as an elderly couple hustled toward him, he won't be alone for a change.

Then he smiled and said, "Good evening, how may I help
you?"

Greta checked her watch and rolled her eyes. "Jeez," she
said, "it's not even midnight."

Beside her, Stu Hockman held up one finger to hush her
for a moment, then continued flipping through the names of
the guests he'd written on 3x5 cards, muttering to himself,
closing his eyes every few seconds, either grimacing or smiling, and opening them again. His nightly routine—an exercise to put faces to every name. The guests loved it. Reno
loved it. His paycheck loved it. When he reached the *M*'s, he
stopped.

"How'd you do?"

He shook his head as a finger stroked a narrow mustache
that would have been in style fifty years ago; today, it only
made his face more like a rodent's. A rodent with thick and
curly red hair, and enough freckles to make him look as if he
suffered from the pox.

"I'm off my game," he said regretfully, and squinted at the
chandeliers. "Bad vibes here, Gret, really bad vibes."

She sighed, but not loudly. "Stu, they don't say bad vibes
anymore, okay?"

"I don't care what they say, it's still bad vibes."

Another look at her watch. "I'm taking my break." She
made for a narrow door in the wall behind her. "I need some
air." Inside the employees' lounge she took a sable coat from

her locker, put it on, snuggled her chin into the sinfully soft fur. "Be back in ten," she said as she rounded the counter.

"Madam," Stu said with a badly faked leer, "your wish is my command."

Not in this life, she thought as she headed for the doors.

"Miss?"

She stopped. It was the old man on the bench; she'd forgotten he was still there. "Yes, sir?"

He pointed at the night. "I wouldn't go out there if I were you."

She liked the old guy, even though they'd seldom passed a word. A harmless nut in a silly fur hat. With a chin that must have been something else when he was young.

"Why not?"

He inhaled slowly, exhaled just as slowly. "If I told you, you wouldn't believe me."

She took a step toward the Boardwalk. "If it's the Ripper you're worried about, I'm just going out for a smoke and some air. I'll only be at the rail." She smiled. "If you see him, you can save me."

His large eye turned to her, sad eyes, she thought, like a sad and lonely dog. "Then it'll be too late, I think."

She wanted to laugh at how glum he sounded, how serious, but that look began to spook her, so she smiled again, polite this time and distant, and went out. Gasped at the slap of cold air against her face. Ducked her head against the wind, and cursed when she realized what it would do to her hair.

Too windy for a cigarette, she should have lit up inside, so she walked over to the rail and leaned against it, looked down, looked out toward the surf, let the cold chill her and revive her, put some color in her cheeks.

Was positive her heart stopped when, from behind her, a hand touched her shoulder and a husky voice said, "Good evening."

Reno was about to lose his temper.

He had checked the restaurants, the high rollers' private rooms, the casino, the closed shops, spoke a few words to the security guards he encountered, and had been on the down escalator when a small man with the worst breath he'd ever smelled accosted him and demanded that he personally check the nickel slots because the man was positive he'd been cheated all night.

The increasingly strained smile hurt Reno's cheeks; the refusal of the man to admit that he might be suffering a really rotten streak of luck produced acid in his stomach; the knowing grins of the gamblers close enough to overhear made him feel like an idiot.

Finally, nearly dizzy from holding his breath, he took the man's arm firmly and led him toward the back entrance. "Mr. Wharton, I believe I have the perfect answer for you."

"Yeah, right," Abel Wharton said, shaking off the grip but following just the same. "A man can't even have a good time at the slots anymore, for crying out loud. You people are a bunch of mobsters, you know that? Just a bunch of mobsters. I oughta write my congressman."

Ah, Reno thought; so you can write, too? Bravo, you little shit, bravo.

He laughed heartily. "You must do what you must, Mr. Wharton. But perhaps an evening—" He stepped up and opened a door, ushered Wharton through, and went straight to Jack Delmonico, the bell captain.

"Mr. Delmonico," he said, and beckoned Wharton closer, "Mr. Wharton here has had a bad run, and feels slighted."

"Slighted, my ass. I've been—"

"So if you wouldn't mind preparing the limousine right away, I'd be grateful." He turned to Wharton without waiting for a reply. "Mr. Wharton, the limousine, courtesy of the Lighthouse, will take you to whatever establishment you wish. It is yours for the rest of the night. As," he said, reaching into his jacket pocket and pulling out a wad of bills that made Wharton's eyes widen. "As is . . ." Reno counted out one thousand dollars in hundreds, put it in Wharton's upturned hand, then smiled and counted out a thousand more. "This."

"Hey," the little man said suspiciously.

"Not to worry," Reno told him smoothly, taking him by the shoulder and leading him to the exit. "This will not be on your bill, and it is not a loan. Win more, lose it all, it's all up to you."

At which point the limousine glided up to the curb.

Reno waited until the man was gone before he turned, lost his smile, and said loudly, "Jesus Christ, Jack, what the hell was I in a former life to deserve someone like that?"

"My old man," Delmonico answered dryly.

Reno faked a smile as he passed. "Very funny, Jack, very funny. And if the driver calls with a complaint, I'm dead, all right? That man's breath killed me."

Leaving the bell captain's laughter behind him, he hurried to the lobby, veered over to the front desk, where he leaned an elbow on the counter's end and said to Hockman, "I'm having a bad night, Stuart. Tell me we're making lots of money."

"Yes, sir, we are."

"Good. And problems?"

"None, sir, none."

He nodded his pleasure and looked down the length of the registration desk. Frowned. "Greta?"

"Break," Stu told him. Nodded toward the entrance. "Smoke."

"Ah. Good." He stifled a yawn, rubbed an eye with a knuckle, and said, "Mr. Hockman, do you envy my position?"

"Honestly, sir?"

Reno nodded.

"Ain't enough money in the world get me to take it. You put up with people I would have killed before they'd gotten another word out." He looked down at his work. "No thanks, Mr. Baron. I'll stick right here if you don't mind."

"Smart move," Reno told him, turned toward his office, and spun around when he heard a woman's short scream and saw Greta run into the hotel, the wind slipping in behind her.

"Police," she said loudly when she saw him. "For God's sake, call the police."

EIGHT

18 February

Detective Lieutenant Granna MacEdan pulled off her wool gloves and unbuttoned her coat. It was good to feel warm again after traipsing around the boardwalk for an hour in a wind that clearly wanted to knock her on her ass, and at least the Lighthouse lobby wasn't entirely devoted to the tacky and gauche. The mermaid was a little much, but everything else was pretty nice.

Outside, a team of men continued to search the beach and the blocks immediately around the casino; cruisers manned the streets, keeping an eye on the searchers as much as searching themselves. Inside the hotel the task force personnel were in civvies. No uniforms, no badges. Discreet searches, to keep the guests from panicking and the suspect from suspecting.

Granna had a gut feeling this was a wild-goose chase, but the way things were, she didn't dare take a chance it wasn't. Over by registration, Sergeant Cox, a stereotypical cop if there ever was one—beefy face, Irish eyes, curly black hair, a gut a dedicated beer drinker would envy—seemed to be having a difficult time with a little old man holding one of those black Russian hats in both hands, like he was begging.

Cox looked over his head and saw her, made a quick face, and put a hand on the old man's shoulders to half turn him so she would see his face.

Oh, hell, she thought, broke out a smile, and walked over.

"Mr. Cobb, how are you tonight?" She held out a hand.

Murray shook it, then shook his head. "Trying to tell the galoot here, Lieutenant, that I'm not crazy."

Granna looked at Cox. "He's not crazy, Sergeant."

"Yes, ma'am, I know that, ma'am," Cox said, trying mightily to keep a grin off his face.

"Look," Murray said, "this is a waste of time. You're not going to find her."

Granna stepped back, the smile gone. "What?"

Murray waved toward the doors. "The lady that scared the other lady. She's gone. I saw her." He snapped his fingers. "Just like that."

"Listen," Granna said sharply, "this isn't another one of your—"

"No, no, please, Lieutenant, no. I saw her. Ask anyone. I saw her."

Granna glanced around the lobby. There was no one else here.

"Lieutenant," Cox said. "Baron is waiting with the woman in his office."

She nodded. "Mr. Cobb, I want you to wait for me, you understand? Sergeant Cox here will take a statement, but I want to talk to you personally when I'm done in there."

Cobb shrugged expressively. "Won't do any good. She's already gone."

She held up a finger and smiled. "Now, now, Mr. Cobb, you should know better than that. All the bases, right? I have to cover all the bases."

Cobb sighed resignation, stuffed his hat into a pocket, and headed for the fountain bench. "Maybe," he muttered, "but you gotta hit the damn ball first."

She and the sergeant exchanged glances as she walked around the counter to the manager's office. She liked Cobb. He was a nice old man who obviously had no intention of retiring no matter what it said on his retirement papers. Every time there was a new corpse, or rumor of a corpse, or a rumored sighting of the Ripper, he was there, hovering in the background, offering unsolicited and unneeded advice. The older guys on the force treated him with respect; the younger guys wanted him put away just to get him out of their hair.

If it hadn't been for the Acmarov incident, however bizarre and unreal it was, she might have been tempted to order him out of town herself.

She opened the office door without knocking.

She waited until Reno Baron and Greta Sanburn broke their clinch, then slipped on the professional smile and said, "I won't keep you much longer, Ms. Sanburn. All I need is a description of the woman you said tried to kill you tonight."

Since Pacific Avenue was one-way north, the Lighthouse limousine drove up to Atlantic Avenue, turned left onto the wide boulevard, and headed south. Another turn a mile later, and it aimed for the ocean and the center of Casino Row.

Abel Wharton wasn't happy.

The limo was nice and all, and the free money was pretty good, no complaints there, but the driver wouldn't answer any of his questions, wouldn't go faster, wouldn't tell him what the hell was in these fancy bottles in the bar, wouldn't tell him a goddamn thing. Finally he picked up the telephone in the armrest, waited until the driver did the same on his end, and said, "You know where the hell you're going, pal? I thought I told you the Sands, huh? Didn't I tell you the Sands?"

The driver nodded.

"Then you gotta go south more, you jerk. Turn up here, go south more, and maybe, if you're lucky, you'll find it."

The driver nodded again and made the next turn. Ten minutes later Wharton stepped out at the Sands' Pacific Avenue entrance.

"Thanks," he said grudgingly. "Wait for me. I'm not done yet."

"Yes, sir," the driver said. "When you're ready to leave, just contact the bell captain and I'll be waiting."

Wharton grunted and went in.

Dumb shit, he thought; I hope he's not expecting a tip.

The desk clerk was hopeless, and Granna quickly let her go after making an appointment to see her downtown tomorrow for an official statement.

She's standing on the boardwalk getting some fresh air,

someone taps her on the shoulder and says something with
some kind of accent, she screams, turns around, and sees . . .
Granna sighed, not moving from behind Baron's desk. She
sees a woman all wrapped up in a fancy hat and coat and
scarf, with piercing—Sanburn's word, not hers—piercing red
eyes. Sanburn immediately knows, she just knows it's the Ripper, and bolts for the hotel only fifty feet away. She looks
back once, halfway there, and the woman is gone.

Yeah. Right.

A woman in a classy coat and hat, the only way she's going
to disappear that fast is by jumping over the railing down to
the beach. A ten-foot drop. In a fancy coat and hat.

Cobb sees her, too. But—and Granna snapped her fingers—
he sees her disappear into thin air.

"I want a vacation," she muttered.

"So do I," Baron said from the doorway.

She started, scowled at his smile, then smiled herself. "I'm
sorry, Mr. Baron, but I think—"

"She's been working long hours this week, Lieutenant," he
said, leaning against the frame. "She took a friend's shift to
make a little extra. I would guess by now she's more than a
bit punchy."

Granna nodded. She understood that. She had done it herself often enough when she'd patrolled the streets in uniform.
That was a long time ago. She rolled her shoulders and pushed
to her feet. "I appreciate the use of your office."

He backed away to give her room to leave. "And I'm sorry
this was such a waste of your time."

"Don't worry about it. I'd be a lot more upset if there was
a body."

Baron cut off the smile instantly. "Yes. Yes, I suppose you
would."

A good-bye nod, and she crossed the lobby to Cobb, who
sat with his hands between his legs, that furry hat on his head.

"Mr. Cobb."

He looked up. "That young woman saw it, too, didn't she?"

Granna touched his shoulder. "Mr. Cobb, that woman has
been working extra time and hasn't had any real sleep in two

or three days. I wouldn't trust her to identify her own mother the way she is now."

"I've been sleeping."

She sat beside him. The doors were closed, bright reflections of the lights and the fountain and the casino doors behind them shimmered in the glass as the wind tried to get in. She watched one of her men walk by, hailing someone she couldn't see. He slipped through, and in and out of, the reflections.

Here one minute, over there the next.

"I know," Cobb said when he saw what she did. "But I don't make mistakes like that, Lieutenant. My eyes are old, but they got good vision still."

"Mine aren't so old," she said, taking out her gloves, pulling them on. "But I wouldn't rely on them to swear what you do when—" She nodded at the doors. "It could be a mistake, Mr. Cobb. You have to admit, it could be a mistake."

"Sure," he admitted as she stood, beckoned to Cox and signaled him to round up the others, send them home. "Sure. But it isn't."

She barely heard him. Already she was home, slipping into bed beside her husband, listening to him snore, feeling his arm automatically drape over her hip to hold her close. This night was over.

"Get some sleep, Mr. Cobb," she said as she headed for the back entrance. "You'll feel better in the morning."

"I saw what I saw," he called after her.

And she heard his fingers make that snapping sound again.

Reno stepped into his apartment on the seventeenth floor, threw his keys onto the hall table, and strode into the living room with its panoramic view of the Atlantic. The scent of fresh flowers pleased him, but it was the silence that made him smile. No voices, no slots, no music, no . . . nothing.

The contrast was almost deafening.

"Greta?"

"Here," she answered.

He turned as she stepped out of a bathroom large enough, in some small cities, to qualify as an apartment on its own.

She wore the sable coat he'd given her for Christmas. Underneath, she was naked. Spectacularly naked.

"I'm cold, Reno." She pouted, one hand drifting over her breasts. "That cop didn't believe me, and I'm cold."

Reno smiled. "At your service, my dear. You'll be warm in no time."

Wharton left the Sands just as the limousine pulled up. The driver opened the door, he got in, and began laughing. Incredible; absolutely incredible. Another grand, for God's sake; he'd won another grand. Proof that faggot manager ran a bum casino.

"The Taj," he ordered. "Drive me up to the Taj. I think I'll take some of Trump's money tonight."

The limousine pulled smoothly away from the curb, rocking slightly in the wind, and he couldn't help thinking of a huge black shark trolling for a meal. All the other cars were like minnows. Tiny. Vulnerable. Meals on wheels. He laughed again.

"Changed my mind," he said loudly. "Let's go to the inlet. I want to go to Harrah's."

The driver didn't respond.

"Hey, you jerk, I'm talking to you. You hear me? We're going to Harrah's."

The driver nodded slowly, and Wharton frowned. He leaned forward so he could see better, and the frown deepened.

"Hey," he said. "You the same guy? That son of a bitch pull a switch on me?"

The limousine pulled off Pacific, into a dark side street with no lighting at all.

"Hey," Wharton said, but it didn't come out very loudly.

The limousine slowed.

"Now, hold on, jerk, don't try no shit on me. I'm—"

The vehicle braked suddenly, and he was thrown off the seat onto his knees. "Jesus H, you goddamn—"

The driver turned around.

Wharton's eyes widened. "Holy shit, you're—"

"Dead," the driver said in a low husky voice. "The word you want, Mr. Wharton, is dead."

NINE

Proctor pulled the living room's oak door shut behind him and passed a hand over a metal plate in the wall. Some fifteen feet down on his left, a doorway filled with light. He walked slowly toward it, massaging the back of his neck, first with one hand, then the other. When he reached the door he glanced into his bedroom, changed his mind, and walked on. He wasn't that tired. And even if he was, he knew he wouldn't sleep.

His eyes would close, and he would once again be wandering somewhere, on that vast obsidian plain.

The next door on the left was closed and locked. He passed a hand over a silver plate in the jamb. The bolt clicked back softly, and the door swung slowly open. A ceiling lamp flickered on.

You shouldn't be doing this, he told himself as he went in; you need to think, not brood.

"Shut up," he said to the empty room, and laughed aloud.

At the central nurses' station in Saddle Hills Recovery Center, a nurse glanced over the bank of monitors on her left: one for each room in the facility. But the only ones in operation were for those whose patients required constant vigilance. Only four screens were lit. All the patients were asleep. Although she was careful to check them all, her particular interest was the football player in 5. One of the handsomest men she'd ever seen in her life. It was unprofessional, she knew it, but she didn't think anyone would really care if she spent a little time watching him sleep, and daydreaming.

In 16, Ellen Proctor stirred.

The nurse watched her roll onto her side, freeze, and roll onto her back again, arms outside her covers, flat against her sides. Twenty minutes later she rolled onto her side again, and the nurse wondered, then dismissed it. People moved in their sleep all the time, and Dr. Browning only wanted her to note if something unusual happened. In this case, she figured that meant if Mrs. Proctor actually sat up, or stood up, or spoke. Something she had never done in all the time she'd been here.

In 9, an old woman moaned in her sleep.

In 11, a young girl with a huge cast on her left leg cried out in a dream, mumbled, and fell still.

In 5, the football player tossed off his covers and snored.

The nurse smiled to herself.

In 16, Ellen Proctor rolled onto her side again and clasped her hands under her chin.

Bored, the nurse thought as she returned to the nightly report. If it wasn't for that football player, she'd be bored out of her mind.

Taped on the back wall of Proctor's private office was a series of sketches he had drawn—a forbidding black castle, a rough approximation of a dragon, a line of guards standing at attention, dressed in black, no faces. A tree without leaves, its branches twisted. A winged creature without form. A plain without features, a plain whose horizon was dotted with leafless trees.

He was the first to admit he could barely draw a straight line with a ruler, and didn't care that the sketches were almost childlike in their execution. He needed them. Not to remember what he saw in his dreams, that was unforgettable, but to help him figure out where the plain was.

He knew, as one knows when traveling through a dream not really a dream, that this place didn't fade when he woke up. It was a real place. He had never been there, but it was real nonetheless.

He dropped into a high-back leather chair with castors on

its lions' paw feet and pushed himself back and forth, away and toward the wall. A lot of things had happened to him on that plain, from tumbling into a chasm when an earthquake struck, to falling into a black river when he reached the edge of an unseen cliff. He had never died, though. He just found himself someplace else, still on that plain.

But he had always been alone.

In England, in the dream, he had heard the same voice he'd heard the other night.

you're not alone

No sex, no age, just a voice.

you're not alone

"Good," he said to the sketches. "So tell me the hell where I am."

No answer, and he stuck his tongue out at them, spun the chair around, and pushed over to a low row of double-steel filing cabinets bolted to the floor. At the fourth one from the door, he touched a finger to a central lock and listened to the locks of each of the six drawers open one by one. He pulled out the second from the bottom, took out a thick file, and opened it on his lap.

A picture of his mother and father on top, the one they used in the newspapers after the accident.

They were smiling, gazing lovingly at each other. He knew it had been taken on their twenty-fifth wedding anniversary, one of the last times they would be together before . . .

"Mom," he said quietly, "what's going on?"

He didn't speak to his father. He had already done that a while ago, in the middle of a snowstorm, in the middle of the backyard. His father had been dead for several years, but Proctor spoke to him anyway, never once questioning his sanity or the reality of what he was doing.

He spoke, but his father hadn't answered, just given him a slow melancholy smile before the snowflakes and the wind took him away.

He stared at the photograph for almost twenty minutes before reluctantly putting the file away, and coasting himself to the other side of the room to a long desk with trestle legs. No computers or typewriters here. Everything he wrote, he wrote by hand. Another folder lay in the center of the deep-grain wood, and he flipped it open, flipped over a few pages until he found what he wanted: a list of events.

It wasn't very long.

An incident in Kentucky, a cult in Kansas; a ghost in England was the last notation. In the margin he had scribbled Celeste Blaine's name. Somewhere else he had printed "amber globe" with a large question mark beside it.

Then he turned another page and stared at a report Doc had given him.

Strange, he thought; very strange.

Standing by the sea, a silent figure dressed warmly, a hood, a scarf, fur-trimmed boots. The waves hiss across the wet apron of sand, curl around the boots and retreat. The voice of the ocean is loud and constant, a series of thunderous explosions that blend into a single sound much like a roar. Spray hangs in the air, a wind-cast mist. Light from the hotels doesn't quite reach this far, and the figure stands in a strip of darkness that has nothing to do with the night.

Its gloved hand moves to hold the coat closed at its throat.

It has traveled a long way to be here, and it still isn't sure it has done the right thing. If it were a believer in anything but itself, it would look for a sign, an omen, something to grant a modicum of reassurance.

The killing certainly hasn't done that.

All that's done is put the scent of fresh blood on the wind.

The figure turns toward the boardwalk, a gust pushes the hood slightly back, and for a moment before a hand drags the hood back in place, there are eyes, and rich eyebrows, a smooth brow, a gentle nose.

Below the hood, in the dark, the face of a woman.

Proctor read the report again, just in case he missed something the first two hundred times.

In Kansas, at the end of a case that had nearly killed him and Vivian, he had retrieved shards of amber he had first thought might be crystal.

He was right.

A team of researchers in Princeton, friends of Doc, had done tests. A lot of tests. They agreed that the pieces were part of a larger amber-colored globe. They agreed that the pieces were indeed a form of crystal. What they couldn't agree on was whether the globe had been hollow or solid; what they couldn't agree on was where the crystal itself had been formed.

There was, they insisted, nothing like it on this planet, and only Doc's smooth talk and fat wallet had insured their silence.

Proctor knew, however, that the silence wouldn't last. These men were scientists, and their curiosity, if they were any part human at all, would soon have them asking questions again, making demands, making threats—tell us or we'll tell the world.

Proctor sighed and closed the folder, leaned back, and stretched his arms over his head, pushing until he felt his shoulders ready to pop.

He tried to think, tried to speculate, and gave up in a few minutes. Lana and the others were right—his mind was indeed that definition of confusion: he jumped on his horse and rode off in all directions.

A yawn, another stretch.

Damn, he hated it when they were right, but it was clear that a weekend in Atlantic City might be exactly what he needed. Diversion; simple diversion.

He grinned as he rose.

And a little Jack the Ripper thrown in for good measure.

What the hell else could a man ask for?

TEN

19 February

Proctor sat on the mermaid bench, his back deliberately to the casino doors. It wasn't an attempt to keep temptation at bay; he wasn't tempted. Not yet. What he wanted was a little peace without having to go to his room. The bars were no good because two were on the casino's periphery, up on the Gallery, and the others played music loud enough to wake the newly dead; he, Taz, and Doc had already eaten, so the restaurants and snack bar were out; and the shops were already closed, so wandering the aisles was no longer an option.

He couldn't go outside because the storm had arrived.

But the lobby, of all places, had proven surprisingly peaceful. The indirect lighting had been dialed down enough to leave its upper reaches in comfortable twilight. Nothing glared off the marble and tiles. The fountain's trickling water was oddly soothing, just arrhythmic enough not to be monotonous. The few guests who wanted something at the front desk kept their voices low. There were no children running around, and no taped music to insult his memory of some fine old tunes.

The voice of the casino itself was muted. With small effort he could still hear the clatter of quarters into their trays, the electronic bells and whistles and snippets of sprightly melodies, the explosions of horns and fanfares and gongs when a winner was pronounced . . . and with equal small effort he could tune it all out. Shift it from irritation to bearable background noise.

The boardwalk, for now, was out of the question.

The storm had hit shortly after they'd arrived, gusty winds became a sustained gale force, and silver pellets of rain cracked against the walls and windows, reaching under the rippling awning to the doors.

There were printed notices in their rooms assuring all guests that in the unlikely event of a power failure, the Lighthouse had multiple backup systems that would insure all necessary operations would continue without interruption.

"Right," Taz had said from the doorway of Proctor's room. "What do you bet the first thing back will be the slots."

Doc had shaken his head slowly. "Such cynicism in the young. I'm hungry. May we eat?"

And in the restaurant on the Gallery level, Proctor was more than a little amused as Taz turned on the charm and soon had the hostess and waitresses practically licking his palms. It was from them that Proctor had learned of the early morning murder, the second Lighthouse victim in the Ripper's string, four if you counted the near misses.

Once the meals were served, Proctor noticed the others looking at him strangely. "What?" he demanded. "Hey, this isn't my fault. The storm, this killer—don't you dare try to blame it on me."

"We're not," Doc said blandly. "We just don't want you to get involved."

He had said nothing more while they ate, and passed on a preliminary excursion to the tables. Instead, he strolled the North and South promenades, hands in his pockets, looking around. Just looking around. Once in the lobby, he settled on the padded bench and watched the storm, the hotel's lights barely reaching the steel railing only sixty feet away.

Perfect weather for a killer, if the killer was determined.

I wonder, he thought, and slowly turned his head toward the front desk; I wonder.

Doc sat at a blackjack table, his chips in precise formation in front of him, one hand in his lap at all times, the other moving only to instruct the dealer. Taz had watched as long as he could, but this wasn't action as far as he was concerned.

Doc won a little, lost a little, never said a word. Neither did anyone else at the table, or any of the tables nearby.

This was way too quiet.

He wanted in on the kind of reactions he heard from those playing craps, from a group settled in at a roulette wheel, or even the nerve-jangling slot machine clatter that floated over the entire floor.

"Later," he said at last, and Doc barely nodded, guiding the dealer to complete his twenty-one.

Restless, he wandered, thinking to place a bet here and changing his mind, place a bet there and changing his mind again. He checked out the waitresses in their low-cut nautical outfits, got a wink from a croupier and a warning glare from her pit boss, passed by the east doors and, squinting through the elaborately etched designs, saw Proctor at the fountain. He almost went out, but the boss's attitude didn't seem to invite company.

"Watch him," Lana had instructed him and Doc before they left. "Make sure he has a good time. I don't care how you do it, just keep his mind from . . . you know."

Great, he thought as he headed for the rear of the hotel; if I push too hard, the boss'll kill me; if I don't push hard enough, Lana'll kill me. If I don't do anything, Doc'll kill me. By the time he finished running through everyone at Black Oak, and included his parents just for the heck of it, he decided there was no way he was ever going to leave Atlantic City alive.

That made him grin as he approached the bellhops standing at the west entrance. Outside, the streets were barely visible. Sideways rain twisted into short-lived braids, rose like mist from the gutters, drifted in thin patches of cloud from one hazy streetlamp to another. Telephone poles seemed to shudder and quiver. Water occasionally slipped in past the doors' rubber seals. The drive curved under a lifeboat-shaped portico, but the overhang might as well not have been there, for all the protection it provided.

"Lousy," he said with a shake of his head.

A car sped past, sheets of water arcing from its wheels.

The bellmen looked at him, saw a guy about their age, and

nodded. "First time I ain't praying for customers," one of them said. "I go out there, I'm gonna drown."

Taz shrugged with an eyebrow. "I don't know. If it's a limo, the tip might be worth it, huh?" It took him a second to notice their expressions. "What? I'm sorry, I say something wrong?" Then he remembered, and winced. "Damn, sorry. I just got here, just heard."

"No sweat," the other one said, PATRICK on his bronze name badge. "It ain't like it was Bruno got zapped, you know?"

Taz didn't say anything. Although he couldn't help wondering who the hell named a kid Bruno anymore?

"Should have, though," said the first one, name tag SAL-VATORE. "He's frigging nuts now, no use to anyone. Baron's gonna fire his ass, I'll bet, soon as he can."

Taz didn't get it. According to the reports, the assigned chauffeur hadn't been located, and there was speculation he had become another victim. So he couldn't help it: "Wait a minute, he's alive?"

Neither man answered. The one called Patrick rubbed an arm as if chilled; the other took out a handkerchief and blew his nose. Taz almost dropped the subject, figured he'd hear about it on the news later, but there was something about the way they almost spoke, didn't, fussed awkwardly in place that made him change his mind.

Listen long enough, Proctor had told him, and sooner or later you'll hear what they want to tell you, whether they want to tell you or not.

Like a pebble; drop a question like a pebble in a pond.

"Wow," he said, watching the rain, hands in his pockets, just hanging out, one of the guys. "Lucky guy. Glad he's not dead."

A patrol car drove by, blurred in the rain.

"Yeah," said Patrick, not sounding as if he agreed.

Taz scratched the side of his neck, pulled at an earlobe. "So, you know, how could he be fired? I mean, the paper I saw said the guy must have been overpowered. Like, ambushed. That's a crime down here?"

The two bellmen looked at each other, each waiting for the

other to make a decision. Then Patrick looked at Taz and said, "You don't know nothing, right?"

Taz held up his hands. "Me? Hey."

Patrick lowered his voice, keeping an eye out for the bell captain. "Fourth floor," he said. "Baron's got a couple rooms up there he lets us have, if we can't get home or pull extra shifts. He's stashing Bruno up there for the cops. They were gonna put him in a hospital or something, but he only showed up couple of hours ago. The roads ain't so good, so they're keeping him here, away from the news guys."

He might have said more, but Salvatore muttered, "Aw, hell," as a pair of automobiles pulled up to the curb. They shrugged an apology at Taz and grabbed for their rain gear. He wished them luck and walked away, into the casino.

Well, well, Tazaretti, he thought; what have we learned here?

He wasn't sure, and right now he didn't care. A bosomy, long-legged redhead in a seaman's costume cut down to breathtaking, smiled and asked him if he wanted a drink.

"Dacey," she said before he answered. "What's yours?"

Doc studied his cards thoughtfully. He supposed that anyone watching would probably think he was bored, that he didn't care about winning one way or another. They would only be half right.

He passed a palm over his cards, and the dealer moved on to the other players. When the hand was done, he had lost; when he cashed in his chips, he was up three hundred dollars. He had indeed been bored; but he cared very much about winning. It was, for him, almost a matter of pride.

He dropped a ten-dollar chip on the table for the dealer's tip, and rose. Stretched without seeming to move, and scanned the huge room for a sign of Paul or Proctor. When he saw neither, he decided to stretch his legs and strode purposefully toward the lobby, checking the other tables as he went, then weaving through the deliberately uneven placement of the slot machine aisles. A step up to the doors, and he spotted Proctor at the front desk, telephone in one hand.

Damn, he thought, and pushed through; if he's talking to who I think he is, Lana is going to be very displeased.

Long before he reached the counter, Proctor held up a wait a minute hand without turning around, and Doc slowed. He wasn't surprised that Proctor knew he was here; nothing the man did surprised him anymore.

Proctor replaced the receiver, folded a piece of paper he'd been taking notes on, nodded thanks to the desk clerk, and turned with a sheepish grin. "Just talking to a friend, Doc."

"Lieutenant MacEdan, I suspect."

Proctor started for the fountain. "Temptation is a terrible thing, Doc. And I am weak."

He didn't smile, although his lips twitched. "As Paul might say . . . bullshit."

Proctor laughed and dropped onto the bench, leaned back with a sigh, crossed his legs at the ankles, and spread his arms along the back. "Interesting case, though."

"Busman's holiday is not what Lana sent us down here for."

Proctor gave him a look. "Doc, I am not going to do anything. I was just curious, that's all." He nodded toward the boardwalk, raindrops like hail. "Hell of a storm."

"Indeed."

"You win?"

"A little."

"Taz?"

"The last I saw, Paul was . . . I don't know the word. Walking around with intent."

"Cruising, Doc," Proctor told him. "Taz is cruising. Trolling. On the hunt, the make—"

"Yes, all right," he said stiffly. "I get the idea."

"Successful?"

"I wouldn't know. I haven't seen him for about an hour."

"Maybe that's my answer."

They watched the rain, watched a poor soul struggling past the hotel with an inside-out umbrella, watched a little man from housekeeping haul a wheeled bucket across the marble and mop up the water that had seeped in under the doors.

Proctor leaned forward and rested his elbows on his knees.

Doc braced himself.

Proctor turned his head, patted his neck. "The throat, Doc. Very interesting. The Ripper tears out their throats."

She watched him from the farthest casino door on the right. The other one was hidden by the mermaid, but him . . . the one with the dark sandy hair and the kind of deep-set eyes that missed nothing, not even inside you . . . *him* . . . she couldn't understand what he said to the bald man with the hooked nose, but whatever it was, the bald man didn't like it . . . *him* . . . she glanced over her shoulder to the casino floor, saw a middle-age man staring at her, and she knew what he wanted. She caught his eye so he would know, and deliberately turned away so he would also know he would be dreaming alone tonight . . . *but him* . . . the one who seemed uncomfortable in slacks and that sport jacket . . . talking with his hands . . . brushing fingertips across his throat, miming not a slashing but a ripping . . .

This was dangerous.

She shouldn't have come back.

She shouldn't have tried to speak to that desk clerk, the one with the fur coat her salary couldn't possibly have bought. The timing was wrong, and she had been . . . anxious . . . too anxious . . . and the poor thing had run as if she'd seen a ghost.

The woman smiled to herself.

Well, of course she had. In a manner of speaking.

She stepped back quickly when *he* glanced idly in her direction, felt something soft give under her heel, heard a grunt, and turned to see the other one, the third one, the one with the long wavy black hair, hop backward off the step with a pained look on his young face.

"Oh, dear," she said, her voice low and husky. "Oh, dear, I'm so sorry."

"That's all right," he said, grinning now, making a game of limping around in a circle, grabbing a slot machine for support. "I think it'll stay on."

"I really am sorry."

"No problem. My fault." He pointed at her feet, and she

looked down, realizing suddenly how close to the edge of the step she had been. "Thought you were going to fall off, see?"

"And you were going to catch me?"

He blushed.

She had to hold back a laugh; the boy actually blushed.

He stammered, flapped his arms, and gave up with a shrug. "No, I was going to tell you, that's all."

"Ah."

Now he seemed distressed. "No, really, I was." He mimed tapping her on the shoulder. "Really."

When she nodded, he sighed loudly and held out his hand. "Paul," he said. "Paul Tazaretti, but they call me Taz."

She shook his hand, felt the veins there, felt the blood. "Nice to meet you, Mr. Tazaretti. I am Petra."

He smiled. He nodded. He spotted something behind her and said, "Look, I'm . . ." He stepped up beside her, moving toward the lobby. "My boss. I . . . sorry about scaring you. I'm . . . maybe I'll see you later?"

The hope in his voice brought him a smile. "Perhaps."

"Sure. Okay. Well . . . maybe later."

And he was gone, doing his best to watch her and at the same time not crash into the fountain. When the others became aware of the fuss, they turned, and she moved swiftly to one side, out of their sight.

This was a complication she hadn't envisioned. Known to one and needing to know the other . . . why not just hang a sign around your neck, Petra? Why not hand out calling cards? Why not shout it so everyone can hear?

Her confusion, and anger at herself, propelled her along the left side of the casino, through the slot machine aisles, past a high, pulpit-like security stand. Several times she sensed someone, a man, weighing his chances, but her speed and bearing stopped them in time. She slowed only when she reached the outer curve of a low dark-plank wall broken in several places for customers to enter a small bar. Then she looked back and was pleased that none of the three were there, looking for her.

She didn't want the three.

She only wanted *him,* and she wanted him alone.

Later, then; it would have to be later. Which was all right tonight. She had patience, and the storm.

Then someone came up behind her, and her eyes widened, a hand snapped to her throat. She turned sharply to face a waitress, whose smile turned puzzled.

"Would you care for something to drink?" the waitress asked, uncertain.

Quickly Petra shook her head. "No. No, thank you."

"Maybe later," and the woman walked away.

Petra watched her, her nostrils flaring slightly, catching the distinctive scent the waitress left behind.

Oh, my God, she thought; oh, my God, the Ripper.

ELEVEN

"I think I speak for both of us," Doc said as he adjusted his cuffs, "when I say that I don't really care if he tears out their hearts and stuffs them in a snuffbox. It is not our concern." He adjusted the knot of his club tie. "It is not the province of our usual cases, and," he added, "it is clearly not one of *your* usual cases."

They sat in the Briny, a North Gallery lounge, part of which projected outward like a balcony over the casino. The lights were dim, the walls dark, all the tables of thick, solid wood topped with glass. The fourth "wall" was a carved railing designed to resemble a ship's rail of brass and mahogany. They could either look over the top or through the fretwork to see the action below.

Proctor, his back to the bar, picked up his tumbler and sipped. Said nothing. When Taz arrived in the lobby, they had discussed the rest of the evening as if he hadn't been there, then practically picked him up by the arms and carried him here.

He still wasn't sure if he was angry or not.

He stared into the tumbler, at the Southern Comfort and the ice, and sipped again. Sweet and strong and, if he wasn't careful, it would have him flat on his back in half an hour.

"Boss," Taz said, one arm resting on the rail, "I'll give you one of mine, okay?"

Proctor looked at him. "What?"

"See?" Taz said to Doc. "I told you he wasn't listening." His right hand held a dark-glass bottle of beer. "I'm talking about the two women I met tonight. Man, it was like I died and went to heaven, you know?" He grinned. "They're gorgeous."

"I wouldn't expect anything else from you," Proctor said dryly.

"There!" the young man said suddenly, and pointed. "There, see her? That's one. The redhead in the whatever you call it, the admiral's outfit."

In spite of himself, Proctor leaned forward and tried to find the woman who had Taz so excited.

"No, over here, Boss," Taz said when he realized Proctor was looking in the wrong direction. "See? By the craps table, the first one. See her now?"

"My," said Doc.

Proctor did see her then and raised his eyebrows. She certainly stood out from the crowd, and suddenly he laughed, had to put his tumbler down. Stood out from the crowd. He laughed harder and leaned back to stare at the ceiling.

"What?" Taz said. He looked to Doc for help. "What?"

Proctor waved a hand. "She . . ." He swallowed. "Stands out." And he couldn't help the eruption of laughter that nearly doubled him over. Knowing it wasn't anywhere near funny, he still felt tears begin to well. His chest began to ache; his sides began to ache. He tried to pick up his drink, and failed. He tried to apologize to the others, and couldn't get an intelligible word out.

"Oh, Lord," he said, and laughed again, this time at Taz's expression.

The younger man wanted to smile because it was his boss who had made the feeble joke; at the same time he wanted to be insulted on the woman's behalf. All without admitting that her figure did indeed make her stand out.

"He can't be drunk," Taz said to Doc.

Doc shook his head. "He's not. It may well be a simple release of tension."

Proctor nodded eagerly, hiccuped, looked down just as she slipped out of sight, and howled his laughter at the ceiling again.

"Or," Doc said, "he might believe he really is funny."

Taz nodded distantly. "I wonder where the other one is."

He scanned the patrons below, frowning, shaking his head. "You should have seen her, Doc. She had this dress on . . ." His hands tried to describe it. "It was really dark green, maybe black, and kind of shiny but it didn't have any of those sequin things on it. It wasn't tight, but it fit, you know what I mean?" He scowled, took a drink of his beer, and put his free hand sideways against the hollow of his throat. "It came up to here, so it wasn't like—"

"She stood out," Proctor said, and howled again.

Taz ignored him. "She had this . . . this thing around her neck."

"A necklace," Doc said, cupping a hand around his glass of wine. "It's called a necklace, Paul."

"No." Taz drank again. "I mean, yeah, I know what a necklace is, but this wasn't like you usually mean. It was like a gold string—a chain, it was a chain—and it had a ruby or something that hung—" His hand moved this time to the center of his chest. He squinted, concentrating on an image he had. "It wasn't really a ruby, I don't think, it was too big. The color was red, though. Like a ruby, though. Very nice. I'll bet it's really expensive."

"And this woman," Doc said. "This is the one who accidentally stepped on your foot?"

"Well." Taz leaned back, tilted his head side to side. "That's what *she* said." He waggled his eyebrows. "If you know what I mean."

"Yes, Paul," Doc told him. "I'm sorry to say that I do know what you mean."

Proctor gasped for air, his mouth wide as he forced himself to blink heavily. He had tried to follow the conversation, caught only a few words here and there, and decided it would be better if, for the time being, he concentrated on not choking to death. The laugh impulse had ended as abruptly as it had begun, and he felt like an idiot, but didn't know what to say, how to make it clear he hadn't intended anything cruel or insulting by it.

Yet he had to admit, the woman's figure—he chuckled, stifled it, chuckled again, and inhaled loudly, loudly enough to get their attention.

"Okay," he said, using a cocktail napkin to dry his cheeks and eyes. "I'm okay." He cleared his throat. He sniffed and used another napkin to blow his nose. He chuckled again, this time at himself, and shook his head. "Gentlemen, I don't know what to say."

"Then, say nothing," Doc advised, raising a hand to catch the waitress's attention.

Proctor nodded, blew out a hard breath, and took a small drink. Grimaced. It was too strong; he should have gone for something a little less potent. A whiskey sour, a Collins. Anything but straight Comfort. He pushed the glass away and propped an elbow on the table, braced jaw and chin in his hand.

"So, Taz, which one is your date for tonight?"

Taz looked at him suspiciously. "Why?"

"Why? I don't know. Just asking." He grinned. "I'm not about to try to steal your thunder, if that's what you're worried about."

"Oh, sure," Taz said. "As if you could."

When his eyes widened and his mouth fell open in reaction to his unthinking boldness, Proctor cleared his throat to kill yet another laugh and widened his own eyes, a suggestion that, yes, even someone as old as he just might still have enough left in him to give the kid a run for his money. Even if there were only ten years and spare change separating him from Taz's twenties.

"I think," Taz said to Doc, "he's feeling better."

Very good, Proctor thought; nicely done, Taz, nicely done.

But he noticed that Doc wasn't really paying attention. Just as he was about to call him on it, however, Falcon picked up his glass and stood.

"I'm sorry, gentlemen," he said, "but as the evening is still young, and I am not, I see some old friends I'd like to sit with for a while."

Proctor exchanged a what-do-you-know glance with Taz, then turned to watch Falcon glide around the tables to the far side, where two women and a grey-haired man sat. Smiling broadly at him. The man rose to shake Doc's hand, the women preened as they made room.

"Well," Taz said. "Would you look at that?"

Proctor faced forward and said nothing. There were, he realized, some things he did not want to know about the private lives of the people who worked for him. Doc, for some reason, especially.

He started, then, when Taz pushed noisily to his feet, finished his beer, and looked down at the casino. After a moment's hesitation he gestured at the gamblers and said, "Is it okay? I mean—"

"Yes, Taz," Proctor told him. "It's fine. Go ahead, have a good time."

The relief in the younger man's face was enough to make Proctor smile, a smile that broadened when the relief was abruptly overtaken by guilt. Taz gestured at the chair he'd just vacated. "I, uh, I mean, I don't have to, you know. I mean, it's okay if I wait a while, that's all right."

Proctor just looked at him and said nothing. When Taz frowned, puzzled, Proctor sighed and jerked a thumb over his shoulder, opened the hand in a small wave when Taz took the hint and, with one last attempt to ease his guilt, left the bar at a brisk walk.

Nothing, then, but the atonal casino chorus rising into the bar, someone trying to laugh quietly and failing, glasses meeting in a toast, and, from a lounge across the way, the muted music of a trio playing effortless jazz.

"So," Proctor said to his glass. "Are we having fun yet?"

She sat in the Tides, ignoring the music and the sometimes comical attempts of a drunk to sing along, and watched *him*. Because of the lighting both in the Briny and the casino proper, his white shirt glowed, but his face was in twilight. On the table in front of her was a black velvet evening bag. She covered it with her hand, feeling paper crinkle inside.

He's alone.

She could be there in less than two minutes if she hurried.

He's alone.

But she didn't move. Something about him frightened her a little, and that was unexpected. No one ever frightened her. She moved through the night under lights like this in every gambling resort in the world almost every night of the year. No one had ever frightened her, not like this.

Disgusted, she sat back, and shook her head apologetically when a waitress asked if she was ready to order. Ridiculous; this was ridiculous. All she had to do was deliver the message. That's it. Go over there, sit down, introduce herself as the friend of a mutual, now deceased, friend, and tell Proctor what she knew. Show him the note she had in the purse. He would have a few questions, most of which she wouldn't be able to answer.

Some of which she wouldn't answer.

Then she would leave, a promise kept, an obligation discharged.

She picked up the evening bag. She put a hand on the table. She watched him and wondered what there was about him that made so many people fear him. She had heard of him, of course. Almost everyone in her world had. Many dismissed him, others thought him an aberration . . . yet there were some who feared him so much that when they learned he would be where they were, they left. As fast as they could.

What was there about him?

Damnit, Petra, she thought; damnit, do it now and be done with it. You have things to do. There's the Ripper—

Yes.

"Yes," she whispered, and stood quickly, left the lounge and hurried as fast as she could without running around the Gallery perimeter.

A few words, hand it over, leave.

She told herself she had nothing to fear from him.

She told herself he was not superhuman and posed her no threat.

Then she called herself ten kinds of a fool when she stepped into the Briny and saw the empty table.

Cursing silently, she made her way across the floor, stretching her neck as if hoping to catch sight of someone down below. A hand on the rail near Proctor's table, and she looked, frowning, shaking her head. Sighing. Then standing straight and lowering her head as if in thought. The check was there. She saw his name, and the room number, and she left.

Do it now, Petra.
Do it now.

Taz leaned as casually as he could against a purple and silver five-dollar slot machine, watching the redhead make her way toward him. And she *was* moving toward him. Deliberately. She wasn't on the way to somewhere else.

"Hi," she said when she reached him. "You winning?"

"Sort of. Maybe." He laughed and ducked his head. "Nope."

"Too bad."

Do it, Tazaretti, he ordered; just do it.

"You, uh . . . are you . . ." He looked at his watch. "I mean—"

She laughed and put a quick hand on his arm. "In an hour, that okay?"

"Wow. You mean . . . I mean, sure, that's fine. Great. An hour."

She winked broadly. "Great. Meet you right here at midnight, yes?"

He nodded quickly, watched her walk away, watched those hips, those legs, and yanked himself upright when she turned a smile at him over her shoulder.

"By the way," she said. "I hope you don't mind, but there's someone I want you to meet, okay? It won't take long, I promise."

TWELVE

A figure in black stood on a balcony with his arms outspread, knowing it was a pose and not caring that it was or that there was no one to see it. What mattered was the way he felt.

And he felt *wonderful*.

The city spread itself out below him, cowering under the weight of the storm, belly-up, like a dog just asking to be beaten; the deserted beach, under constant assault from the rain, looked like tired concrete; and the ocean, angry white crests spitting foam at the shore, crawled its way toward him, punching the sand, each punch another slam of thunder.

It was perfect.

No other word for it.

It was perfect.

So unbelievably right, so amazingly filled with every cliché in the book, so utterly and deliciously gothic, he was almost disappointed he hadn't thought of it before and called the storm up himself.

With his dark coat open and his arms outstretched, it was as if he wore a cape, and the wind billowed it behind him as he raised his face to the night sky, felt the rain try to blind him and flay his skin, and he laughed in delight. Curled his hands into fists and lifted them, shook them to tempt the lightning that lashed over the rooftops.

Wonderful; it was wonderful and it was perfect.

It was nearly midnight, and he was hungry.

*   *   *

The twelfth-floor room was too large for one person.

Proctor stood at the window, its heavy dark drapes drawn aside to let in the night. Parts of the room were reflected in the pane, shimmering as the wind slammed against it.

A massive king-size bed with elaborately carved head- and footboards extended from one wall, its sheets soft, blanket thick and warm, the coverlet embroidered in blue and gold to match the wallpaper. Facing it against the opposite wall was a long couch with end tables and brass lamps, two armchairs, and a tinted-glass coffee table with brass legs and rim. A tall armoire stood beside him, with drawers below for clothing, doors above to hide the television. An alcove near the door held a half-size refrigerator and wall cabinets, a two-burner stove, and enough paraphernalia to make coffee or tea for several dozen people. A tiled serving shelf had been cut into the wall, with cabinets above and a liquor cabinet below on the bedroom side.

He figured there were probably people out there who didn't have apartments this big. He definitely didn't want to see the bill come Sunday.

The view was south, and on a clear night there would have been the long dark gap of an undeveloped site before the Showboat's profile, the Taj Mahal's multicolored Ababian Nights towers, and the others farther down. Incredibly bright lights that spilled onto the Boardwalk and out over the sand.

Tonight the lights were there, but they were dizzying to look at—sometimes sharp, sometimes blurred, fingerpaints running when the rain grew too heavy.

He didn't have to touch the glass to feel the cold, and supposed he was lucky the temperature wasn't low enough to turn it all to snow.

He glanced at his watch; not quite midnight.

A glance at the bed; he wasn't that tired.

Tore their throats right out, Granna had told him. *You want to have a look?*

He had declined with a laugh, even when she suggested, with a laugh of her own, that he might well be passing up the chance to catch a vampire.

Vampires, he told her, don't tear out whole throats. Just enough to get at the blood.

What blood? she'd answered, and eventually laughed heartily into his startled silence. The thing is, Proctor, we don't know if we have all the bodies. People go missing down here all the time. They get dumped in the ocean, dumped in the Pine Barrens. We got eight, but I'm betting the way this guy is, there's at least that many more we don't know about yet. Hell, we don't even know if he's from the city, or just comes in for the kill.

He turned around, left hand unconsciously pulling at his throat. He stared at the telephone on the table beside the couch, at its twin on the nightstand.

A woman says another woman accosts her on the boardwalk right in front of the hotel, but by the time she reaches the hotel's entrance, the other woman is gone.

A woman says a man who came up through the boardwalk in a mist nearly caught her, even though she had been running, and he was not.

The cop who found Charleen Caje said there were little bits of mist still floating around the blacktop. He had almost missed them. And the woman who had been with Charleen had claimed there was a man in the street, and fog came out of his clothes so fast they were covered by it in less than a couple of minutes.

Proctor laughed without opening his mouth, sounding almost like an old-time movie villain.

If he did this, if he sniffed around a little, maybe had another talk with Granna—off the record, of course—Lana would never let him live it down. On the other hand, he was supposed to have fun. As a producer of great times and memorable moments, the Lighthouse wasn't exactly living up to Lana's hopes. Granna, on the other hand . . .

He laughed again, and shook his head.

No; another time, maybe, but . . . no.

A last glance at the view, and he opened the armoire doors. The television was large, and he automatically reached for the remote control sitting on top.

Stopped before he picked it up.

"Now, think," he ordered the dim reflection on the screen. "You've got a theater downstairs with dancers that are only half dressed, if that. You've got a couple bars, one with a jazz trio that isn't half bad, another with a singer and piano player who are better than average. You've got slots and craps and roulette and about forty kinds of poker." His voice rose. "And you're going to watch a goddamn TV?"

Proctor, you jerk, let's face it, you're worse off than you thought.

He had to face something else—he was beginning to feel a little sorry for himself. Taz already had lines out to two women, and Doc had bumped into some old friends. Yet he, the one who was supposed to be benefiting most from this weekend, had ridden elevators up and down since leaving the Briny, reading the menus and advertisements, stopping at random floors and wandering around the long, softly lit corridors, sighing, looking out at the storm from the high and narrow end windows, half hoping one of the mock-stateroom doors would suddenly fly open and a bevy of gorgeous women would reach out and drag him inside.

"Oh, brother," he muttered, and grabbed his sport jacket from the back of an armchair, checked to be sure his electronic card key was in the breast pocket, and headed for the door. Now it was a challenge. Now it had become personal. He was not about to be beaten to good times by a straight arrow bald man in his fifties and a kid in his twenties.

Pride, he told himself; now it was a matter of pride.

He reached for the doorknob, the telephone rang, and someone knocked.

When he looked through the security peephole, all he saw was the dark blonde hair on the back of a woman's head.

Hungry.

Defiantly he put his back to the storm and returned inside. Multiple shadows of himself radiated from his feet like the spokes of the Wheel of the Damned.

Hungry.

He closed his eyes and sensed the time, curled a lip in a

snarl and decided to give it ten minutes more. If his partner didn't bring someone by then, he would hunt on his own.

When Doc realized it was ten minutes shy of midnight and Proctor hadn't yet returned, he excused himself from his friends, promised to be back as quickly as he could, and walked over to the low outer wall. He scanned the area below carefully, but saw no sign of him. Or, for that matter, any sign of Tazaretti.

He left the lounge with an apologetic wave to the others, and located a brace of house phones nearby. No one answered Proctor's phone. If Paul was in his room, he wasn't answering, either. He glanced around, then wandered over to the pair of escalators in the middle of the Gallery, one of which led to the casino floor. He hesitated before riding down, chiding himself for being such a mother hen but unable to shake the feeling that all was not right tonight. This bothered him. This kind of foreboding more properly belonged to Proctor, not him.

Good heavens, he thought; maybe it's catching.

The lights flickered, and the room went briefly silent.

He couldn't hear the storm, but he could see in some faces a subtle sort of fear, in others a forced gaiety. An overheard conversation told him Absecon, and thus Atlantic City, was cut off, that flooded roads and collapsed road surfaces had temporarily severed all ties to the rest of the state. That didn't seem like much to him. After all, it wasn't as if they were miles out at sea. Nevertheless, it clearly unsettled some and upset others.

The lights dimmed, and stayed that way for several seconds before returning to normal.

He quickened his pace, taking to the huge room's perimeter so he wouldn't miss anyone slipping away behind him. He couldn't see Paul, nor the waitress the young man had so enthusiastically described. The other woman, though . . .

He had seen her in the lounge, standing at the table, and had a definite suspicion she'd been looking for Proctor. Why he thought that, he wasn't sure, but as soon as he caught her staring at the signed bar tab, he'd known he was right.

Suddenly he smiled.

Maybe she found him anyway.

Taz paced the length of the South Promenade nervously. Several times he ducked into the men's room to be sure he still looked okay, that nothing had sprouted on his face since the last time he checked. He glanced at his watch. Twice, surreptitiously, he pinched the inside of a wrist to make sure he wasn't dreaming, that he was really about to spend who knew how long with a redhead who couldn't possibly be interested in a guy like him, and was.

He tried, he really tried to concentrate on an image of her face, to prove to someone, if not himself, that he wasn't solely interested in those incredible legs, those incredible breasts, those incredible full lips.

He took a deep breath to calm himself.

He took another and started walking again.

Soon.

Ten minutes, maybe less, and since he didn't want to appear too eager, he tried to time his arrival at the Employees Only door in the back corner to just after she stepped through. It had occurred to him only once that she might be putting him on, and he'd dismissed the notion instantly.

She was real, she really wanted to get him alone, and he would do everything he could to make sure she got exactly what she wanted.

What a night, he thought; oh, boy, what a night.

The phone stopped ringing, and Proctor opened the door, and wondered if he looked as stupid as he felt.

She was beautiful, but there was nothing classic about her, nothing ordinary.

"Mr. Proctor?" she said, a faint accent there in the low and husky voice. "Mr. Ethan Proctor?"

She came up to his chin, her hair thick and rolling to just above her shoulders. Her eyebrows were dark, her eyes dark brown with a hint of another color, her face perhaps a little wide for some tastes, her nose perhaps a little sharp for others'. The dress was an expensive one, just as Taz had described it—a scattering of metallic threads in the dark green cloth winking even in the hall's subdued lighting. Taz was right about the pendant, too; red, but not a ruby, in a setting of what looked like serrated dark silver, and he realized he'd been staring at it when she repeated his name.

"I'm sorry," he said. A quick smile, one-sided. "Yes, I'm Proctor."

She clutched an evening bag to her stomach. "I have something for you, Mr. Proctor."

He didn't get it. "I'm sorry, but I don't know you, do I?"

"No." She held out a hand. "Haslic, Mr. Proctor. Petra Haslic."

"And . . . what is it you have for me, Miss Haslic?"

"Well, for one thing," she said, "I think I can tell you who killed Shake Waldman."

THIRTEEN

The man began to pace.

He didn't like being made to wait. Obedience to his command had to be certain, had to be exact. He should have known his partner would be difficult. For all her appearance, she was a very strong woman. She would have to be, to do what she's done for so long with only a few complaints, only a few rebellious moments with a conscience she very quickly managed to strangle.

Yet he was reasonably sure this tardiness was not an act of defiance. She was too smart for that. She understood the consequences.

So what kept her?

Why must he wait?

Didn't she understand?

He was *hungry*.

Doc left the gaming floor by the back exit, and found himself watching the storm through the tall glass doors that opened onto the hotel's Pacific Avenue drive. No one waited at the bell captain's stand, there were no bellmen that he could see. Under the lifeboat a blue-and-white van waited, exhaust torn from behind it and blown into the rain.

He winced at the sound here, sound that hadn't been able to override the casino's noise—high whistles and higher keening, and under it all a throbbing subterranean rumbling.

He frowned.

The storm had grown worse.

The lights dimmed for a second, just long enough for him to know he hadn't imagined it.

From the casino, high-pitched laughter, decidedly nervous.

He was tempted to open one of the doors a little, to hear the storm's full throat, but voices to his left distracted him. He saw Paul and the redheaded waitress coming toward him arm in arm. She wore a light sweater caped over her shoulders, one almost as red as her hair.

"Hey, Doc," he said, grinning broadly. The grin wavered. "You . . . are you looking for me?"

Falcon paid no direct attention to the waitress's face, although he thought he could see something there, a ghost of anger. "As a matter of fact, yes. I am."

Taz laughed and hugged the woman's arm closer to his side. "Well, sorry, Doc, but I'm off duty, remember?"

The woman laughed shrilly. "Yeah, off duty. Come on, Taz, I haven't got all night, you know." She rested her hand briefly against his shoulder. "And I'm getting chilly here, you know?"

Taz seemed uncertain now, his smile more strained, as he tried to read Doc's expression.

The woman tugged on his arm petulantly. "Come on, huh?" Still holding on, she leaned toward the North Promenade. "Look, he's waiting, okay?"

"Hang on a minute, Dacey," Taz said. "Give me a second here."

"What? This guy's your father or something?" She leaned up and kissed him soundly on the cheek, pressed into his arm. "Come on, hon, let's go."

Taz's cheeks flushed, and his smile became a grin as he finally allowed her to lead him away. "Sorry, Doc," he said. "You know how it is. See you later."

Doc said nothing, didn't try to detain him. He had neither the desire nor the inclination to interfere in the young man's love life, but he didn't think it wise, given Proctor's current mood, that either of them be out of touch for very long. Yet he could think of no good reason that would convince Paul to stay. He could only watch as they turned the corner, undoubtedly heading for the elevators.

That feeling again, the Proctor feeling.

He frowned, told himself not to be foolish.

Yet the temptation to follow the couple was strong. So strong that he required very little debate to overcome his reluctance. He slipped a hand into his pocket and ducked into the casino, hurried diagonally across to the North Promenade exits, reaching them just in time to see Paul and the woman swerve into the elevator alcove nearest the lobby. He waited several seconds to be sure they wouldn't reappear, then walked as quickly as he could without breaking into a run, taking the corner with mentally crossed fingers, and smiled when he saw that only one elevator was in motion. With a nod to the security guard, he watched the numbers above the door light up until, to his surprise, they stopped at the top floor.

Which, as he understood it, was usually reserved for the biggest spenders, or guests who have more money than sense. So who would that woman know up there?

"Sir?"

He turned his head.

"May I help you, sir?"

Doc took his hand out of his pocket, examined the bills he had folded into a money clip. "No," he said. "Thank you, but I think I'll try again."

"Good luck," the guard said as he walked away.

Doc nodded without looking back, and once on the Promenade, wondered what, if anything, he should do now.

The simple fact was, the man the papers called the Ripper didn't need anyone to find him prey. He could do that well enough on his own, and had been doing so for more years than he cared to remember.

This way, however, was more enjoyable.

It enabled him to test the limits of the procurers he chose, to see how far he could push them before their greed was finally overwhelmed by either their humanity or their horror. More often than not, they lasted quite a while . . . as long as they didn't see the fruit of their labor.

So far, Dacey was only one of a handful to continue after seeing what was left of his victims.

That, in fact, surprised him.

And pleased him.

As far as he was concerned, that made her almost as much a monster as he was. It made more tempting her tentative request to become one such as he. More tempting because, he hated admitting, he had grown a little lonely for a permanent companion.

He laughed to himself, bowed low to the city that had spawned her, and lifted his face. Tested the air for scent and spoor.

And laughed again.

Once the initial glow of excitement faded, Taz began to wonder what he should do now.

He glanced up and down the long corridor, which to him pronounced wealth and privilege in its generously thick carpeting, its subdued wallpaper and walnut wainscoting, and the gleaming sconces that held candle-shaped bulbs quietly burning at what Doc would probably call a restful level; not to mention the waist-high brick walls topped with planters that separated each section to give those rooms their own semi-private elevators, the gilt-edged mirrors between each gold-and-white door, and the Chippendale-styled sideboards in each section, which held multipurpose telephones, writing pads and utensils, and a gold crystal vase holding fresh flowers.

What didn't fit was the slight tremor he felt each time the wind slammed into the hotel.

"Hey," Dacey whispered loudly.

He raised an unenthusiastic hand to acknowledge her, but didn't move.

She stood to his right, at corridor's end, at the brushed steel door of a small private elevator that, she'd explained, used to go all the way down to the ground floor, but now only moved between here and the closed restaurant and observation balcony four stories above. She had scanned a copy of the key required to work it.

She stood sideways now and beckoned, her eyes slightly closed, hair falling over half her face as her smile promised much more than she'd given him during the ride up.

There was no sound here, and that unsettled him. He thought

he should at least hear something of the storm, however muffled, however distant, but there was nothing but Dacey's increasingly impatient voice reminding him that she only had so much time on her break, and if he didn't hurry it up, he was going to miss out on something really special.

Mistake, man, he warned himself when he finally got off the mark and walked slowly toward her; this is too good to be true, it's gotta be a mistake.

"Where is he?" he asked, not understanding why, suddenly, he was whispering, too.

"Up," she told him, pointing at the ceiling.

"But I thought . . ." He stopped, raised a palm. "Hey, wait a minute, this isn't one of those . . . you know, those . . ."

She giggled. "Jesus, you think he's a voyeur? He's gonna watch?" She laughed, reached out, and grabbed his hand. "Don't be silly." Tugged him closer. "Just you and me, Taz." Placed the hand on the rise of her chest and pressed it into her. Lowered her voice. "Just you and me."

She leaned into him as her free hand slipped the key into its star-shaped slot and turned it.

She kissed his chin.

The doors whispered open, onto a wine-and-brass car.

Now he did hear the storm and, when he allowed himself to be pulled in, something else.

Quickly he snapped out a hand to keep the doors from closing, and tilted his head. Listening.

"Taz," she complained, and tried to slap his arm down. "Come on, huh? This isn't funny, okay?"

He listened, and heard it again. Just under the roar of the wind, just under the keening—someone laughing. A full-throated, deep laugh that stirred the hair on the back of his neck. Hastily he stepped out and backed away. He had no idea who this guy was or why Dacey wanted him to meet him, but he wasn't going to do it. It didn't feel right, and Proctor had told him a hundred thousand times that feeling something like this was worth paying attention to. He needed a lot more information before he'd go back into that elevator.

"Taz!"

"Sorry," he said. "I don't care who he is, I'm not going." He glanced at his watch. "Come on, Dacey, let's go down to my room, okay? There's no—"

She yanked down her top, cupped her hands under her breasts. "You're telling me you're giving up these because you don't want to meet my friend?"

He swallowed, only barely able to concentrate on her face. "No," he said, hating the way he sounded—not strong at all, but tentative. Weak. "Just introduce them to me in my room. No big deal."

The doors began to slide shut.

She looked down at her breasts, looked up at him. "Are you sure?"

Jeez, Taz, are you an idiot or what?

He nodded.

The doors closed just as she swung at the wall in anger, her obscenities cut off before they barely got started.

He waited to see if she'd change her mind, to see if the doors wouldn't open—now!—and she'd come running out to tear at his clothes as he half carried her, half dragged her down to his floor.

He waited, and laughed bitterly, and as he waited for the regular elevator to come get him, he thought, *Doc, I can't figure it out, but this is your fault. I don't know how, man, but this is your fault.*

"Idiot!" he said miserably, and kicked the wall. Hard.

Proctor stared at the woman in the hall—Shake Waldman? How would someone like this know Shake?—and stepped aside to allow her room to come in.

She didn't move.

"Well?" he said.

Her smile was mockingly coy. "A lady likes to be invited."

"Then come in, Ms. Haslic, please."

And she did, brushing a finger lightly over his chest as she passed him. "Thank you."

He nodded and closed the door behind her. Watched as she moved about the large room, touching the bedspread, the backs of the chairs, before turning to face him.

"You should be careful," she said, "who you ask into your home."

Proctor would have responded with a joke then, but couldn't help noticing the woman wasn't smiling.

FOURTEEN

In the first-floor ladies' room, Dacey huddled in the last stall, her sweater pulled tightly over her bare shoulders. She was angry. She was frightened. After she'd stopped the private elevator and returned to the eighteenth floor, realized Taz was already gone, she had panicked. Took the next car all the way down and seriously considered stealing a coat from somewhere and getting the hell out.

But she couldn't.

He would find her, no matter where she went.

The only sanctuary she could think of was the ladies' room, and on the way she had run into Delmonico, who told her she'd have to share one of the fourth-floor rooms with some other women because he was sending the hotel van to the garage and the escort guards home.

"Baron don't want Salvatore driving anymore tonight. He half drowns or crashes, he'll sue our asses off. You're stuck, Logetta."

That figures, she thought; Baron's more worried about legal stuff than people getting hurt.

She stared at the stall door, wishing the cleaning staff hadn't been so diligent. Without graffiti to occupy her, all she could think of was how pissed he would be that she hadn't brought someone to him.

She punched the door lightly, lifted her head, and glared at the ceiling. She had almost had him, that Tazaretti guy. All she had to do was stick out her chest, and he was hers. She couldn't believe he'd refused her.

Now *he* was going to be mad.

Really mad.

Oh, God, she thought; oh, God, what am I going to do?

And the lights went out.

"You have no idea," Taz said miserably, standing beside Doc as the bell captain swept down the hall, grabbed a huge umbrella from behind his stand, and went outside. Instantly he was shoved to one side, and had to tack against the wind to reach the idling van. He opened the passenger door, said something to whoever was inside, and stepped back when the van pulled away almost before the door closed again.

Once back inside, he dropped the umbrella against the wall, and noticed the two men.

"Sorry, he's outta here for the night. You gentlemen aren't waiting for a ride, are you?"

Taz shook his head, unable to keep from smiling at the prayerful hope in the guy's voice.

Delmonico pressed his palms together, looked skyward, and said, "Thank you, thank you," and with a tip of his cap, swept away again.

"Only an idiot would go out on a night like this," Taz said.

Doc nodded. "Exactly."

Taz looked at him, looked away, tried not to sound sullen. "He's going to be all right, you know. It's not like we have to baby-sit him."

"No. That's true, Paul, that's very true."

"Yeah, well . . ." He sidestepped into the casino, pulled two five-dollar chips from his pocket, bounced them in his hand, and put them back as he returned to Doc's side. "I don't see him, and I don't feel like going in. If Dacey's in there, she'll pour drinks all over me."

Doc checked his watch. "My friends," he said thoughtfully.

Taz checked his. "There's a show in an hour. Maybe I could see that?"

"Whatever you wish, Paul."

"What I wish, you screwed up, Doc, thanks a lot. I don't know how you did it, but thanks a whole lot."

Doc smiled briefly. "You're welcome."

"What about the boss?"

"Oh, I think Proctor might well be occupied."

Taz couldn't believe it. "He is? You think?"

Doc shrugged.

"You know who?"

"I might."

Taz shuddered at a draft that slipped up his pants legs. "Come on, Doc, who?"

Doc checked his watch again. "I am pretty sure a woman who came into the lounge earlier was looking for him." He turned his head slowly. "I also believe it was the lady who stepped on your foot."

"What?" Taz realized he had shouted, and lowered his voice to a disbelieving stage whisper. "Petra? He's with Petra?"

"I didn't say that, Paul. I merely said it's possible."

"Oh, great. Now, that's just great. Two gorgeous ladies in one night, and I get aced out of both of them." His expression turned sour. "That's just great."

"You're young," Falcon said as he walked into the casino, heading for the escalators. "You'll get over it."

"Sure I will," Taz answered, knowing Doc couldn't hear him. "Oh, yeah, sure I will."

With hands stuffed in his pockets, he watched the storm for a few minutes, shivering even though he couldn't feel the cold.

There were moments when the rain seemed to stop, and the night became astonishingly clear; there were moments when the rain seemed to mix with streaks of fog; and he wasn't at all surprised when, as he finally decided he might as well catch that show, all the lights went out.

Murray Cobb groaned when the television and lamps snapped off, leaving him in complete darkness until his vision adjusted to the watery glow that came through his eleventh-floor window. That much was a relief—the whole city hadn't gone out, thank God. And just his luck that he decides to stay at the Lighthouse, being cheaper than a lot of other places he could mention down here, and which is the one that loses power. He sighed, wriggled his toes, and pushed out of the chair, a groan this time for the aches in his knees.

He stretched, considered chucking the night and going to bed, considered how perfect a night like this was for a monster like the one crawling around out there, and instead padded in stocking feet to the kitchenette, where he pulled a bottle of beer from the refrigerator. It was only his third of the night, third since seven o'clock, but he still felt a little guilty as he twisted off the cap. Maybe he shouldn't drink it. Maybe his mind needed to be sharp tonight. Maybe that nice lieutenant will need his help. Maybe, he thought, nobody gives a damn.

Reno Baron, for just the first second after the lights went out, lifted his arm to throw the champagne bottle against the wall. Was anything else going to go wrong today? Immediately, he pulled his arm down and looked for some wood to knock on, found it at his office door, and rapped it three times with a knuckle. No need tempting the Fates, not today. As he fumbled for the doorknob, he could hear the night clerks cursing, and when he opened the door, he also heard the dreadful silence in the casino, the moans and groans and nervous laughter of his guests.

"Where the hell are the candles?" one of the clerks asked.

Reno leaned against the jamb, noting how spooky the lobby looked with only the faint glow from a boardwalk streetlamp. "Fifteen seconds, the backup will be on," he said, and grinned when the clerks jumped. "Sorry." He wasn't. It was the best thing that had happened to him all day.

First, the storm—larger and slower moving than forecast; then trouble in housekeeping as the maids refused to work on the fourth floor because of Bruno, who seemed to have no end of energy when it came to weeping loudly, screaming once in a while, moaning like a banshee, and swinging back to weeping again; then a counter had been caught at one of the blackjack tables; and that damn Lieutenant MacEdan had called twice, to see if the Acmarov woman remembered anything sensible about her encounter, to which Baron could only say, honestly, that he didn't know, that he wasn't a cop, and that maybe the lieutenant should come to the hotel if she wanted more answers.

"It's been more than fifteen seconds," one of the clerks said nervously.

Tell me about it, he thought; then shoot me.

The garage was only a block away, but it felt like ten as Sal fought the wind and rain heading back to the hotel. His slicker was a waste, his shoes were heavy, and he could barely see, so he walked with his head down, staring at the pitted sidewalk.

And he was cold.

There wasn't a part of him that didn't feel like it had turned to ice.

Patrick, he figured, was laughing his ass off, nice and dry in his apartment. Laughing because Sal had foolishly volunteered to drive the van this week, take staff to homes too far to walk to, just to earn a few stupid extra bucks. Now he was drenched to the skin, definitely in line for a hell of a cold if not outright pneumonia, and because he lived down in Margate and his car was up on blocks, he'd have to use one of those stupid fourth-floor rooms again.

He hated those rooms.

Too crowded, too smelly, no way in hell he'd ever get laid, and Delmonico forever dragging him out for one thing or another. While Patrick sat home, laughing his ass off.

He blinked rain from his eyes, hunched his shoulders against the wind, and cursed halfheartedly when a gust nearly toppled him off the curb. A patrol car sped past, and he was caught by the wave it threw over the pavement. Not, he thought as he trod dismally on, that he was any wetter than before. That was impossible. Hell, this whole goddamn night was impossible. Just his luck it'd all turn to snow and he'd freeze to death before he got back.

A glance up to get his bearings, and he sighed when he realized he was across the street from the Lighthouse. He didn't bother to check for traffic; he moved as quickly as his stiff legs would carry him, thinking about changing clothes and heading for the nearest bar.

Halfway across, all the lights went out, those that rimmed the overhang, and inside as well. No windows lit up. The place so abruptly dark he couldn't even see the gulls on the obelisks.

Despite the wind and rain, he stopped.

Out here there was still some light; in there was nothing.

Sal, he thought, I know what you're thinking, but you gotta go in before Delmonico fries your ass.

But he didn't want to.

He did not want to go in there.

The lights went out.

And Petra Haslic said, "Don't move."

FIFTEEN

The Ripper howled and raged as the scent of fresh prey faded. He snarled at the storm, daring it to break in and challenge his power; he whirled and put a fist through the wall that encased the elevator shaft; he whirled again and picked up a heavy chair he hurled across the room, following it with long strides to pick it up again and fling it one-handed in the opposite direction.

How dare she!

Again, and once again, moving in time to the lightning strikes over the sea, he threw the chair and chased after it, stopping only when there was nothing left to pick up but splinters. By then, he had reached an equilibrium between his anger and his hunger, a delicate temporary state that allowed him, for the time being, to think reasonably clearly. Dacey would have to be dealt with; that was a given. Unfortunately it would have to be later, when he was finally sated and in a much better mood.

He nodded. Yes, a lesson would have to be taught. First, however, he needed to marshal his wits in order to conduct the lesson properly. To do otherwise would mean time wasted because she'd be quite dead and no use to him at all.

First things first.

Right now he wanted . . . he needed his nourishment. Without it, all else was moot.

He stood at the elevator's burnished door and fussed with his clothes, straightening his suit jacket, his tie, brushing palms across his trousers, smoothing his lapels. He liked this suit. It wasn't a perfect fit, but he liked the way it made his shoulders seem a little wider, his waist a little more narrow. If he was able to keep it clean after tonight, he decided to find a tailor who could duplicate it. Different colors, of course. Brown really didn't suit him.

Once satisfied, and after a single pass of a hand over his hair, he touched the keyhole with a fingertip, and after a long moment felt the car begin to climb toward him.

Rage held hunger in check.

The storm couldn't reach him, and that made him smile, lightened his mood.

Perhaps, he thought, one finger brushing a stray hair away from a temple, this situation won't be so bad after all.

Perhaps, just perhaps, this was one of those so-called blessings in disguise.

Lightning turned the room a vivid white, snapping shadows into place before they vanished when the room blackened again.

Perhaps, he thought as he stepped into the car and the doors closed behind him, it was high time he stopped relying on others. Stopped playing the games that, if truth be told, really didn't amuse him anymore. Stopped blaming people like Dacey Logetta for his own foolish faults.

He faced the door, considered for a moment, and pressed a button. Felt the car shudder faintly, as if reluctant to move before it finally did.

Perhaps it was at last time for a new game. New rules.

Halfway to his destination the car juddered to a halt, the interior lights dimming until they were out. He shook his head in disgust and pressed the button again, harder this time, and amid the hollow voice of the wind in the elevator shaft, the car moved downward.

Perhaps, he thought a few seconds later, as the doors slid open and he stepped into the dark . . . perhaps it was time to stop being so insufferably solemn and just have a little fun.

SIXTEEN

Proctor's chair faced the window. When he looked down at himself it was as if he had turned grey; even his skin looked bloodless. Petra sat on the far side of the coffee table; he couldn't see her at all, save for an occasional glint of silver thread when she shifted, a pale, ghostly hint of skin, once in a while a pinpoint of light where her eyes watched him.

He leaned back and crossed his legs. He almost smiled. So far, this weekend escape wasn't turning out anything like Lana had planned. It was a lot more interesting.

"Talk to me, Miss Haslic," he said quietly. "What about Shake?"

He heard her dress shift, heard something snap, and a tightly folded piece of paper was tossed onto the table. He picked it up, but he didn't open it; it was too dark.

"I am a professional gambler, Mr. Proctor," she said, in an accent he was unable to identify, in a tone that made no apologies for her life. "Not big stakes. Enough to keep me from starving, and buy me nice things once in a while. I travel quite a lot. I come here once a year or so, and that's how I knew Shake. We were ... not friends, exactly. Colleagues." The sense of a smile. "Not competitors, colleagues. Small-timers, Mr. Proctor. As Shake used to say, we're small-timers."

"Proctor," he said. "Please call me Proctor."

"Very well. But how do you know Shake, Proctor? I've seen your friends, and with no disrespect to his memory, he doesn't seem to fit."

It wasn't the first time someone was surprised or puzzled by the company he kept and the people he knew; and, like all those other times, he offered no explanation. He met people on cases—in this instance, one he had worked on with Granna MacEdan long before she made lieutenant—and he remembered them, and they, for one reason or another, remembered him.

"A long story," was the only answer he gave her, and added quickly, "Where are you from, Miss Haslic? Your accent . . . I can't quite place it. Familiar, but I still can't . . ."

"Everywhere," she told him, and he sensed the smile again. "As I said, I travel quite a lot. In my profession."

"As a small-time gambler."

"Exactly. As a small-time gambler."

He wished he could see her face, her eyes. Except for those instances of implied humor, he could tell nothing from her voice except that he was beginning to enjoy listening to it. Even if she had ducked the question. He also had a strong feeling he should never play cards with this woman.

He held up the paper. "Miss Haslic—"

"Turnabout," she interrupted. "It's Petra. If it does not make you uncomfortable, then please . . . call me Petra."

A one-sided smile and a nod. "Sure. So, Petra, what's this?"

"The night before he was murdered, we spoke. I was leaving town. Moving on. For someone like me, it doesn't pay to be noticed, and if I stay too long in one place, like Shake and the others in our little community, I am noticed. I had no specific plans, but I was heading west. Time to leave, nothing more."

He knew what she meant, but he couldn't help thinking that she'd undoubtedly be noticed no matter what.

"We were on the boardwalk, saying our good-byes, when he gave that to me. He told me to keep it, the paper, and it had your name on it."

"Then, why didn't you call me when he was killed?"

"I was long gone by then, Proctor. I didn't know about his death until quite recently."

"Ah." He scratched behind one ear. "So this is what, a pleasant coincidence? My being here the same time you are?"

"There are such things as coincidences, Proctor, you know.

Predestination notwithstanding, it is a natural occurrence, no precedents required, or interventions of the Divine."

He nodded; but if coincidence was natural, so was suspicion.

The wind pulsed; rain slapped against the pane.

"You doubt," she said into the silence, and he was startled. She laughed, a low and husky laugh deep in her throat. "You may even suspect I have something to do with this Ripper person. Coincidence, you see."

"No," he said. "I really doubt you have anything to do with this Ripper."

"You think a woman is not capable of such things?"

His smile told her he didn't buy that one for a minute. For all the books and essays, all the theories and psychological profiling currently in vogue, he knew firsthand that some women can easily be as physically ruthless as some men. They can easily be just as monstrous.

When they kill, however they kill, their victims are just as dead.

Silver winked and cloth rustled as she got to her feet and moved to the window. Her arms hugged her stomach. Her head was slightly bowed. Seeing her, however faintly, for the first time since the lights went out, he was struck once more by her curious beauty. And, he noted in mild surprise, that she'd taken her shoes off, that she wore no stockings.

She lay a palm against the pane. "The night," she said quietly, almost covered by the wind. The palm slid downward. "I've seen many sunrises, many sunsets, but . . . but there's nothing like the night, Proctor. Nothing like a storm in the middle of the night."

"Ah," he said with a grin, "the children of the night, how sweetly they sing."

She turned her head, half her face in shadow. "You have no idea, Proctor, how true that is."

Dacey cowered in the stall, slipping to the floor, legs curled tightly beneath her. Tears coated her cheeks; she was cold, the sweater doing her no good at all; she couldn't move except

to turn her head, aiming one ear, then the other, at the sounds
she thought she heard.

Please, she prayed; please please please.

She didn't stop praying until she heard the outer door swing
open.

A soft voice, and urgent: "Bellman."

No sooner had he gotten inside than Sal had been handed
a flashlight and stationed midway along the South Promenade,
next to the men's room. It was his job to make sure none of
the guests broke a leg or got lost or became hysterical.

"Bellman."

He had no idea where that fat toad Delmonico was. Probably in one of the bars, trading stories and beers with the bartender. Patrick, of course—

"Bellman, I need your assistance."

"Sure thing, sir," he said as he turned, wincing at the feel
of wet socks in his shoes. "What seems to be the problem?"

"I believe someone has had a heart attack in the men's
room."

Well, shit, he thought; now ain't that just my luck.

"Please, come with me. I'm a doctor, it's all right, but I
need your assistance now, and your light, or we're going to
lose him."

"Right behind you, sir," Sal said. "Right behind you."

Proctor wasn't sure how it happened.

The room had grown stuffy, and a damp chill made even
the chair unpleasant to the touch. Rumblings in the hall as
guests gathered to complain about the lack of power. He half
expected someone to knock on the door and request his presence at the manager-burning in the lobby, as if Baron were
personally responsible for the outage. And assuming any of
the guests were going to tramp down fourteen flights of stairs
in the dark.

He wasn't sure how it happened, but he dropped the note
onto the coffee table and was on his feet and standing beside
her, watching grey strips of clouds twist out of the dark over
the hotels, and boardwalk, the irregular strip of sand he could

see. Her hand somehow found its way to his arm. A light touch, palm against the outside of his biceps. Not an invitation, but more intimate than anything he had felt in a long, long time.

Without her shoes the top of her head just reached his chin, and if he'd wanted to he could have lowered his head without effort and kissed her hair.

He blinked and looked away quickly.

Jesus, Proctor.

She wore no perfume, but he could smell it anyway.

Damn.

"Who?" he said, aware he was whispering when there was no need. "Who killed him?"

"It's in the note."

"Tell me anyway."

The hand slid away, not leaving his arm until it reached his elbow. Unmistakable regret.

Proctor, what the hell's going on here?

"He was in Resorts, I think, Shake was. Maybe it was Caesar's. I really don't remember. He was very tired"—a small smile—"he told me the jacks were winking at him. You must understand, Proctor, that sometimes we get a feeling. We get a hunch. We think maybe we're about to get a little more lucky than our skill usually allows. Shake sat in on a high-stakes game that night. Only a couple of hands, just enough to know that his hunch was wrong, that he was in much over his head. But—"

The lights flickered, and they started, turned toward the lamps just as they went out again.

"Ah, well," she said with a shrug, and looked back at the city.

"The people at the table," he said carefully. "Didn't they notice him? I mean, if—"

"We are invisible to most," she said, a statement of fact, no plea for sympathy. "It is how we survive. As I said, it doesn't pay for any of us to get noticed, and we make sure we don't. The right clothes, the right expressions, not winning too much, not losing too much when the games turn against us . . . to most, Proctor, we simply do not exist. In a very real sense, we're a strange kind of ghost. Shake knew this, and knew—he *hoped* they wouldn't remember him, those players at the table.

"While he played, they spoke as if he weren't there. Not very much, as I understand it, but enough to make him leave. I think, in a hurry. I think, that's why he was noticed. He left too quickly. He forgot the rules of our world, and he drew attention to himself.

"Coincidence, Proctor. These players, they were talking about you."

He stared at her, hard, but he didn't interrupt.

"Shake was not too specific to me about this, or in the note. It was written so he would have someone to share what he had learned, not as a report. I am doubting these players used the exact words, but Shake was convinced that they were planning to kill you."

"Over here, bellman. Hurry. Flash your light over here."

Taz remembered the notice card in his room, the one that claimed the hotel had a state-of-the-art backup system that would not let its guests suffer inconvenience for too long. Although he couldn't see his watch, he was pretty sure the power had been off for nearly twenty minutes. In the casino he heard complaints begin to overtake the jokes. Once, he heard a sharp voice, a commanding voice that suggested someone might have tried to help himself to a couple of extra chips.

He had stayed where he was, at the gambling floor's rear doors, figuring there was no use moving around, since there was, right now, no place to go. His room was on the tenth, the show on the Gallery level, and the dealers and pit bosses— sorry, he corrected to himself; floor managers—were concentrating on protecting the hotel's assets. From the ceiling battery-powered spotlights had been lowered to shine on each table, and he could see the staff hovering at the edges of each pale white cone. The way his luck was running, if he tried to move elsewhere he'd trip over something and break his neck.

Oh, the hell with this, he thought and made his way carefully through the casino to the escalators on the right, climbed up to the Gallery, and tried to remember which way the Sea Cruise Theater was.

When the lights flickered, he saw a large poster directly in front of him, an arrow at the bottom pointing to his right. A shrug at such luck, and he started in that direction; when the lights went out again, he took two more steps before someone collided with him, sending them both to the floor, him on the bottom.

"God *damn*," a woman's angry voice said in his ear. "Why the hell don't you look where you're going?"

"I don't see anybody," Sal said, sweeping the flashlight around the tiled floor. He scowled. He didn't have any time for this kind of crap. "What's going on here, huh? I don't see anybody."

A soft footstep.

The faint scent of cloves.

"Damnit, is this some kind of joke? Where is he?"

"I'm right behind you."

Proctor sat on the corner of the bed and stared at the floor. At the shadow-drops of rain, the stop-and-go trails of them as they slid down the window, how they simmered in the wind.

Her bare feet gliding across the carpet, the slight tremor in her voice, low and husky: "Proctor, are you all right?"

Being threatened was nothing new. He had been that, and much worse. He had seen things this woman would not believe possible, not even in nightmares within nightmares within dreams.

A gentle hand on his shoulder: "Proctor, what's wrong?"

When he looked up, she backed off a step, but quickly, her hands not sure what they should do.

"Shake died last year," he said flatly. "Last fall."

Her hands finally met in a clasp, an almost schoolmarm stance.

"You knew this all along, and you didn't try to find me."

"I was away."

"You could have come back."

"You could have been dead by then."

"You could have come back."

The lights came on. Went out.

She returned to the window, her back to him, and straight. "Shake . . . dear Shake was . . ." She shrugged.

"Unreliable," he suggested.

She nodded. "To be kind. I didn't know if I should believe him or not."

He shook his head. "You believed him, Petra."

"How do you know that?"

His smile, just a corner of his mouth, would not have made her smile in return. "I know."

She bowed her head; her arms moved to hug herself just under her breasts. "Yes," she said at last. "That I do believe."

"Then, why didn't you come back?"

She turned on him then, one hand in a fist at her waist, her face contorted with anger, and something else. "I did! Isn't that enough that I did?"

"You said it yourself—I could have been dead. If I had been, you'd be a little late, wouldn't you say?"

Silver threads flaring, winking, as she walked stiffly away from the window, back to her chair, back to the dark. "No," she said once she was settled. Her voice was calm. Confident. "No."

He didn't know what to do. This woman, this clichéd, beautiful, mysterious stranger, comes to him in the middle of the night in the middle of a terrific storm and claims that a group of unknown people are plotting to kill him, for reasons also unknown. Except that this so-called plot was overheard last October, and he's still alive four months later. There have been no assassin's bullets, knives, or hit-and-runs; no bombs, no nothing.

If these men, whoever they are, are his executioners, they're pretty damn inept.

Assuming Shake was right, that is. Assuming this woman . . . what, Proctor? Assuming what? You don't even know if she is who she says she is.

Yet Shake was murdered. Gunned down in the middle of

the city, daylight. Everyone, Lieutenant MacEdan included, believed it had been a deadly fight between gamblers. And maybe it was, but not the way anyone had it figured.

The lamps began to glow.

Slowly, like stage lights rising, they brightened, and he couldn't help watching her as the light filled in the details. Watching so hard, in fact, that it took him a second to realize she was smiling at him, just one step away from laughing aloud.

"You're taking this awfully lightly," he grumbled, pushing off the bed. He grabbed the note from the coffee table, stuffed it in his pocket, and reached for his jacket.

"You," she countered, "don't seem to be taking it seriously at all."

He watched her for a long time, long enough to force her to lower her gaze to her lap, to her hands. Then: "I'm hungry. I'm going to grab a sandwich or something before the power goes again. Would you like something?"

She looked up at him without raising her head.

He saw that smile again, barely there.

As she slipped on her shoes, a silent affirmative, he couldn't resist: "Tell me something."

"If I can."

"Who are you, Petra? No more stories about gamblers and traveling around. Who are you, really?"

SEVENTEEN

Like New Year's Eve, Proctor thought.

The elevator had been packed all the way down, all those caught in their rooms fleeing to lower ground. Forced and genuine laughter, jovial conversations between strangers, one indignant elderly couple who apparently considered themselves an official delegation to the manager to redress the wrong.

By the time they reached the Gallery, he was pinned in the corner, Petra pressed against his arm, by her expression amused at all the fuss and bother. He, on the other hand, couldn't wait to get out. Disturbed by the closeness and the dozen increasingly raucous people jammed in with him, he was also bothered by her touch, and the idea that he shouldn't be, yet was.

By the time they reached the Gallery and all but the elderly couple had hustled out, he was ready to shoot someone.

"Claustrophobic?" Petra asked as she left ahead of him, not waiting for an answer.

That smile again. Knowing, and amused.

He followed her to the open perimeter, where he was pummeled by the noise—human voices, the casino's voice, and somewhere deep in the background the constant voice of the storm. Reno Baron stood near the entrance to the Briny, assuring a quartet of well-dressed women that his men, even as they spoke, were making sure the backup generators would not fail again. Proctor touched Petra's arm, and they walked west to the end, turned the corner, and followed the chest-high wall south toward the Davy Jones, a burger and sandwich shop tucked into the far corner.

As they walked, taking their time, he glanced into the shop windows on his right, gifts and clothing and jewelry. A hair salon. A travel agent. All of them dark. At the same time he watched her reflection, frowning once when it seemed to shimmer and vanish, and he had to check to be sure she was still there.

"Like a party," she said. A wave of her left hand toward the casino floor. "They've turned it into a party."

"Until the power goes again," he answered. "Then they'll be a lynch mob."

She laughed silently. "Such optimism, Proctor." A nod then. "There—isn't that one of your friends?"

The wall to the left of the Davy Jones was covered with gold-framed posters announcing the stars and theme of the next Sea Cruise presentation. Taz stood in front of them, talking animatedly with a young woman. Her hair was black and curly, her figure slight; she wore a sweatshirt and tights, and he pegged her for a dancer.

"A nice young man," Petra said as they approached.

Proctor shrugged. "He is, most of the time. But you make yourself sound old."

"Older than I look, Proctor. Older than I look."

The way she said it, with an almost palpable melancholy, made him stare until she turned her head and stared back. Just for a second. Long enough for him to wonder, and look away.

Taz spotted them and waved them over, to the clear consternation of his companion. "Hey, Boss. Hello again, Petra. Thought we'd lost you. Guys, this is Suze. Suze Acmarov. She's in the show. Pretty neat, huh?"

Proctor nodded a polite greeting, and Petra asked her how long she'd been a dancer, stepping aside to bring the woman with her as she answered.

With a sly grin Taz said, "Nice," and poked him with an elbow. Closed his eyes briefly and said, "Sorry."

Proctor just looked at him, watched at how easily Petra befriended the girl, and wondered again. "We're grabbing a sandwich. You want in?" His tone indicated more than a polite request and Taz, after a moment's visible temptation to argue, nodded reluctantly.

"Thanks." Proctor stepped back, drawing Taz with him, and in a low voice explained what Petra had told him. "I think—"

"Work," Taz said sternly. "That's work, Proctor, and you're not supposed to, remember?"

"Taz, we're talking about some people who maybe want to kill me. I don't think Lana would mind if I thought about that for a little while, do you?"

Taz wasn't sure. "That was months ago. Even if it's true, and I kind of doubt it, they'll be long gone, don't you think?"

Proctor moved to the wall, a crooked finger summoning him to his side. "They're here every day," he said, pointing with his chin at the crowds swarming the casino floor. "Or their types."

He pointed again, this time along the Gallery and beyond the escalators, indicating a number of red velvet ropes attached by hooks to brass stanchions—the understated division between those who played below, and those who played up here, for stakes far higher than any of the others could possibly afford. From their angle neither could see into the high-roller enclaves, but if the velvet ropes didn't do the job, a man in a tuxedo in front of each was there to make sure the only people who went in were the people who could manage the ante.

"They," he explained, "are hunters, Taz. They hunt each other, and they hunt suckers with fat wallets. It doesn't make any difference how they dress, they're still hunters, and as ruthless as any predator you'll ever meet."

Taz frowned and rested his arms on the wall, looked down, looked to the velvet ropes. "Okay. So . . . what?"

"This is their hunting ground. If they were here before, they'll be here again. The easiest bet you'll ever find in this place."

"Boss—Proctor, you're paranoid."

"So? I'm still alive, aren't I?"

Slowly, painfully, Dacey struggled to her feet. Her legs wanted to cramp; her arms wanted to cramp. She'd been so still for so long, when she finally made it to her feet she was forced to grab the top of the stall wall to keep from falling. Yet she didn't leave until she heard voices on the other side, lots of voices, most of them complaining about the hotel and the power. She opened the door and stepped out; no one looked at her. A toilet flushed. A faucet ran full. She had no idea who had come in earlier, and she didn't care. She wanted people, tons of people around her, and she headed straight for her station in the Dunes, the ground floor casino bar. As she did, she glanced up and saw the kid, the one with all the hair, the one she almost had in the elevator. She wanted to scream at him, give him the finger, for doing this to her. It would have been all right if it wasn't for him. Everything would have been all right.

Now *he* was probably furious, tearing things apart as the hunger took hold, as he had done before when she hadn't come through for him. Maybe taking someone in one of the rooms, a violation of his primary rule—never foul your own nest—which would make him very angry at her indeed.

She had to make it up to him.

She didn't know how, but she would make it up to him.

If she didn't, all the money in the world wouldn't be able to save her.

Bruno Gladman sat on his bed in T-shirt and boxers, huddled against the wall, knees drawn to his chest, arms wrapped tightly around his shins. He was a large man, as large as his name implied, but not nearly as strong. Every time one of the cops assigned to guard him came in, he jumped and tried to push himself into the plaster; every time the wind slapped rain against the window, he whimpered; every time he heard someone in the hall, he closed his eyes and prayed as hard as he could.

When the lights went out, he didn't scream; he bit down so hard on his lips that he bled. When the lights returned, his shirt and legs were speckled with blood, but he didn't leave the bed to clean himself. He stayed where he was, licking his lips until the bleeding stopped.

Bruno was twenty-eight.

He had the absolute conviction he would not live to see twenty-nine.

He shuddered as he exhaled, whimpered when the rain slapped at the window, moaned when the wind moaned, and he prayed.

As hard as he could, he prayed.

There was nothing else he could do.

Not after what he had seen.

The Davy Jones was brightly lit and not very crowded; food of any kind was not high on the list of things to do after being trapped in a room or an elevator for a good half an hour, and the brightness level was so high, it discouraged lingering. Some thirty square tables, most barely large enough to seat two, were scattered around the white-tile floor, half of them pushed up against a padded bench that ran the length of the left wall and among most of the rear. On the right was the serving station—order your sandwich or burger, push your tray along a stainless-steel shelf, pick a dessert from the display, pick up your order, turn the corner, and pay at the register.

Cheap, efficient—eat quick and get out.

The walls were a reflective white, except for a colorful mural that ran around its middle—ships and mermaids and fish, swimmers and divers, all headed to the bottom, for, Proctor presumed, Davy Jones' locker.

He chose the back wall and pushed two red-topped tables together. Petra immediately sat on the bench, and Taz volunteered to get the food, after first making it clear that Proctor was not to sit on either of the chairs.

Before he walked off, Proctor grabbed his arm. "Doc," he said.

"Aw, come on, Boss—Proctor, have a heart, huh?"

Proctor looked at him.

"All right, all right, but he's not going to like it."

"He doesn't have to."

Once Taz was gone, Proctor, feeling almost childishly spiteful, took the seat opposite Petra. When their knees touched, he eased back, trying not to make his sudden discomfort appear too obvious. Behind him a group of women chattered in shotgun Spanish; chairs scraped across the floor; an old man muttered loudly to himself between slurps of soup; off to the right, one of the short-order cooks sang enthusiastically and off-key.

Proctor leaned back, the chair too small to be really comfortable, and shifted his gaze from Petra to the mural, this section depicting an underwater pirate ship manned by skeletons heading straight for a cave in which he could see two bright green slanted eyes. He looked back to Petra and thought, yes, sir, pal, you really know how to treat a lady right.

"Before the others return," she said suddenly, making him blink, forcing him to focus.

He tilted his head. Waited.

"Shake told me some very little of what you do."

"Did he now," he said without smiling.

She nodded. "It is making me wonder, then, why you are not interested in this . . . this Ripper murderer. I would think this would be something you're interested in, yes?"

The clutch of Hispanic women rose in laughter; the old man muttered more loudly; one of the servers yelled at the cook to shut the hell up.

The rabbit hole, he thought; I've fallen down the damn rabbit hole.

Her eyes widened slightly, a silent repetition of her question.

He touched his neck with two fingers. "He tears out throats. That makes him bizarre, probably sick, certainly disgusting. It doesn't make him interesting. Not to me, anyway."

"The mysterious fog?"

He looked over his shoulder. Where the hell was Taz?

Gently: "Proctor."

"Ice," he said impatiently, and instantly, and instantly regretted it. "Dry ice. A magician's trick. Simply, he wears an insulated belt or straps that have pockets of dry ice with vents he controls with strings or zippers, depending. There are chemicals, too, that produce the same effect, but the delivery's the same. He can make it look as if he's steaming, on fire, or even melting. I saw one who had some miniature fans, and I do mean miniature, so he could pretty much get the stuff to go where he wanted, for a limited time within a limited area." He lifted a hand. "Simple enough."

"Those women who were attacked, the one who survived said the street was covered with it, they could barely see where they were going when they tried to run. And that woman on the boardwalk, she said—"

"Terrified," he explained impatiently, looking over his shoulder again. "Terror can make you see, and do, very strange things." He rapped a knuckle thoughtfully on the table. "You seem to know a lot about this stuff."

"To me," she answered, "it is interesting."

The noise level increased when a group of young men in jeans and college sweatshirts spilled into the shop, going over each roll in a craps session as if they were reliving every play in a championship football game. Proctor winced at their boisterous entrance, winced again when some, still loudly, began flirting with the servers. When he returned his attention to Petra, he didn't feel much better. He couldn't figure this woman out, he couldn't figure out why Taz was taking so long, and he wondered why even perfect strangers seemed to assume he would automatically look into every oddball crime that came down the pike.

If she only knew the kind of things he really took an interest in.

"The interrogation is late."

He frowned. "What?"

"Your friends," she said mildly, gesturing toward the entrance. "They are late for the interrogation."

"They're not going to interrogate you. What gave you that idea?"

"They will want to know what I know," she answered. "You can tell them yourself, but you want at least the bald one to hear it directly from me." Her face darkened. "I think I'm not happy with that."

He reached across the table to take her hand. "Look, Petra, if I've insulted you, forgive me, I didn't mean to." Her fingers folded around his, a gentle squeeze before they relaxed.

"Honestly, I didn't mean it. But if there's someone after me—"

"Not if, Proctor," she said stiffly, freeing her hand, sliding away from the table so she could stand. "Not if."

Startled by her change in mood, he shoved his chair back so hard in order to get up before she left, that it toppled, and when he turned to reach for her arm as she passed, his feet caught in the legs and he fell sideways, grabbing the nearest table as he went and pulling it down on top of him.

The room went abruptly quiet.

He watched helplessly as she left without looking back, then swore at himself as he shoved the table away. Looked up and saw Taz and Doc standing over him.

"Smooth," Taz said sadly. "Real smooth, Boss."

Doc stretched out a hand and hauled Proctor effortlessly to his feet, his expression carefully neutral. Proctor dusted himself off, ignoring the looks from the other customers as he pushed between the two men and headed for the exit. Once on the Gallery he hesitated, not knowing which direction to go. He couldn't see her, couldn't believe she could move so fast, that she was gone already. He stepped over to the wall and looked right and down, but she wasn't on the escalator, nor was she anywhere on the floor that he could see.

Doc came up beside him. "Paul told me about these men."

He nodded absently.

"What do you want to do?"

"I want to find Petra."

"Proctor," Taz said, "I think that ship has sailed."

"I need to find her."

Doc tapped his arm. "There are more important matters at the moment."

"No, in fact there aren't." Leaning back against the wall, he ran his fingers along his jaw, pulled at his nose. "She told me she knew something about what I did. About the special cases, I mean. She said Shake told her a couple of things about them, and that's why she wanted to talk to me. Not just about the message the poor jerk gave her to give me, but about this Ripper guy."

Taz spread his hands—*so?*

"All Shake ever knew was that I'm an investigator. I never said a word to him about anything else." He checked the corridors again. "She lied to me, gentlemen, and I want to know why. I want to know how she knows so much about me."

Petra stood just inside the theater's wide entrance, trying to lose herself in what few shadows there were, hoping Proctor wouldn't come this way, wouldn't look this way if he did. She scolded herself for wearing this ridiculous dress; it caught every stray bit of light and turned her into a beacon. It was a foolish choice, chosen by a foolish heart.

She dared a peek around the corner, and saw them clustered at the wall. Proctor looked angry. No, he looked determined. She ducked back and moved deeper into the lobby, keeping against the wall, doing her best to appear as if she were waiting for someone.

But she couldn't wait much longer.

As soon as her pride-driven temper had taken her from the food place, her nostrils had widened.

The scent.

He was here.

She had fled to avoid being stopped by Proctor, and to give herself a chance to think about what to do next. Knowing that whatever it was, she wouldn't be able to do it alone. He was here, in this hotel, and all these people were going to be his victims unless . . .

Her eyes closed.

Her breathing eased.

. . . unless she got to him first.

EIGHTEEN

"Haslic," Proctor told the desk clerk. "Petra Haslic, and before you ask, no, I don't know how to spell the last name."

"I'm sorry, sir," Stu Hockman told him, making no move toward the keyboard or his terminal. "She's not a guest at the hotel."

Proctor said, "Check."

"I can assure you, sir, that—"

"Check," he said again, and nodded sharply at the keyboard. He didn't care how good this guy thought he was, he wanted to be sure. Besides, how could he trust the memory of a grown man who wore admiral's braids on his stupid desk clerk jacket? He scowled when the younger man made a mistake and had to begin his search again, realized he was scowling and took a step back, the fingers of his left hand rubbing over the ball of his thumb.

This wasn't like him; this wasn't like him at all.

Yet when someone tapped his shoulder, he turned slowly, knowing full well what his expression was like. Even if he hadn't, he could easily have guessed by the way Taz stepped back hastily and Doc stiffened.

"Do not push me on this," he told them quietly. "Do not push me."

Taz started to say something, and Doc grabbed his wrist to shut him up.

"Then what," Falcon said, "can we do to help?"

"Sir? Mr. Proctor?"

He turned back, and the clerk's eyes widened. "I . . . I've

checked, sir. Like I said, she's not registered as a guest, and I'm ... well, I'm pretty sure she's not ..." He swallowed, glanced nervously at the manager's office door, and lowered his voice. "I'm pretty sure she's not a special guest, sir. Of the manager, I mean. Unregistered, I mean."

"Thank you," Proctor said, and turned his back to him. "Find her," he told the others. "You want to help, find her."

Neither man argued. With a glance at each other, they headed immediately for the casino, entered by two different doors, and were gone.

Proctor waited for the doors to swing shut, for the noise to be muted, then slipped his hands into his pockets and wandered over to the boardwalk entrance. The rain had eased, the wind stopped completely. It was almost peaceful out there, the surf popping fragments of pale white out of the dark, water dripping from the awning's scalloped edge; almost peaceful.

someone wants you dead

Almost peaceful.

He wouldn't have been a bit surprised to see the White Rabbit racing up the boardwalk toward his appointment; that's about how much sense any of this made.

It wasn't surprising that someone wanted him dead. Over the years he had made more than a few enemies in the aftermath of the schemes he had exposed, and had been threatened with death more times than he could count. Most, however, were the sort of threats made in the first few days immediately after the bad guys had been uncovered—bluster and short-fuse anger, humiliation and impotent rage. Only a tiny percentage had ever tried to carry them out. None had ever come close to succeeding. The contacts who sent possible cases his way also granted him protection.

And he had never, as far as he knew, angered anyone who walked in the circles Shake had so inadvertently infiltrated that night.

A part of him felt the thrill of vindication—someone really *is* after me—but the rest of him couldn't figure out how a high-stakes card game in Atlantic City connected to a small town in Kansas and an even smaller one in England.

That's the part that threw him.

Pieces; he had pieces of a blind puzzle.

Not to mention a beautiful woman who knew a hell of a lot more than she was telling.

A laugh slipped out before he could stop it. Lord, he sounded like the hero in an old black-and-white movie. Richard Widmark. Robert Mitchum. Victor Mature. Walking the mean streets, slicing off bits and pieces of a conscience, intensifying rather than solving the moral ambiguities of this action and that belief.

He laughed again and shook his head, because that made no sense, either.

Face it, Proctor, you are a mess.

"Pardon me," a rasping voice said. "Pardon me, I don't mean to interrupt your thinking, but do I know you?"

At first he didn't realize he had been the one spoken to, but when the voice said, "Pardon me," again, he looked over his shoulder, than half turned to face an old man sitting on the fountain bench. He wore an old suit that didn't quite fit but looked comfortable enough, an unbuttoned vest that didn't match the suit's dark brown, and suspenders that might once have been bright red.

"No, sir," Proctor said politely. "I don't think you do."

The man waved at him. "You're right. I meet a lot of people over the years; sometimes I think I still know them years later." He forced a cough to clear his throat. "Didn't mean to bother your thinking." Another wave—go ahead, turn around, it's all right, I'm not offended."

Proctor did, with a smile, which soured when he saw that the rain had picked up, and the wind with it.

No peace out there now.

And no White Rabbit, either.

The knuckles of his left hand brushed against Waldman's note in his pocket. He started to bring it out, to match it against what Petra had told him, when the old man said, "David Proctor. Am I right? Your father. David Proctor."

Sergeant Cox yawned so widely he felt his jaw pop. Beefy hands rubbed hard over his face, and he shoved himself out of the chair he'd dragged into the hall. This was not what he'd signed on for when Lieutenant MacEdan asked him to be on the Ripper team. He was supposed to be chasing the state's premiere killer, not sitting in a hotel hallway, baby-sitting a loon. The next time he saw her, lieutenant or no lieutenant, he was going to give her a damn big piece of his mind.

He stretched, he yawned, he marched down the long hall to wake his legs back up, he returned to the loon's room, looked in, and saw him—thank you, God—sleeping on the bed. Sitting up in the corner, but the loon was sleeping.

He had just closed the door again when he heard the soft chime of an arriving elevator. He stiffened and waited, hoping it was one of the dancers, lovely flirts, every one, rolling his eyes when he saw who it was.

"You okay, Sergeant?"

"Yes, ma'am," he said. "He's okay, too."

"Think I'll have a talk with him."

Jesus, lady, he thought, don't you ever sleep?

Proctor remained by the door as he studied the old man, sifting through memories and finding none that matched.

"Cobb," the old man said, smiling broadly. His hand in the air again. "Murray Cobb. You don't remember me, you were too young—I don't know, ten, maybe eleven. About what, twenty-five years ago? A little less. Nah, you wouldn't remember."

Proctor had to admit it—he didn't.

"Long time ago. Your father, before he got that job in Jersey, he worked my precinct for a while. A couple or three, four years, maybe." Cobb smacked his lips once. "Hated it, you know. Couldn't stand the city."

Intrigued, Proctor checked the storm once more before moving over to the bench. He didn't sit; he stood in front of Cobb, trying to remember.

"Left as soon as he could," Cobb said, leaning right so he could see the boardwalk. Smacked his lips again. Ran a large-knuckled finger over his mustache. "Smart boy, though. I think he left right after he got his gold shield, am I right?" He nodded. "Yeah, right after. Said, Murray, you can have this hell-hole, I'm going back home." Finally he looked up. "So, how is he, your father? He make Chief yet? Still catching the bad guys?"

Proctor's expression didn't change. "He's dead."

Cobb's mouth opened, shut with an almost audible snap, and he shook his head. "Son of a bitch. Dead? Son of a bitch. Line of duty? I mean, dead is dead, it's a terrible thing, but it's not so terrible in the line of duty, you know?"

"No," Proctor said. "It wasn't."

Cobb slapped a thigh. "Worse. Damn. Worse. I'm sorry. Genuinely sorry. I liked your father. He was a good man. A smart man." He shook his head sadly. "Damn. Hell of a good man." He looked up again, one eye closed as if the light were too bright. "So what do they call you?"

"Proctor," he said.

Cobb shrugged. "You a cop? Keep it in the family?"

"No."

Another shrug. "Too bad. Good cops are hard to come by. Guys get in, they do the minimum without breaking a sweat, they get out with a pension keeps them from eating dog food, you know what I mean?" He leaned forward, resting his arms on his legs. "Damn shame, Proctor. He was a good man." Awkwardly he reached around to pat the bench beside him, trying to get Proctor to sit. "I lost a friend, you know. Last month. Right here in Atlantic City. Right under my feet practically. Son of a bitch killed him practically right under my feet."

Proctor frowned. "What?"

Cobb patted the bench again. "Fred. Fred Dailey. That Ripper, you heard of him? Fred was one of his first victims. Right under my feet."

Proctor sat, slowly.

"I said I thought I saw somebody lying under the boardwalk, Fred thinks I'm crazy, he goes to look, next thing I know he's dead." Cobb pulled at the loose flesh under his chin. "Tore his throat right out. Damnedest thing. I was sitting on the bench, practically right over him." He turned his head. "You know, I never heard a sound. I'm not that old I can't hear. Practically right under my feet, and I never heard a sound."

"So you're looking," Proctor said quietly. "For the Ripper, I mean."

"Hell, yeah. What kind of friend would I be, I didn't look? They don't want me to look, but I look anyway."

"Find anything?"

Cobb snorted. "They aren't talking to me. That lady—"

"Lieutenant MacEdan."

Cobb raised his eyebrows. "You know her? Personally, you know her?"

Proctor nodded.

"Nice lady, very smart." He touched the side of his nose. "Doesn't always listen, though. She doesn't always listen."

"To what?" Proctor asked carefully.

"To me, for one. Sometimes to the survivors. She has—"

"Survivors?" Proctor felt a stir in spite of himself, and a silent message asking Lana to forgive him. "What survivors?" He shifted until he was seated nearly sideways, stretched an arm along the fountain's lip. As he did, he spotted Taz leaving the casino, Doc right behind him. He beckoned, and when they arrived, introduced them to the old man.

"They work for you?" Cobb said, impressed. "What do you do, Proctor, you got people like this working for you?"

"He is an investigator," Doc answered formally. "We are his associates."

Cobb turned to Proctor. "So. You're not a cop, but you investigate? Like Sherlock Holmes, yeah? Something like that?"

Taz started to speak, but Proctor hushed him with a look. "Mr. Cobb," he said, "let's just say I don't think Sherlock Holmes would approve of my cases. Or, for that matter, my methods."

Cobb looked at him intently, gauging him, the tip of one finger scratching his cheek. Then, slowly: "I saw a woman disappear out there." He snapped his fingers. "Right on the boardwalk. I was here, she was out there." He snapped his fingers again. "She was there, she wasn't there." A look to Doc, to Taz, and he frowned when he saw the faint smile.

"You think that's funny, kid? You think this old man is going—" And he twirled a finger beside his temple.

"Mr. Cobb," Proctor said, before Taz could respond, "I think Taz is thinking about what my office manager is going to say when she finds out what I'm doing."

"Oh? And what is that?"

"Right now? Listening, Mr. Cobb. Listening."

While waiting for the bartender to fill the order, Dacey adjusted her neckline, a little tug to keep things from getting her arrested. She was feeling good. Much better.

Hey, she'd say, I can't help it the guy was gay, you know. It's not my fault. You can't blame me for this.

The perfect excuse.

Until she turned around and saw him in the entrance.

Smiling at her. Winking.

She couldn't move.

Walking up to her, a hand in his pocket, so damn casual she wanted to scream. Standing near but not beside her, surveying the handful of customers at the tables. Most of them alone.

She couldn't move.

"I don't know about you," he said quietly, "but I'm having fun."

Granna stood in the doorway, watching Bruno sleep, once in a while a limb twitching, once in a while a tic pulling at the corner of an eye. All the lights were on, including the bathroom, all the draperies closed.

Behind her Cox whispered, "Thought you were going to send a doc out to see him."

She backed into the hallway, closed the door, but not all the way. She could still Gladman through the crack. "Can't get one to come out this late, in this lousy weather." Her shoulders lifted in a sigh. "Half the force's out digging people out of accidents. A storm like this, you'd think people would stay home, for God's sake.

"Lieutenant," he said gruffly, "meaning no disrespect, but

why don't you go back home and get some sleep? He's not going anywhere."

"I know." She leaned a weary shoulder against the frame. "My husband said practically the same thing when I left the house." A wry smile. "I haven't listened to him since we got married, why should I start now?"

Gladman moaned in his sleep.

She saw Cox take a short step back. "He spook you, Tobius?"

"A little," the sergeant admitted. "He's a loon, you know? but all that stuff he keeps babbling about . . ." A shake of his head.

"I know what you mean." She tapped a finger against her chin, straightened abruptly and said, "Sergeant, what I'm about to do goes against regulations. I'm telling you this now so you can ask to be relieved."

Cox stared at her, puzzled.

"I'm going to bring in a . . . I guess you'd call him an expert."

"Aw, Jesus, Lieutenant, not that old guy."

She smiled. "No, not him. But I know he's at the hotel, the man I'm thinking of, and this just may be right up his alley." She looked at him, waiting.

Cox shrugged. "Whatever you say, Lieutenant. I ain't going anywhere."

"Good. Watch him, then. I've got a call to make."

Hockman replaced the receiver in its cradle, checked the length of the front desk, and decided that the first chance he had, he was going to complain to Baron. Greta was already ten minutes late returning from her break, and he'd be damned if he was going to do everything himself.

Like, for example, going over there to that Proctor guy to give him the cop's message. That guy was damn spooky. His eyes kind of looked right through you, and that voice . . . he shivered. He checked the telephone to be sure none of the lights were lit, then hurried around the counter's end.

Last time, he vowed; last time I do that bitch's job.

The bald one turned as he approached, but said nothing.

The kid didn't even bother; he was too busy listening to something that ex-cop was saying.

Nuts, Hockman thought; we're filled with nuts tonight.

"Mr. Proctor?"

Proctor barely turned his head.

"A message from Lieutenant MacEdan, sir. She, uh, she says she wants to see you as soon as possible."

Proctor looked at the others before saying, "All right. Where?"

"Fourth floor, sir. She said she'd be waiting in the hall for you."

Proctor nodded, said, "Thanks," and Hockman left as quickly as he could without seeming rude. Those eyes again . . . jeez. Absently he rubbed an arm as if he were cold, saw that Sanburn still wasn't back, and slapped the counter angrily. That's it; he'd had it. He rounded the corner and headed straight for Baron's door.

He raised a hand to knock, and behind him a voice said, "Excuse me."

"Jesus!" he said, spinning around, a hand clapped to his chest. "Jesus H, you scared the shit out of me."

"I'm so sorry," the man said. "Forgive me."

Hockman winced then, realizing what he'd said. "No," he said, slipping on his best professional smile. "I'm sorry for the language. You . . . you startled me, that's all. I wasn't expecting—" He shut up; he was babbling.

"I understand. The weather, the power . . . I quite understand."

Training drove Hockman behind the counter, still smiling. "And how may I help you, sir?"

The man looked embarrassed.

Hockman nodded knowingly. "Room key, right?"

"Yes, and there doesn't seem to be anyone who can help me."

One of Baron's rules was never to leave the front desk unattended. On the other hand, Greta was supposed to be here, and if Baron showed up . . . his smile became a grin. "No problem, sir. If you'll just give me your name, I think we'll have you back in your room in no time."

"I'm staying with a friend."

"Not a problem. All I need is a name, sir. Yours, and your friend's."

"Excellent. It's Valknir. My name is Emile Valknir."

NINETEEN

Proctor stepped off the elevator and, as he had been the first time, was momentarily startled by how tall Lieutenant MacEdan was—at least six feet, with sharp features and coloration that announced an Indian heritage. Less than her height, however, was her bearing that commanded attention, a straight spine and a way of looking at you from those narrow dark eyes that made you feel as if you'd somehow stumbled into the path of some ancient royalty. He also knew she could beat the crap out of just about anybody, which didn't hurt when it came to commanding respect.

"Proctor," she said, grinning, holding out her hand.

"Granna." He took the offered hand and held it. "My friends here—this is Doc Falcon, that's Paul Tazaretti—think you're corrupting me, ruining my vacation."

She smiled. "You don't take vacations, Proctor."

"That's what I keep telling them."

He nodded a greeting to the sergeant standing by someone's door, noticed this hall was more brightly lit than the others he'd wandered around earlier.

"I replaced the bulbs," she explained. "I want to see, not trip over my own feet."

From down the hall he could hear faint music, and a dealer popped out of one room, took one look at the group, and popped back in. She explained the staff use of the rooms, then began to explain about the man she wanted him to see.

"I already know," he interrupted, and couldn't help grin at her expression. "Taz here told me. He, uh, . . . hears things."

She wasn't pleased, and that widened his grin before he

said, "It's going on two, Granna, and I'm fading here. It's been a long day. What do you want me to do?"

"Talk," she said, leading up the hall. "And listen." She gestured Sergeant Cox aside. "It's weird, Proctor. But I can't shake the feeling this guy's not as nuts as we think he is."

It didn't take long for the lieutenant to convince Gladman she had someone willing to listen to his story. In fact, all he did was see Proctor in the doorway, and he agreed without any conditions except one: "Alone, okay? I want to talk to him alone."

"No problem. I'll be right outside if you need me."

Once the door was closed, Proctor tossed his jacket onto a love seat, and walked slowly around the room, turning off one of the two lamps and the bathroom light as well.

"You won't need them," was all he said.

Bruno said nothing.

Proctor pulled aside the drapes, winced as he said, "Lousy view, Bruno," and made sure the two halves overlapped in the middle. Then he dragged the room's only easy chair over to the bed, sat, and propped his feet on the edge of the mattress. Bruno, backed against the wall, knees up and gripped by his hands, looked everywhere in the room except at him. Gasping quietly once when a gust roared past the window.

Proctor, in turn, watched the chauffeur carefully. A young man, not yet thirty, about as afraid as he'd seen anyone be. He pushed a hand back through his hair. He checked the room as if making sure they were actually alone before he said, gently, "Whatever it is you saw, Bruno, you can believe me when I say that I've seen stranger."

Then he waited. Not smiling. Not staring. Watching, shifting to make himself more comfortable. A couple of guys in a hotel room, nothing more, nothing less.

Bruno inhaled slowly, deeply, and just as slowly allowed his legs to straighten, his hands to rest on the bed.

"He flew," he said, obviously expecting either derision or skepticism.

Proctor only nodded.

i've seen stranger

Bruno swallowed, swallowed again, abruptly scooted off the bed, and hurried into the bathroom. The sound of running water, and he returned with a glass, sat next to Proctor's legs.

"He flew."

Proctor nodded.

stranger

"I'm not crazy."

"Sure you are," and Proctor gave him a lopsided smile. "Me, too."

Bruno glared for a second, then shrugged, lips tugging into a reluctant smile of their own. "Yeah, maybe. But not then, I wasn't. He flew, Mr. Proctor."

"You've said that already." He gestured. "You know *Alice in Wonderland*? Like it says, start at the beginning, keep going until you reach the end, then stop."

The chauffeur emptied his glass, took a few seconds to decide to put it on the floor.

I drive the Lighthouse limo, you know? About three years already. Mr. Baron tells me take this guy here, those people there, I drive them. That's all I do. This guy, he's a real pain in the ass. He acts like he's been cheated out of a million bucks, and Mr. Baron, he gives him the treatment—he gets him out of the hotel, pretty much dumps him on someone else's turf. I've done it a million times. Jerks; they're all jerks, and they never tip, the cheap sons of bitches.

So I drop this guy at the Sands, and I park down the end of the street, out of the way. Nothing to do but wait, but I always got a book or something, like a crossword magazine, to kill time. Never leave the limo, Mr. Proctor. That's my rule—I never leave the limo.

But this guy—Wharton, Barton, something like that—he really pissed me off. I couldn't concentrate, couldn't even listen to the radio, so I got out. Figured I'd walk around a little, you know? Just around the limo, that's all, let off some steam.

Now, you gotta understand, I was parked on the other side of Pacific, away from the other limos and cabs. It wasn't totally dark, but it was pretty dark, not all the streetlights working, and if you were standing there at the casino, you probably couldn't see me. It was cold, too, but I didn't feel it much. I guess I was too pissed off.

So I was walking around . . . hell, I guess it was like I was marching or something. It was pretty quiet, late and all, so when I heard this noise, it was pretty clear. I looked around, didn't see anything, I figured I was hearing things. But I kept hearing it, so I looked around some more . . . Christ, Mr. Proctor, you're gonna think I'm nuts.

I'm standing by the door, you know? and I look down the street, and I see this . . . I see something flying toward me. It was too big to be a bird, anything like that, and I don't know if it even had wings. But it came down out of the sky and right down the middle of the street and . . . it was . . . it was like I didn't believe what I was seeing, you know? Like those guys in the movies, they rub their eyes and look again? I did. I did the same thing. And it came down the street and over the sidewalk and it . . . I couldn't move . . . it landed right in front of me. I mean, it was a man, Mr. Proctor. At least that's what I thought at first, that it was a guy in a dark coat. And he kind of smelled. Not bad, not like that, but there was this smell, I don't know what it was. And . . . aw, Jesus, he looked at me, I couldn't move for anything, and his face . . . it was kind of dark, but his face . . . I don't know . . . it twisted and he wasn't like a guy anymore and his . . . they were like this really dark red, his eyes they were this really weird red, and I couldn't move and he was smiling at me, and I think he was laughing at me, and I think . . . I think . . .

I'm a big buy, right? I go six-foot-four, I'm around two-seventy, two-eighty, okay? I go to get in the limo and he grabs my shoulder and it's like I can't move. It's like he's got me pinned there, I can't move, and he's still laughing and he shows me a hand like this . . . holds it up so I can see his fingers, and he . . . the nails, they . . . I couldn't move and I couldn't look away 'cause of the way he was looking at me, I don't know, so I saw those nails, Mr. Proctor, it wasn't that dark, I saw those friggin' nails *grow*. But it was like they weren't nails anymore, they were like claws or something and

I knew I was gonna die. I mean, I just knew it, you know? Aw, Jesus, Mr. Proctor, I just knew I was gonna die.

Proctor leaned over and rested a hand on Bruno's leg, squeezed it until the young man looked right at him before sitting back again. "You didn't die."

Bruno, trembling as if the temperature had suddenly dropped through the floor, nodded shakily. "Yeah."

"What happened?"

For a moment the young man looked as if he were going to cry. "I don't know. I mean, I don't remember. I swear it, Mr. Proctor, I don't really remember. I saw those claws or whatever, and he must've taken a swing at me, because the next thing I knew I was flat out on somebody's front steps, not even the same block, and all—" He stopped and laughed, a quick snap of a laugh. "I was in my underwear, and the limo was gone. After that"—he shrugged helplessly—"I swear, I don't know. I just ended up here, that's all I remember. Except that . . . that guy's gonna kill me 'cause I saw his face, man. I saw his face."

Again, he refused to meet Proctor's gaze. After a brief hesitation he picked up the glass and wandered into the bathroom to refill it, not bothering to turn on the light. Proctor stared at the wall, hands clasped loosely under his chin, listening to the water, listening to the fading voice of the wind. He felt sorry for the guy, and didn't know what to tell him. He was right that this man would probably want him out of the way, although he doubted the Ripper would be in any serious hurry to take care of it. It had already been over twenty-four hours and not even a hint of an attempt yet.

What was worse, however, what would haunt Bruno Gladman for the rest of his life, was the sudden knowledge that the world wasn't as cut-and-dried as he'd once believed. Childhood stories weren't always simply stories. Movie monsters weren't always confined to the screen, to the back row of a dark theater, where boys protected their dates with a simple arm around a shoulder.

Once in a while there really was something in the closet.

Once in a while there really was something under the bed.

Once in a while, on a dark street, on a dark road, there really was someone back there, and it wasn't always human.

Eventually Bruno would build a wall, a high and thick wall, and find the rationalization that would satisfy him. That would allow him to function in what he used to believe was the real world. That would wither the nightmares like a waterless flower, because belief would no longer be there to feed them.

"I'm not crazy," Bruno insisted from the bathroom doorway.

It wasn't a question, but it sounded like pleading.

"No," Proctor said. "No, you're not."

Bruno inhaled sharply, stepped back, and closed the door. Despite the insistence of his sanity, that wasn't the answer he wanted to hear.

At the same time, the hall door opened. Proctor lifted a hand and waved a "come in" over his shoulder, then pointed at the bathroom when Sergeant Cox asked a silent *where is he?* Granna sat on the edge of the bed, her coat open, hands on her thighs.

"Well?"

"He saw what he saw, Granna."

"Meaning what?"

Proctor ignored the question. "What haven't you been telling me? What do you know that I don't?"

She glanced at Cox, who was leaning against the wall, concentrating on listening to what was happening in the bathroom. Proctor didn't see what look he gave her, but she hesitated before reaching into her coat and pulling out a manila envelope folded in half. She dropped it into his lap and looked away.

Oh, man, he thought; I am not going to like this.

As he lay the envelope flat, he heard Taz and Doc come in. Taz he knew would be all right with what he was about to learn—the kid wouldn't like it, but he'd been through one of these cases before. Doc, on the other hand, even after all these years, had never been in the field like this. All his work was done in research labs and photo labs, libraries and the shelved knowledge of his mind. All theory, no practice outside the office.

He opened the clasp, lifted the flap. Inside were a half dozen photographs.

"That's only one," Granna said. "Charleen Caje. The others are the same."

"Boss?" Taz said.

"Later."

"Sure."

He slipped out the first picture, black-and-white, the woman's body on the street. Black blood on the black tarmac, black blood on her chest.

"Told you there was blood," MacEdan said, the smile on her lips, not in her voice.

"No vampire."

"Shoot. I was hoping."

He looked at her.

"You know." She made a pass at her throat. "Tears it out to cover his tracks."

Proctor grunted. "If there's no blood left, MacEdan, wrecking the throat is kind of superfluous, don't you think?"

"What the hell are you guys talking about?" Cox demanded. "Jesus, he's a maniac, okay?" He rapped on the bathroom door. "Come on, Bruno, let's move it, huh?" He rapped again. "Vampires. God Almighty."

Proctor held the picture up to catch the faint light, caught his breath, and held it closer to his eyes.

I'll be damned, he thought; son of a bitch, I'll be damned.

He took out the second one. "My God, I don't believe it." No one spoke.

Cox knocked again, harder, and opened the door a crack. "Move it, Bruno."

The chauffeur answered, his voice muffled.

"Tough," the sergeant told him. "I want you out here. Now." He shook his head. "Ain't doing nothing stupid on my watch," he said to the room.

The other photographs were the same—all of Charleen's face, two from the street, the rest from the morgue. He held one up. "Taz." And waited for him to take it.

"You gotta be kidding," Taz said as he took it back to show Falcon.

Proctor didn't hear what reaction Doc had, if any. His was to turn facedown what remained in his lap.

There were holes, deep holes, where the dancer's eyes had been, blood like black tears frozen on her cheeks. Her mouth was open, the right corner slit so it would open wider than normal. He saw teeth, gums, the roof of her mouth.

She didn't have a tongue.

It had been sliced off near the base.

Bruno left the bathroom just as Cox said, "Like I said, a nutcase. A razor, right? Some kind of hospital thing, surgeon's instrument, right?"

The chauffeur sat on the foot of the bed, shivering, and Granna said, "Find him some clothes, Sergeant. It's time he was dressed." After Cox left, she looked at Proctor. "So? Was he right? A psycho with medical knowledge? A—"

"Maybe," he said quietly, doubtfully.

She closed her eyes. "Shit."

"That girl. The one who saw this man, the Ripper, on the boardwalk. Can I talk to her?"

"Nope," Taz said.

He scowled and looked around the side of the chair.

"She's in the show, remember?" Then: "Oh. You didn't know. Oh, well, yeah, Suze is the one you're talking about. And she's in the show." A glance at his watch. "She won't be done until nearly three."

Nearly three. Proctor thought, and I'll be too tired to blink, much less think.

"Fix it for me, will you, Taz? Early lunch or something. Whatever she'll agree to."

Taz nodded.

Proctor sat back, pushed his heels against the mattress. "Doc, I need that woman. Petra. See what you can do, okay?"

"Of course."

When Granna asked him what he was talking about, Proctor waved her off, nothing to do with this. Then he looked at Bruno and smiled. "Hang in there."

Bruno's expression told him that was easier said than done.

"Hey," Granna said, shaking his leg to regain his attention.

"So it's not a bloodthirsty psycho. So what am I dealing with? I mean, you do know, don't you?"

He took a long time before he finally said, "I think so."

"Like last time?"

He wanted very much to tell her that, yes, it was like the last time, the first time they'd met, when he'd accepted a case that purportedly had the Jersey Devil as its centerpiece. What it ended up being was a scheme by a former King of Prussia cop who had been fired for brutality; by saving the world, or at least the central part of the state, from the Jersey Devil, he'd hoped to be either reinstated, or given a position on another force. What he got was Proctor in his Pine Barrens cabin, and life at Rahway for murdering three teens.

"Proctor."

He looked at the photographs one last time before returning them to their envelope. Tapped it several times against his chest and handed it over.

"No, Granna. No, I don't think it's like last time at all."

TWENTY

They stood by the elevator on the fourteenth floor. A bulb had burned out near Proctor's room, that part of the hall marked now by a dark grey haze. When they spoke it was in whispers.

"I'm going to bed," he told them, rubbing the heel of a hand against one eye. His exhaustion had arrived not in stages but abruptly. "I can't think anymore." He noticed Doc fussing with his tie when it didn't need fussing at all, and that surprised him. A sign of uncertainty, and about as nervous as he'd ever seen Falcon get. "Been a long day."

Taz checked down the hall. "You going to be all right?"

He nodded. "Sure. Just need sleep."

"Then, I'll go down to the theater and see if I can't catch Suze before she leaves after the show."

"Thanks."

Doc kept silent.

Proctor poked his arm lightly with a finger. "It's too late to think so hard, Doc. Go find your friends, or go to bed."

Falcon inhaled slowly. "I'm wondering something."

Proctor groaned silently. This was not the time, and he wished the man would just go away for a while—like until tomorrow morning. It wasn't as if there was any urgency here. It wasn't as if he could just reach out and touch the Ripper, expose him, and give chase. Tomorrow would do just as well, and at least he'd be able to function properly.

"All right," he said, resigned and making sure they knew it. "What?"

"It isn't like you to admit that you've got a . . . case here.

Not so soon." The hand to the tie. "You have apparently accepted the existence of this Ripper as something not ordinary. Unless I've missed something, you haven't examined the possibilities. The alternatives."

Proctor squeezed his eyes shut as tightly as he could, then snapped them open, an old trick to clear his mind. Except this time it didn't work.

"Lieutenant MacEdan will think about what I said, and she'll decide that I really didn't give her a straight answer. Which I didn't." He scratched at an ear. "As soon as she figures that out, she'll be a little ticked and probably come at me again tomorrow. By then, maybe I'll know something more." He rubbed his chest, passed a hand over his face. "There are alternatives, Doc. I had a conversation about coincidence earlier"—a wave of his hand, it didn't matter with whom—"and who knows, this just might be one—a killer with a thing for eyes and tongues. Or it might be someone who actually knows what I do and is playing copycat for his own amusement."

"Copycat of what?" Taz asked.

Proctor ignored the question. "Or it might be the real thing."

"Which is what?" Taz asked.

"Not now," he said.

"But—"

"Taz, not now."

"But *you* think it is," Doc persisted. "Whatever you're thinking of, you think it's real."

Proctor shrugged. "I'm not sure. Really. I'm not sure. That's why I'd like to talk to this Suze woman, but only when I'm more awake." He yawned abruptly, his jaw popping loudly. "I don't get it." He frowned. "It's not like I haven't been up all day before."

"A number of factors," Doc said.

"I'm sure there are," he answered sourly before Falcon could begin to list them. "And right now, no offense, I don't care. I just want to sleep, okay? You guys go on, do what you're going to do. I'll see you in the morning."

He walked away without waiting for a response, heard a muttered "Good night, Boss," and nearly turned to make the correction, decided with a weary smile it wasn't worth it, and fished his room key from his shirt's breast pocket. Once inside, he undressed quickly, was in and out of the bathroom in record time, and finally stood at the window. Watching the city.

Watching the storm.

It wasn't New York, wasn't Chicago, but it was big enough out there. Big enough to hide in, big enough not to be found no matter how hard the police looked.

He looked above the lights, to the dark band of night between city and sky, and saw Charleen Caje's face, the different angles of what was left of it frozen by the camera.

The eyes.

The ruins of the mouth.

"Mahjra," he whispered, and lowered his head, shook it slowly, and rubbed the back of his neck with a weighted hand. Sometimes he honestly believed he knew too many things, and wished, often fervently, that he were normal, that he was like everyone else, even those gamblers down there who talked to their cards, or the slots, or the dice. Everyone else who was positive to the point of religious belief that such things that lived in shadow did not now and never did exist.

It was a far simpler world that way.

It was a world far safer than the one he lived in.

A glance to the bed, sheet and blankets folded down, a foil-wrapped mint centered on his pillow. For a moment he thought he saw Petra there, hints of silver outlining her figure. His breath caught. His stomach tightened against a brief fluttering there. Until he realized he was only looking at the shadows of the rain as they slid down the wall and across the covers, their outlines sharp, and sometimes marked with faint silver.

It startled him, and made him nervous, how disappointed he felt.

He yawned. He stretched, then pulled the drawstring to bring the draperies together, fussed a little until there was a gap between the halves, a couple of inches to let in the light no matter how pale it was.

He went to bed.

Cursed loudly and got up again, shuffled to the door and hung the "DO NOT DISTURB" sign on the outside knob, turned the extra lock over, and put on the chain.

Back under the covers, and he was asleep in seconds.

The storm weakened, but it didn't move. It lurked off the coast, goading the sea to claw at the beach, holding tight rein on the wind, holding the rain to an easy fall. No thunder; no lightning.

For almost an hour there was no rain or wind at all, and for the first time since Friday afternoon, those on the boardwalk could hear the angry surf.

A break in the clouds showed the city the stars.

When the clouds merged again, they were stitched together by lightning.

He sat straight up and practically yelled, "Tiger's eye? Jesus Christ!"

He rolled onto his side and reached for the bedside telephone, changed his mind when he saw the red-numeral time on the nightstand's clock radio. First thing, he told himself as he fell back onto the pillow; first thing tomorrow he would call the office and leave a message, tell RJ and Eriko they wouldn't have to search the answering tapes anymore.

Tiger's eye.

According to one witness, that was the last thing Shake Waldman had said before he died. Granna had called his office with the information, and it had meant nothing to him at the time. How the hell could he have forgotten something like that, after Browning had told him what Mom had said?

Tiger's eye.

The obvious questions trampled each other, trying to gain his attention, but he shoved them all back where they belonged. For the time being. Later, when he was awake he would consider them. Right now he needed rest, sleep, more than he needed answers. Able to think once again, that's when he'd work on turning answers into pieces to fit the puzzle.

His eyes fluttered closed as lighting slashed over the water.

Tiger's eye.

Good Lord, Mom . . . tiger's eye.

She stood at the foot of the bed.

His eyes only half open, he could see her in the thin slant of light that slipped through the gap he'd left between the drapes. Silver threads winking as she reached down to prop her evening bag against the footboard.

He couldn't see any lower than her knees, but he knew, somehow, she wasn't wearing any shoes.

Why are you here?

To see you.

What do you want?

To see you.

Their voices were quiet in the lull of the storm, the hotel itself in one of those rare moments when nothing moved and no one spoke and even the machinery ran softly for a while.

He frowned, unable to drive sleep completely away.

How . . . how did you get in? I locked the door.

Her smile.

It is amazing, Proctor, what a few dollars and a smile will get a woman.

The chain—

—wasn't seated properly. It fell when I pushed in. You must have been very tired.

Where have you been? Where did you go? I wanted to apologize for—

That's all right. It doesn't matter. I should have trusted you more.

Why? You don't know me.

Her smile; it brought the flutter back to his stomach.

You don't know me, he repeated.

Well enough, Proctor. Well enough.

He pushed himself up on his elbows, watching as she hiked up her dress until it cleared her knees, then tipped forward until she could kneel on the bed. Shifted until she was far enough on so she could settle back on her heels, next to his right leg, palms smoothing the wrinkles out of the silver-darted cloth before resting on her thighs.

He was right; she wore no shoes.

Out of the light now, he couldn't see her face clearly at all.

They didn't speak for a long time, and his head tilted to one side, then the other, as if listening to sounds only he could hear. He wanted to change position, the weight on his elbows began to pull at his shoulders, but he didn't want to move for fear she would move, too—away and off the bed.

She was too far away to touch.

Lightning struck somewhere outside, and because the gap was behind her, she became a solid black silhouette, outlined in silver.

Her right hand slipped slowly off her thigh, came to rest on his shin. She did not squeeze or brush or caress it; the hand simply lay there, barely any weight at all. A gesture he wasn't sure was casual, or deliberate.

It certainly didn't help him decide if he were dreaming or awake.

Thunder rumbled faintly.

Eventually his muscles complained, so he rocked to his right and grabbed the other pillows, dropped them onto the one behind his back. Reluctantly he scooted backward until he could sit up. His leg moved under her hand, until her hand was at the juncture of shin and foot. Not squeezing, or caressing, or brushing—just resting.

Which made him abruptly aware that he was naked to the waist, aware even more that what she could see in the not quite full dark wasn't the body of a man who worked out, pumped iron, walked or jogged twenty miles a day, ate only healthy foods, didn't smoke or drink. An ordinary body, with the hint of a pouch and a stomach that was anything but rock hard.

Suddenly he yawned.

She giggled.

Sorry, you were right, I'm really tired.

That's fine, Proctor, no shame in being tired.

He wanted to pull the covers up a little, but doing that would draw attention to what he was doing, so he lay his hands across his stomach, fingers laced.

Casual; half naked in front of a beautiful woman, and he was trying to be casual.

Proctor, he thought; you are a real jerk.

Petra . . . why are you here?

I think it is possible you need some help.

Nuts. And I thought you might be here to, I don't know, seduce me.

She giggled again, slapped his foot lightly with her palm.

Be serious, Proctor. I may be able to help.

With what?

He sensed her displeasure.

No games, Proctor. There is no time for games.

I'm sorry, but I can't really see how you can help. What I'm involved in has nothing to do with Shake.

What I can tell you has nothing to do with Shake. At least I am perhaps sure it has nothing to do with Shake.

Then what is it? What has nothing to do with Shake, maybe?

Emile Valknir.

He frowned. Shook his head. Lifted a shoulder.

Mahjra, Proctor. He is the mahjra you think may have killed all those people.

The light patter of rain against the window.

In the hall a man singing not quite loudly but very drunkenly. It didn't last very long; soon enough there was only the rain.

You know this for a fact? About the mahjra?

Yes.

You know this for a fact, and he hasn't killed you?

Yes.

Does he know you know this?

I do not . . . perhaps, but I doubt it. I am, as you say, still not killed.

This makes no sense.

No, Proctor. What makes no sense is that you haven't once asked me how I know that you believe these things. That you have not once asked me if I believe this thing. And if I do, how I know this to be true.

This is . . . I can't think. Wait a minute. Give me a minute here. I can't think.

Poor Proctor. You have what they call overload, yes?

Petra, I don't know what the hell they call it, but I can't think. This is crazy. I'm not supposed to—

She sighed her sympathy and moved on hands and knees across the bed. He still couldn't see her face, but he could smell the scent of her, could hear the dress rustling. She lay a hand against his cheek and, this close now, he could see that smile.

Poor Proctor. Perhaps I have not done this properly. I think so. I think I should have waited.

She nodded.

Yes, I should have waited.

She leaned forward, hesitated for a look into his eyes, and she kissed him. A feather-touch kiss that both soothed and tickled his lips.

He wanted to move his hands. He wanted to touch her, hold her, but all he could do was kiss her in return, and close his eyes, enjoy the sensation, and feel her pull away much too soon for the way he felt.

When he opened his eyes a moment later, she was gone.

There was no one in the room but him, no movement but the jump of shadows on the walls when lightning struck again.

TWENTY-ONE

Proctor opened his eyes, groaned at the bright light that punched between the drapes into the center of the room, and tried to burrow deeper into his pillow, pulling the covers up over his shoulders, almost over his head.

Dozed for several minutes, using that half-sleeping state to direct a dream about flipping a five-dollar chip onto a roulette number and watching it grow to a pile, two piles, the five-dollar chips replaced by ten-dollar ones. Twenty-five-dollar ones. A man in a new but not expensive suit asking politely if he would like his room comped. A woman flirting with him. Another candidly looking him over without apology.

The piles grew, and he tried to figure out how much it was, but in that half dream he couldn't add, or multiply, so he gave it up and concentrated instead on directing the little white ball into the proper number's pocket so he'd keep on winning.

It was fun for a while, but he saw no end to it, no rousing cinematic ending that would clear him of all debts and fatten his bank account, just numbers adding up, one thousand at a time. So he let them go, the chips and the wheel, the women checking him out, and let his mind skate randomly, waiting for it to latch onto something he could use. But he kept going back to the wheel, the blur of red and black, the rattle and bounce of the white marble—

Tiger's eye.

"Son of a bitch."

Tiger's eye.

"Damn!" and he rolled over to face the nightstand, the red

numerals telling him it was only a few minutes shy of noon.
"Son of a *bitch*."

He snapped the covers away and swung angrily to his feet.
Raised his hands in frustration, and stomped into the bathroom, slamming the door behind him.

Son of a bitch, he thought in the shower.

"What the hell were they thinking of?" he demanded of
his reflection while brushing his teeth.

"Idiots," each time he yanked an angry brush through his
hair.

Noon; goddamnit, those idiots, it was now past noon, for
crying out loud.

As he grabbed a pair of jeans and a dark shirt from the
closet, he could imagine the rationalizations: let him sleep, he
needs his rest; he'll get up when he gets up and thank us for
it; if he's going to stick his nose into Lieutenant MacEdan's
case, he's going to need a clear head. He's going to have to
be able to *think*.

He yanked the drapes open, squinting until his eyes grew
accustomed to the daylight. What there was of it.

The clouds didn't seem as low as they had been the day
before, or as dark; the rain fell in fits and starts; and the wind
was barely a wind at all. It had no voice. Yet it was still grim
out there, more like November than February, everything
washed of its color.

As he buttoned the shirt, still muttering to himself, he
switched on the TV, used the remote to find a local newscast,
and tossed the unit onto the couch. The weather report, the
anchorwoman assured him, would follow the next commer-
cial, then proceeded to a solemn narration over a series of
scenes that proved how a few well-placed accidents and a hell
of a wet and blustering storm could cut the city off for hours
at a time.

Although he wasn't surprised at the havoc the storm caused,
the report was a disturbing reminder of how insulated the
Lighthouse's guests were from the real world out there. There
could have been a war, and no one at the tables would have
ever known it.

Finally he did what he had been avoiding since leaving the bathroom—he looked over at the bed.

"Well . . . hell," he muttered. "Nuts."

It was easy to see which side he had taken—the covers tossed back, the pillow shoved against the headboard. The center was only slightly disturbed, the other side not at all. Those pillows were still tucked under the coverlet.

He hadn't used them at all.

Not to sleep on, and definitely not to prop behind his back so he could sit up in the middle of the night.

Instead of the obsidian plain, he had dreamed of Petra Haslic; and even as he half closed his eyes to bring the dream back, it slipped away, and all he could remember was the way she had knelt beside him, the touch of her hand on his leg, and the way she had kissed him.

He could almost see her lips moving; he couldn't hear a single word she said.

Disappointment tasted sour, turned bitter, and he cursed. Glared at the TV and tapped an impatient foot until the weather report told him that his luck hadn't changed—the storm wasn't about to leave the area anytime soon, and experts predicted that the lull they enjoyed now would probably last only an hour or so longer. Certainly no longer than the dinner hour that evening.

Air, he decided even though his stomach rumbled. He wanted fresh air. He grabbed a fleece-lined denim jacket from the closet, stared for a moment at the chain snug in its groove, and left.

He walked south along the boardwalk, his collar snapped up, hands jammed in his pockets. The rain had weakened into a light mist, and he welcomed its touch on his face. Cold, but it felt fresh. Smelled fresh. The surf thundered. A pair of black-face gulls hung over the beach, calling to each other. Far below he could see other people taking advantage of the break. The boardwalk benches were empty.

Head down, staring at his feet, he walked past the Showboat and the Taj Mahal, swerving to avoid collisions, just as often forcing others to swerve around him. His earlier anger had subsided to a simmering irritation, and he used the exercise and the distractions to settle him the rest of the way down.

A mile, give or take, and various parts of him revolted, demanding immediate fuel before he fell on his face.

In a delicatessen in Resorts, he had eggs and a sandwich, juice, a glass of milk, and a slice of cardboard apple pie.

Except for the pie, it all tasted the same.

When he reached into his jeans for the money to pay the bill, he found what looked like a red roulette chip among his change, one made of stone. He frowned, then realized it must have come from the welcome package they'd received when they'd checked in. Whatever it meant, however, he'd forgotten; he'd ask Taz or Doc later.

As he made his way back to the boardwalk, he told himself that his mood was a result of a lingering, and unreasonable, disappointment. A dream; nothing but a dream. But that was kid stuff; a touch of adolescent-like longing. He then suggested his disappointment actually had nothing to do with the dream at all, but instead was a result of Doc's and Taz's misguided attempts to force relaxation on him, when they should have known better. That it had been done with the best of intentions didn't change the fact that he had lost an entire morning.

For what, Proctor?

For what?

Once outside, he zigzagged to the iron railing through a vocal pensioner crowd and headed north. Taking his time. Watching the surf. Watching an agitated man out on the sand wave his arms at a cop, while a small dog trailing a leash yapped around their ankles. Watching another pair of gulls, which brought his gaze to the cloud cover that was thin enough to allow the light through, close to the shore while over the Atlantic it was solid and near black.

For what?

He squinted into a spray of mist and finally admitted it probably wasn't disappointment at all, but a mood born of wishing he had never seen those pictures of Charleen Caje. Because if, God help him, he was even close to being right, that the Ripper *was* one of the mahjra, then he could be walking behind it right now and never know it. Or had already walked past it. It could have been the one playing the horn. It could have been his waitress in the deli. Hell, it could be Lieutenant MacEdan for all he knew. There was no way of telling by simple observation, and it sure as hell wouldn't be wearing a sign.

If, that is, he was right.

He needed something more.

Then don't forget the dream, he told himself; you've got a name—Emile Valknir—remember?

He paused for a moment to lean against the railing, give his walk-weary legs a respite before moving on. Slightly short of breath. Brunch sitting heavily in his stomach. This, he decided when he realized how far away the Lighthouse still was, was a really dumb idea.

The wind picked up, amplifying the steady rolling roar of the surf.

Valknir.

He shook his head; it was only a dream.

Emile Valknir.

But if it *was* a dream, where did he get the name?

He used a palm to wipe mist from his face, dried the hand on his hip, and stuck it back in its pocket. Almost immediately his cheeks were wet again, and he lengthened his stride, checking on the progress of that black wall of clouds as it lumbered toward shore. When someone tapped his shoulder, he spun around, still moving, and scowled when Doc Falcon held up an it's-only-me hand.

"I've been looking for you," Falcon said, effortlessly matching Proctor's pace.

"You could have found me in bed no problem," Proctor told him shortly.

Ordinarily Falcon's expression would have been apology enough, but Proctor wasn't in the mood to let him off the hook. "What is it?"

"Another body."

"Damn. Who?"

"A bellman. A Salvatore Visconte. He was found in the

men's room on the first floor—" He checked his watch. "Almost two hours ago now, tucked into the last stall and the door jammed so anyone in there would think it was locked. In use, that is. Apparently he's been missing since last night's blackout."

"Does Granna know?"

"A bit of luck for her. It was her Sergeant Cox who found him, so keeping it quiet, thus far, has been relatively easy. Mr. Baron, the manager, is quite pleased with that. They're just saying it was a fatal heart attack."

Proctor checked the black clouds again. "Right. Whatever you do, don't bother the guests." He looked skyward, and to his left—the thin patches over the city had begun to fill in as the other clouds were pushed against them.

He moved faster, close to a trot.

"Paul was unable to arrange an early meeting with that young woman."

"Which is why you let me sleep."

"No. Which is why she's agreed to talk to you later this afternoon. There is a stipulation, however."

"Good Lord, all I want to do is ask her a few questions, make sure the story Cobb told us is accurate." He adjusted his collar, swiped at his hair. "All right, what is it?"

"She will talk to you, but only if her cousin is with her."

Proctor shook his head. "What is he, a lawyer?"

"No, a composer who moonlights as a hotel maintenance man."

Proctor couldn't help a grin. "You're kidding."

"She insisted, Paul agreed. Evidently, it was the only way."

"Fine." He veered around a middle-age woman who pushed an old man in a wheelchair. "What about Petra?"

"I have not seen her. No one else has, either, or they're not talking."

"Everyone talks to you, Doc. It's part of your charm."

Falcon gave him no satisfaction by either altering his expression or issuing a remark. In his sleek expensive topcoat, the scarf carefully set under his chin, and the bearing he carried, he looked like a man who could buy and sell any one of these hotels a few times over. If he looked at all unhappy,

Proctor figured it was because he probably wished he'd worn a hat to protect that bald dome.

"Proctor," he said as they rushed past the Showboat, "this woman."

"Don't ask, Doc, because I really don't know. She lied to me. I want to know why."

"If I may say so, you're in danger of splitting yourself off again."

"Say it all you want, Doc. I still want to find her and have a quiet word."

He said nothing about the mahjra, about the name.

if it wasn't a dream, Proctor, how did she get in and out?

The brief flurry of pedestrians was gone. Aside from a handful of women swinging into the hotel from the other direction, there was no one near them. They could hear nothing but their own breathing, their footsteps, and the waves striking the shore.

He didn't expect that the body would still be there, but he wanted a look at that men's room before Granna turned her lab boys loose. She would be concerned about contamination; he wanted to see if an ordinary man could have done it.

A glance up at the beacon. Pale near the hotel itself, it brightened as it reached the ocean. Even as he watched it shimmered from blue to green.

As they approached the entrance, the light inside was so much brighter that he felt as if he were watching a theater screen. Guests floated through the lobby; a bellman pushed a cart piled high with luggage; a half dozen young men sat around the fountain; two men without coats stood just outside under the awning, smoking, shoulders hunched against the cold.

Proctor nodded to them as he pushed the nearest door open, already pulling at his jacket's zipper. Doc went through another door, his scarf unwound, a hand working to open his topcoat.

"Get Taz," Proctor told him, angling toward the South Promenade.

Doc nodded.

"First chance I get," he added, "I'll give you the whole story."

He didn't wait, he kept moving, pushing at his hair, wiping his face, rounding the corner and slowing when he saw Granna halfway down.

Oh, boy, he thought.

There was a scowl on her face, and when she spotted him, it deepened.

TWENTY-TWO

Aside from an expressionless patrolman standing guard at the men's room entrance, there were no indications this was a crime scene. No curious onlookers, no press, no technicians at work, no yellow tape. All very low-key, all very . . . ordinary, and that bothered Proctor as Granna walked up to meet him.

A man had died, brutally, viciously, and the games went on as if nothing had happened.

Life in the fast lane.

"I just heard," he said when she was close enough to hear.

"Good for you. What do you want?" Her topcoat was open, her hands in its pockets.

He didn't hesitate: "To help, if I can."

"What, to track down Count Dracula?"

He ignored the sneer. "No, to eliminate him."

"Oh, please," she said. "You gave me a load of bullshit last night, Proctor, and I don't appreciate it. It *is* the same as last time, and you know it."

He didn't know that at all, but this wasn't the time to attempt a conversion. "There'll be talk, though," he said, keeping his tone neutral. "It's already started in the papers." A nod toward the Promenade's casino doors. "Sooner or later, they're going to start talking, too."

"Heart attack."

"Sure. Until tonight's news."

She turned sideways to him, staring at the wall. Thinking, and clearly not liking what it was she thought.

"So you put me in your report," he suggested reasonably.

"I was in town, you happened to see me, you decided to put out the brushfire before it got worse." A quick smile. "Serendipity, and a preemptive strike. Whatever the media comes up with, it'll be dead before they can get much out of it."

Her shoulders rose and fell. "My people have already been through. Finished just a couple of minutes ago." A pained expression, almost apologetic; she knew what he was thinking, and helpless against the power of the hotels and the political fallout. "They worked fast, okay? In and out. No fuss."

"And?"

"What do you think?"

"I think they didn't find anything they can use. Not until they get their microscopes working, anyway." He turned as well, facing the casino. "No weapon, that's for sure."

She grunted.

A pair of waitresses stood in one of the doorways, voices low and unhappy, one of them pointing, the other nodding. A troublesome customer, he reckoned, or a bitchy shift boss. When they saw him watching, they hustled away.

"Security tapes," he said suddenly.

"Already looking, but it won't do any good."

"Too easy?"

A grudging half smile. "Yeah. On the backup system, the cameras concentrate on the casino. Everything else is secondary. Like the john."

"Tough luck."

He waited. She would either let him have a look, or she wouldn't. Not terribly complicated. And she knew, or ought to know, from the last time that he had no intention of talking to the press.

She studied the floor. She studied the wall. She turned, and together they watched the gamblers, unconcerned and uncaring.

He spotted Murray Cobb. The old man put a quarter into a machine and pulled the arm. Stared at the tumblers, scooped some money from the tray. Looked straight at Proctor and walked away, out of sight.

"Five minutes," she said.

"Fair enough."

"More than that. Cox goes with you."

"Jesus, Granna, I'm not going to steal the damn toilet."

She didn't react. "Cox goes with you."

"Whatever you say."

She turned to him then. "Damn right, whatever I say. And if by some miracle you do find something, you tell me right away, no screwing around."

He nodded. To add anything now might set off an explosion. She was right: He could only imagine the pressure she was under, from a hundred different directions. Bad for the city. Bad for the hotel. Bad for the image. But the Ripper kept killing, and the pressure kept building.

Another reason to be absolutely sure—he didn't want Granna to lose her job.

He shifted to tell her he was ready, and she said, "Wait," and walked over to the guard. He gave Proctor a puzzled glance, then spoke into his shoulder radio. Proctor looked up toward the lobby, down toward the shops. He didn't see Cobb, but he had a feeling the old cop wasn't very far away.

A few minutes later Sergeant Cox popped through a casino door. Proctor stayed where he was until he heard his name.

"One thing," MacEdan warned, long finger pointing at his chest. "One little thing, and I know it."

"Sure."

"Let them in," she ordered the patrolman, who stepped aside, still puzzled.

Cox went first, pushing open the swinging door, holding it for Proctor, who was right behind them. They were in a small anteroom, muted red wallpaper, a table with vase and flowers, a chair, galleon on the high seas print on the wall. The smell wasn't strong, but it was there—antiseptic perfumed soap and cleanser.

"This is nuts," the sergeant complained. "You're not a cop."

"That's right," Proctor agreed, and pushed into the main room.

Stopped on the threshold, and shook his head in wonder. "Now, that," he said, "is amazing."

*   *   *

Someone shook Dacey's shoulder, hard, and she sat up abruptly, swallowing a scream. A second's disorientation, and she remembered that as soon as her shift was over, she had taken refuge on the fourth floor. The bed had been taken from the room, replaced by ten roll-away cots; with the exception of the television, it made the place look like a barracks or a hospital ward.

The woman who had awakened her was already on her way into the bathroom; three women still slept under light blankets, one of them snoring lightly. The other cots were empty.

Oh, God, she thought, and rubbed her face hard, scratched through her hair, and put her feet on the floor. On one wall was a long wardrobe, and she padded over to it, opened one of the doors, and rubbed her eyes again. The rail had been divided into ten sections by four-foot pieces of plywood. Lockers without doors. She found her uniform and street clothes, and seriously considered grabbing the latter, dressing, and taking the first bus out of the town.

But if she did that, she'd lose all that money, all that payment money in the suitcase back at her apartment.

Jesus, Dacey, she thought; what the hell kind of woman are you?

She knew, and at the moment she just didn't give a damn.

A shower, take the uniform to Housekeeping and replace it with a clean one, get something to eat, and by then maybe she'll have thought of something to keep him happy. And if not happy, at least keep her alive.

The other woman came out of the bathroom, muttered, "Your turn," and shouldered her away from the wardrobe.

By the time she was dressed, she still had no firm plan, but the water and the towels and the image of the suitcase made her feel a lot better. Something would come her way. She knew it; she just knew it.

All she had to do was wait for the right time.

Reno Baron carefully replaced the receiver onto its cradle, pushed back from his desk, cupped his hands behind his head, and stared blankly at the ceiling. His lips pursed in a silent whistle. His gaze shifted across the ceiling's surface. He did not yield to the urge to take the gun from the lower left-hand drawer, go into the lobby, and shoot someone. Anyone. He didn't give a damn who.

The owners were not happy.

He had spent an hour reassuring them that the bellman really had died of a heart attack, knowing the whole time that sooner or later the truth would get out, and his ass would be grass.

"I do not deserve this," he said to the ceiling. "I do not deserve this."

First the Caje woman, now this. Next thing you know, they'll find out the Ripper is a registered guest.

At least the damn backups had been repaired.

He sighed.

He decided it was time to grab some lunch and get out there among the sheep. Snip a little wool. Then go up to his rooms, wake Greta up, and screw her brains out.

He grinned.

"Sounds like a plan," he said, and kept grinning until he left the office and one of the day clerks said, "Mr. Baron, do you know if Stuart Hockman is coming in tonight? Greta wants him in early, but no one seems to know where he is."

"It's like I said to the mayor," Cobb told the bell captain. "I said, Your Honor, you get rid of half the cars in this city, you get rid of half your problems."

"Yeah." Delmonico was behind his stand, elbows on the ledge. "I grew up in Staten Island, I know what you mean."

"Pah," said Cobb with a grin. "Staten Island isn't real New York, you know that. It's like I said to the mayor—"

Delmonico gave him a look, and Murray laughed aloud. Smacked his lips and watched a car pull up to the curb. Patrick Whatshisname—Malley, O'Malley, something like that—hurried outside to open the passenger door, and Murray watched carefully.

Strange how these guys can be subservient and snotty at the same time. Like the butlers in old movies, who thought they owned the mansion, everyone else just renting space. Heck of a way to earn a living.

Certainly not stressful enough to earn a young guy like Sal Visconte a heart attack in the middle of the night.

Strange.

And then that Proctor kid shows up, talking to Lieutenant MacEdan. He's an investigator he says, so what's to investigate about a heart attack in the john? Happens all the time.

Strange.

He sniffed, nodded a good-bye to Delmonico, and wandered into the casino. There weren't a lot of people around just now. Some out on the boardwalk getting a little air in their lungs, others testing the other casinos, others in the restaurants. He was hungry himself, but he didn't want to eat. Eating meant getting out of the stream of things, things happening he couldn't see. Like if he'd been eating, he wouldn't have seen that Proctor kid talking to MacEdan. About a heart attack victim?

Strange.

He paused midway down the row of roulette tables.

Now, that is strange, he thought; somebody here has aftershave that smells just like cloves.

"Amazing," Proctor said again, and Cox crowded in behind him.

The room was large, the tiled walls a soft white and gold, the ceiling white but darker. Against the right-hand wall were the sinks and soap dispensers, hot-air drying machines, paper towels, and one long mirror, edged in ornate silver. The urinals were on the left, and ten stalls were tucked into an alcove in back. The floor was smooth, white-and-pale blue, and clean enough so he could see a vague reflection when he looked down.

"Which stall?" he asked.

Cox pointed to the one on the end, on the right.

Proctor didn't move.

"You're not gonna look?"

"I'm already looking."

Cox snorted. "Yeah? At what?"

"At no blood, that's what."

The room was clean. It even smelled clean, lemon and soap, not a hint of the scent of blood.

He walked slowly over to the stall, examining the floor as he went, knowing it was a waste because the techs had already gone over the place with everything they could carry. He veered toward the sinks, saw faint residue of fingerprint powder at the edge of one chrome faucet.

"Your guys are good," he said, his voice carrying a slight echo.

"Damn right." Cox remained by the door.

"They the ones who cleaned up?"

Cox rolled his eyes. "Well, yeah. Once the lab boys left, the lieutenant had some guys in. The maids sure as hell weren't going to do it." He chuckled. "Union would've shit a brick."

"Bad, huh?"

The sergeant gave him a look, and he shrugged an apology for asking a stupid question. "So Housekeeping hasn't been in yet. Or whoever takes care of this place."

"Not that I know of, no. They'll be in later, probably, when the lieutenant gives the okay."

Proctor stared at the toilet, looked up at the ceiling to see if there was a convenient vent up there, one large enough for a man to slip through after he'd finished tearing out someone's throat. And since there wasn't, he would have had to kill poor Visconte, take his eyes and tongue, and walk out of here without being seen.

Easy enough, considering the blackout.

"Hey," Cox said impatiently.

Proctor sighed silently.

Nothing here. He saw nothing, felt nothing. Too many possibilities either way, and without a security tape there was, now, no chance of an explanation that would convince MacEdan she wasn't dealing with another phony Jersey Devil. Especially since, despite the dream, he still wasn't completely convinced himself. He needed to talk with that woman, the one who saw the Ripper on the boardwalk, to see how much of her story was influenced by her fear.

"That's it," Cox told him.

"Sure," and followed the big cop out.

"Well?" MacEdan asked as soon as he came through the outer door.

"Nothing."

She didn't say I told you so, but it was in her expression.

Which was when Taz ran up and said, "Boss, come on, you gotta see this."

Proctor nodded, crouched, stood, nodded again. "So he was in here? This one?" He pointed at the door; Cox nodded. "How'd you know he was there?"

"Saw his feet."

"Ah. Tried to start a conversation, right?"

"Nope. Smelled the blood. Looked under and . . ." He shrugged and made a face.

Proctor could imagine it; the overwhelming stench of blood and death. He had a strong feeling the sergeant had had to think twice before he stuck around to investigate.

"I wonder," he said, "why someone else didn't find him before you?"

Cox rested a shoulder against the jamb. "The guy was smart. He put an out-of-order sign out there." A thumb jerked over his shoulder. "You know, on one of those chrome post things."

"But you came in."

"Hey, when a man's gotta, a man's gotta, you know?"

Proctor nodded to show he did know, then pulled open the door. Toilet, toilet paper in a smoked-glass container, one hook on the door, one on the wall. He kept his voice conversational. "So how come you didn't use the one in Bruno's room?"

Signs of powder here, too.

"I do get a break now and then, you know, Proctor. Stretch my legs. Hey, you gonna take all day or what? The lieutenant said five minutes."

TWENTY-THREE

A handful of people hovered at the lobby doors, whisper-ing, one or two pointing. As Proctor passed the fountain, he spotted Falcon over by Registration, speaking to a tall, well-tanned man in a dark suit.

"Manager," Taz whispered. "Reno Baron."

Proctor didn't ask why. Nor did he speculate on why there were a couple of lines of guests at the checkout counter, bag-gage at their feet, impatience preventing them from standing still. Instead, he followed Taz to the nearest door, and saw a faint flickering outside. A frown, and he followed Taz onto the boardwalk, zipping up his coat as he went.

"What do you think?" Taz asked, pointing unnecessarily.

No wind; the clear scent of approaching rain mingled with the salt air; the cloud cover overhead still thin, with streaks of black snaking through it; groups of tourists spread along the railing as far down as he could see, many with video cam-eras up to their eyes. Excited. Nervous. Their breath in puffs, smoke signals as they spoke.

Beside him, Taz whispered, "Something, isn't it?"

Proctor didn't deny it.

Spider-leg lightning walked across the surface of the ocean. Not occasional single bolts, but patches of them scattered up and down the coast. Rapid and fierce, their numbers so great the thunder they produced merged into one rolling, distant cannonade. Although he wasn't good at such things, Proctor reckoned them to be at least a mile or so out.

"That's not natural," Taz said.

Tentatively Proctor agreed. "But I'm no expert," he cautioned. "Maybe it is, I don't know."

Taz shook his head. "You don't have to be, Boss. That's not natural."

Spontaneous applause from some folks down the line, as if the display had been arranged just for them.

Every so often a bolt traveled horizontally through the clouds, and he saw how thick the cover was out there, how black and heavy. He also had an idea why some guests were leaving—if they had seen this, they knew that the storm to come would be considerably worse than the one they'd just experienced.

He also suspected they hadn't a prayer of reaching the mainland before it struck again.

Taz gripped the railing with both hands. "Closer," he said, fascinated.

"Yeah."

"Gonna get nailed."

"I think you're right."

More applause, and laughter this time.

"So, Boss," Taz said, slowly turning his head, "you gonna keep it a secret or do we get to know?"

The way Proctor looked at him, Taz thought for a second he had overstepped his bounds, but the bellman's murder and the weird story that poor chauffeur guy had told last night weren't doing much for his nerves. And the lightning sure as hell didn't help.

Then Proctor said, "You're right," and moved up the boardwalk, passing under the beacon that aimed gold at the lightning. Taz followed, flipping up his collar to try to block some of the cold. A glance left, and he saw Doc leaving the hotel with Suze Acmarov, his hand at her elbow to guide and support. The cousin wasn't with her.

He nodded when they joined him, couldn't help noticing Suze's apprehension. "He won't bite," he whispered with a conspiratorial smile and a nod toward his boss.

She licked her lips nervously, and smiled back weakly. Said

nothing. Hugging herself against the easy wind as she watched the lightning walk the Atlantic's surface.

When a good fifty yards separated them from the nearest storm-gawkers, Proctor leaned against the railing and faced the hotel. His collar was up, hands in jacket pockets, and when the beacon passed overhead, its glow never touched his eyes. Doc stood beside him on his right, his expression neutral, and Taz wondered what he was thinking. He himself had been on one of these cases before, and although, in retrospect, it had been kind of a neat adventure, he never wanted to do it again.

It told him too much about what he didn't know.

Doc cleared his throat.

"Oh," Taz said, feeling a little stupid, and made the introductions, doing his best to sound professional, fully aware he was trying to impress the woman beyond his actual status.

"Where's, uh, Mike?" he asked.

"Working, I guess." She shrugged as if to say she was used to this, his not showing up when he was supposed to. A sigh, and she looked at Proctor. "I think," she said hopefully, "what I saw was some kind of magician's trick, right?"

He lifted one shoulder. "Probably."

"What else could it be?" a voice asked, and they looked up the boardwalk, Taz frowning when he saw the old man, that retired New York cop waddling toward them, a big smile on his face. He nodded a greeting to Proctor and made a tipping-his-hat gesture to Suze. She grinned, and his smile widened. "Old friends we are," he said to no one in particular. "Your hands all right?"

She nodded quickly.

"Good. You may be a dancer, but your hands are important, too." He squinted up at Taz. "You ever think about getting a haircut, kiddo?"

Taz didn't answer.

"No matter. You look good. Like whatshisname, the guy who danced in the white suit, except he's got all puffy these days, all that rich food he can afford now." He moved to the railing, faced the sea. "I thought maybe I'd listen in," he said to Proctor. "If that's all right. Maybe she forgets something she told me, I can tell you what it is." He coughed into a gloved fist. "If that's all right with you."

Taz watched Doc stiffen in annoyance, but Proctor only nodded, once, very slowly, not taking his gaze from Suze's face.

Behind him the lightning walked, and the thunder grew more insistent.

Taz felt Suze take a breath then, grow tense, and he took a chance, put a palm lightly on the small of her back. An encouragement. He figured she needed it the way Proctor studied her, those eyes not even he liked to look at too long.

They saw too much.

"Tell me," Proctor said quietly. Gently.

When Suze finished no one spoke, and she lifted a hand in question, squinting against the wind. "I wasn't drunk, if that's what you're thinking." Defensive, clearly wondering why she'd agreed to talk. She looked up at Taz. "I wasn't. Mr. Cobb can tell you."

"I didn't say you were." Proctor shifted.

The lightning crackled audibly, its thunder gaining echoes, and Taz watched as most of the people standing at the rail began to drift away uneasily.

Proctor shifted again, adjusting his collar, swiping at the hair the wind snapped around his face. "Maybe we should—" he said, and lifted a chin toward the hotel.

Taz was surprised when Suze shook her head emphatically. "No. I want to know now, Mr. Proctor. If we go inside, something will distract us, and anyway, Baron will be on me to get back to work. Taz told me you would understand. He said you would explain." Her voice began to tremble. "You don't know the nightmares, Mr. Proctor. So please now, okay?"

"Mahjra," he said.

She blinked in astonishment, lowered her head, looked up. *"Mahjrachin,"* she told him, wonder in her tone. "Russian. That's the Russian. I remember my grandmother, she used to . . ." Her voice faded, lips moving until at last she shook her head quickly. Hard. "A story. You know, scare the kids with spooky stuff. It's been so long since I've heard it."

Taz had no idea what they were talking about, but he saw the way Proctor's mouth pulled at one corner, not quite a smile. Doc was no help, his face gave nothing away, and the old cop only coughed and spat over the rail.

"A quick course," Proctor said then, looking up at the beacon, looking away, but not at them. "If there's any such thing as a rare . . . let's call him a creature, this is it. Very little written down. Most of it oral history, and not much of that, either. Some claim he's a form of vampire, or some low-order demon." He looked up. "He's neither of those. Mahjra. He is what he is."

His voice was low, yet it carried through the thunder, the growing anger of the surf, the growing roar of the wind.

"He is, to coin a cliché, mostly a creature of the night. Sunlight weakens but doesn't kill him. Much stronger than most men. No wings, but he can fly in some limited way I can't remember. Gliding maybe, I'm not sure. According to the stories, his nails can elongate into razor-sharp claws. Think of the fingernails you've seen in pictures of those old Chinese emperors. He uses them to scoop out his victim's eyes and cut out the tongue. Then . . . he eats them."

"Jesus," Taz said, shuddering. "He can't just drink blood?"

Proctor gestured at his eyes, his mouth. "The eyes see, the tongue speaks. I don't know exactly how it works, but they sustain him, and it's the way he learns about the time he's in. As well as keeping the victims from describing him."

"But they're dead," Taz protested.

Proctor looked at him. "This time, yes. But not always."

"Aw, jeez, Boss."

Doc touched a gloved finger to his chin. "He's immortal?"

"No, just extremely long-lived. He ages, but very slowly. He's not the Living Dead, a walking corpse. He's not a ghost. Like I said, he's not a denom. He is, however, as vicious as any demon you've ever heard of. He doesn't care about anything except surviving."

Cobb coughed, and spat again. "So you're saying this thing is real?"

Proctor didn't answer.

The spider-leg lightning was replaced by single broad

flashes, the cannonade by explosions so loud Taz felt them in his bones.

When Proctor spoke again, it was to Suze, patiently, carefully explaining the gimmicks used to produce what looked like mist, or fog. "You weren't running as fast as you thought," he said gently, "and his illusion made him seem that much faster. He counts on that, the distortion of perspective and time, for everything to work. You were angry, and in a hurry." A faint one-sided grin. "You can do pretty weird things to yourself in a state like that."

She shook her head in confusion. "That's what Mr. Cobb said, too, but I don't know. It seemed so real, you know?" Fingers pushed back through her curls. "I wish Mischa were here." Her smile was almost rueful. "He's more Russian than me. He remembers these things better. He knows the stories."

"It wouldn't make any difference," Proctor answered in the same careful tone. "A mahjra isn't Russian. Like a vampire or a were-beast, it crosses cultures." He inhaled slowly, deeply. "The most important thing is, Miss Acmarov, that the Ripper is *not* one of these things your grandmother told you about. He probably doesn't even know about it." His voice hardened. "Believe me on this, he's nothing more than a brutal killer. A butcher. Playing games, that's all. The eyes, the tongue, he's playing games." He nodded sharply. "You were very lucky, Suze. Very, very lucky."

Cobb gripped the railing with both hands and leaned back, face to the strengthening wind, cheeks and forehead reddening. "He can't be a woman?"

Proctor hesitated. Then: "Yes, it can."

The old cop nodded, bowed his head, grunted.

Abruptly Suze held out her hand, and Proctor took it. "Thank you," she said. "I've got to get to rehearsal, but thanks. Really."

She was gone before Taz could have a word, but he watched her hurry into the hotel, head up, one hand holding her coat closed at the throat. When she was gone, he said, "She's not sure."

"I know." A pause. "But she will be."

Taz realized then that his teeth had begun to chatter, that

the temperature had continued to fall. Flares of silver darted through the beacon as it swept over the beach, and he couldn't tell if they were rain or snow.

"Correct me if I'm wrong," Cobb said, putting his back to the wind, "but the way you talk, you talk like this thing is real. Like it walks around like a normal person. Like we can't tell the difference."

Doc snorted.

Proctor blew out a breath, a temporary veil before his face. "You can't," he said.

"Tough fella." The old man took off his hat, scratched through his hair. "Could be me even, just standing here, listening to you talking."

Proctor nodded.

Cobb replaced his hat, adjusted it with both hands. "Very entertaining, Mr. Proctor, I enjoyed the story. You helped the girl, and that's important. She doesn't realize it yet, but you did." He started for the hotel. "But it doesn't help me find the man who killed Fred."

Taz shivered violently when a surge of damp cold passed through him. A check over Proctor's shoulder, and he saw that the lightning had stopped. So had the thunder. His watch told him it was only a few minutes after three.

He looked at Proctor. "Not many people know about this mahjra thing, right?"

Proctor nodded.

"So what are the odds?" he asked.

Doc looked at him strangely; Proctor didn't look at him at all.

Taz shook his head, his right hand out to indicate the length of the boardwalk. "For something that hardly anyone knows about, what are the odds that two—no, maybe four people who know about this . . . I don't know, this rare *thing,* are in the same place at the same time?"

Proctor pushed away from the railing and headed for the entrance. Not a look, not a sound.

"That's what I thought," he said in whispered resignation. "Son of a bitch, that's what I thought."

TWENTY-FOUR

What are the odds?

Proctor sat in the Briny, a glass of ginger ale and a small basket of tiny pretzels in front of him, jacket hung on the back of his chair. Except for the bartender, he was the only one here.

He had left the others on the boardwalk, knowing from their expressions that they would, for the time being, keep their distance. Time to think was what he needed, and a place to do it in. The room was no good—present or not, Petra would be distracting, and wandering the halls as he had the night before would sooner or later alert Hotel Security. It was too cold outside, the lobby slowly degenerating into mild chaos. The Briny, however, once he saw it was empty, promised a few minutes of paradoxical peace, since the casino below provided him with sufficient white noise not to bother him.

What are the odds?

He sat so he could rest his arm on the carved wall's flat top, watching but paying little attention to the gamblers. Not that there were all that many. The middle of Saturday afternoon, and less than half the tables were open, and the ones in use weren't filled. He suspected that, storm or no, this wasn't unusual. Southward, the density of casinos promised continuous excitement—you don't get it in one, walk next door to the next, or the next, often through connecting tunnels. Here, walking next door was, for many, too much of a hike. While there were some who probably appreciated the relative lack of electric tension, most apparently didn't.

Come on, Proctor, what are the odds?

He sipped; he ate; he stirred the ginger ale with a cocktail straw and listened to the music of the ice cubes as they ricocheted off each other and the side of the frosted glass.

Got a better question for you, Taz, he thought; what are the odds that I had a dream about a woman, and she told me the mahjra's name?

Mischa's fingers hovered over the keyboard, his eyes closed, his lips moving silently as he played and sang without a sound. In his head it was great, this latest song of his. A ballad, a hymn to unrequited love. Touching without being maudlin; clever without announcing it; the voice deliberately sexless so anyone could sing it.

Dacey was his muse.

Beside him, a square piece of scrounged plywood balanced on the tops of four folding chairs. It held blank sheet music and a half dozen pencils, but not a note, not a word had been written yet. He wanted to learn it first; he wanted to make sure.

What he wanted was Dacey Logetta; what he wanted was to be one of those guys he'd seen with her at the end of her shift, sneaking off arm in arm, smiling, laughing, bumping hips . . . promising.

Nothing he'd done so far had changed a thing. He was still "cute," the unoffensive piano guy with the black curly hair. The safe one.

He growled softly.

You are pathetic, Acmarov, you know that, right? You are goddamn pathetic.

The door opened, and someone said, "Oops, sorry."

He looked and smiled. "Hey, Zach."

Zach Berls, the maintenance crew's afternoon chief, grinned through his heavy brown beard. "Doing the genius thing?"

"Trying."

"You'll get it, no sweat. Need you, though."

He could have argued, but didn't feel like it. Part of his job was helping out the crew when needed. It had been made to seem as if he had an actual choice; the reality, reflected in his paycheck, was something quite different.

He closed the keyboard lid. "What's up?"

"Damn storm's ready to blow again. Gotta make sure the backups are okay."

And you couldn't do this alone? Mischa thought as he followed the stocky man into the hall. A glance at his watch, and he groaned. He was supposed to meet Suze upstairs in a couple of minutes; she was going to kill him.

They swung right and took a service elevator that only moved between this floor and those below. When they reached the next stop, Berls handed him a bulky, high-intensity flashlight, warning him not to aim it at his eyes, or look too long at the beam. "Damn thing'll louse up your eyes, kid."

Mischa had been down here several times before, and didn't like it. A series of vast rooms lined with pipes and bundled wires, machinery whose purpose he could only guess at, lighting from caged bulbs that didn't quite do the job. The only sounds, the clank and constant hum of engines. All it needed was dripping water and escaping steam, and he'd feel as if he stepped into a cheap horror movie.

"Meet you there," Zach said, giving him a playful shove toward a small area on the far side of the room, blocked off by a ceiling-high wall of thick-wire mesh framed with pitted iron. Red warning signs. The mesh-and-steel door boasted an electronic lock. He wondered if a simple pair of wire cutters would do the job anyway.

Back in the shadows Zach cursed.

Mischa rolled his eyes and switched on his light, passed it over the array of monitors and squat generators on the other side.

"Holy shit," he said.

"What?" Zach yelled. "You say something?"

"Yeah," he called, still working the light. "You'd better get over here, man. I think you got a problem."

Lieutenant MacEdan said, "Mr. Gladman, you'll be happy to know there'll be a car waiting for you downstairs in a couple of minutes. Sergeant Cox here is going to take you someplace we think is better for you right now."

Bruno shook his head. "I want to stay here. That man, that guy, he knows."

Please, Granna thought; please, I'm too tired for this crap.

"I'm sorry, Mr. Gladman, but you don't have a choice."

Cox gestured at the floor. "Put your shoes on, pal. We're outta here."

Bruno shook his head again. Stubborn, like a child.

"I ain't gonna tell you again," Cox said, and jerked a thumb toward the two uniformed cops in the hall. "Do it, or we'll do it for you."

"No."

Granna's patience, already thin since her encounter with Proctor, signaled wearily to her sergeant to get it over with, and stepped into the hall, nodding at the uniforms as they hurried past her to assist Cox. She rolled her eyes at the high-pitched protests and the curses, steeled herself against the scuffling and grunts of blows landed, had a bad feeling she'd have to answer for every damn bruise the chauffeur suffered, and whirled when she heard a shout of alarm.

"No," she said calmly, when she saw Bruno swaying in the doorway. "This is foolish, Mr. Gladman. We're not the bad guys here, remember?"

Gladman had a gun, and he wasted no time. Keeping the weapon trained on her heart, he sidled along the wall toward the elevators. "You don't get it," he said, voice tight with fear. A small scratch on his brow seemed larger against his pale skin. "I'm not going with you. I'm finding that guy. He knows, you don't."

From the corner of her vision, she saw Cox struggling to his feet, one of the others unmoving on the bed, the second uniform fighting his way clear of the legs of a chair.

"Mr. Gladman—"

"Swear to God, lady," he said, "one step, and I'll shoot."

She took it, a hand out.

He fired.

Doc and Taz stood against the lobby wall, the mermaid between them and the milling guests. Harried bellmen rushed their packed hand trolleys toward the back entrance, many guests carried their own bags, and the noise filled the room like an old-fashioned train station.

"What should we do, Doc?"

"I must confess, Paul, I'm at a loss."

"I have to tell you, I don't get it. One minute he acts like this mahjra thing is for real, the next he's making like it's only some nutcase." He snorted a laugh. "I didn't mean 'only' some nutcase. I meant—"

"I know, Paul, I know."

"So what do you think? About the nut, I mean."

Doc shook his head. "Again, I'm at a loss."

"You want to know what I think?"

"It would help."

"I think the boss believes it, only he doesn't know it just yet. I think . . . I think I do, too. Like I said, the odds. And . . ." He shook his head. "Never mind, it's not important."

Doc glanced at him sideways. "Paul."

Taz slumped a bit, stared unhappily at the floor. "I think, Doc, you don't like this very much. You and Lana, all those hours in the office making me look at pictures and things, finding the fakes and stuff, making me concentrate . . . that's a whole 'nother thing than this, and you really don't like it."

Doc didn't respond beyond the touch of two fingers to the knot of his tie.

"Doc, I didn't mean to insult you. Honest to God, I wasn't slamming you or anything."

"I understand." Doc straightened his shoulders. "It is, as you say, entirely different out here." He adjusted his pocket handkerchief, stared at his hand for a moment, and let it drop to his side. "Another confession, Paul, about which you will tell no one."

"Cross my heart, swear it."

"I had no idea, Paul. I had no idea it would be like this."

The odds, Proctor thought with a glance at the gamblers, are too damn long.

A sound effect below made him start, reminding him of the walking lightning, and he frowned for a moment. Taz had been right about that, too—a display like that couldn't possibly be natural.

"You know what your problem is?" he whispered.

No, he answered silently; what?

"You're thinking too damn much."

A sardonic grin for his pronouncement of the at-long-last obvious, and he picked out four of the small pretzels and placed them in a row in front of him. Used the straw to poke at them, shift them around into meaningless patterns. Trying to clear his mind, not to think but to *feel*. To see beyond the logic of things to the sense of them. Scowling, grunting softly, shaking his head slowly in frustration because there was something in the way. Something blocking him. Something that would not allow him to take that last step, the one through the Looking Glass, *his* Looking Glass, into the world too few knew.

He didn't look up when someone took the chair opposite him.

He didn't move when a slender finger appeared over the pretzels, and a long clear nail hooked one and lifted it away.

He heard the first crunching bite, he heard the chewing, and he heard a friendly voice say, "Mr. Proctor, I understand you're looking for me. My name is Emile Valknir."

TWENTY-FIVE

Under the lifeboat portico departing guests gathered with their luggage, waiting for their automobiles, snarling about the time it took a taxi to arrive, arguing with the bell captain, who looked to commit murder. Every few seconds one of them, usually a man, would step into the open and stare at the sky, shrug, and step back.

The wind was constant, neither weak nor strong; they could see their breath, puffs and plumes of it.

They could feel the cold.

"This is the Shore," one man complained. "It can't snow here, can it?"

"Stick around," someone answered grumpily. "You'd be surprised."

A minor fender bender between a van and a jitney made them groan at the anticipated delays; a one-legged gull scolded them from atop one of the obelisk globes; an ambulance siren cried; someone's brakes squealed; three patrol cars slammed to a halt at the curb, and a dozen cops climbed out and hustled inside.

No one asked why, they only demanded faster action.

The afternoon darkened.

And they could all feel the cold.

"I don't know about you," Valknir said amiably, "but I'm enjoying myself immensely this weekend." He took a pretzel from the basket and studied it as if he'd never seen one before popping it into his mouth. He smiled as he chewed. He swallowed. "Aren't you?"

There was nothing sinister, and certainly nothing dramatic, about him. His narrow forehead was a rectangle of smooth corners and barely perceptible edges, his brown eyes had a faint Oriental cast, but his nose and lips were nondescript, his teeth when he smiled neither filed nor fanged. Slightly swarthy skin. Thick fair hair brushed straight back, just reaching the collar of his ordinary dark brown suit.

"Of course," he said, "as soon as I heard about you, I just had to meet you."

Proctor sat back slowly, sliding his hands off the table—one settled on the armrest, the other slipped into his lap where it shifted in and out of a fist.

Valknir ate another pretzel and made a face, an exaggerated shudder. "Too much salt. Bad for the heart." He half turned and signaled the bartender for a drink, making it clear all he wanted was a beer. Looking at Proctor, he said, "I never drink . . . wine," and guffawed, slapping the table with a palm, wiping an invisible tear from his eye. "Damn, I've always wanted to say that."

Proctor picked up his ginger ale and sipped it, not because he was thirsty, but to see how badly his hand would shake. It didn't, no sign at all of how he felt—still startled, and definitely still off balance. Fear, if it came, would come later.

He wished he had his gun.

Whatever doubts he might still have had about the mahjra's being in the city faded when he replaced his glass and caught a clear, distant scent of cloves.

When the beer was delivered, Valknir held it up to the dim light, turning the glass slowly. "The sad thing about vampires is, Mr. Proctor, that they can dress up all they want, they can live a thousand years, but they can never truly enjoy the good life. Pleasant company, a fine meal, a decent beer. Cheers." And he drank half the glass without once taking his gaze from Proctor's face.

When he was finished, he set the glass down. "Are you going to live a thousand years, Mr. Proctor?"

Proctor shook his head. "I doubt it."

"Me, too, Mr. Proctor. I doubt you will, either." He wiped a trace of foam from his upper lip with the side of a finger.

"But you haven't answered my question yet, sir. Are you having a good time?"

Proctor felt it then—a curious cold calm settling over and within him. A comfortable, familiar sensation that allowed him, after a moment, to answer, "Not yet. But I will."

"Wonderful. That's great. But I think you're wrong there, as well."

"Really."

"But of course. Having a good time requires . . . well, it requires life, Mr. Proctor. Life in all senses of the word." A quick toothsome smile. "You won't be living that long."

"Maybe. Maybe not."

Valknir grunted, traced the side of his glass with the edge of his thumb. "You doubt my prophetic abilities?"

Proctor shrugged; he didn't care one way or the other.

The mahjra laughed silently without parting his lips. "Amazing. You sit there without a quiver, and yet you know what I've done. Well, not *all* that I've done. But you know. And still . . . nothing. I like that, actually. A man resigned to his fate. It makes it all so much easier."

Deliberately Proctor looked away and down at the gambling floor, noticing a few people in open topcoats, unable to leave without making one last bet. He spotted Reno Baron across the way, traveling up the escalator, back too rigid, arms too stiff. From the Tides he could hear, faintly, the jazz trio, the song unknown.

He blinked slowly, realizing for the first time how relatively quiet the place had become. Only a few slots ringing, no commotions at the tables, just a few murmurs of conversations rising toward the ceiling. It was more like three in the morning than three in the afternoon.

At the corner of his vision, he saw Valknir drag the pretzel basket toward him as he signaled languidly for another beer. On the Gallery opposite, he saw Baron standing at the top of the escalator, and from the manager's expression he guessed the man had received some unpleasant news.

The second drink was delivered.

The trio played on.

Again deliberately, Proctor turned his head and, keeping his tone flat, said, "Why?"

Puzzled, Valknir cocked an eyebrow. "Why what?"

"All those people. You don't need them. Not all of them."

"True enough."

"Then why?"

"It pleases me."

"But you bring attention to yourself. I wouldn't think that would be wise."

Valknir hooked another pretzel; the nail had grown. "They haven't caught me, have they?" A shrug. "Not for a very long time." He drank, wiped his lip, leaned forward, holding up an index finger close to his chest, so no one else could see. The nail had grown again, six inches now and sharp. His expression remained perfectly bland. "You realize, don't you, that I could, if I wanted, reach across this table and open your throat before your heart took another beat."

Proctor nodded carefully, at the same time making sure he didn't stare directly into those eyes. He had seen what looked like tiny points of fire there, or pinpricks of light that were not reflections. Whichever they were, he made sure they would not entrap him.

Valknir's eyes narrowed. "That I choose not to do this should please you."

Proctor only smiled coldly. "The point being?"

Valknir tapped the finger against his chest; the nail withdrew. "The point, Mr. Proctor, is that I am in control. I am always in control. You would do well to remember that."

"You sound like a cheap movie."

"Life is a cheap movie, Mr. Proctor."

Proctor couldn't help it; he barked a laugh. "Jesus, that's awful."

Valknir's expression didn't change. "Please, don't tempt me."

Proctor raised a hand in a blatantly insincere apology, picked up his own glass, and drank, abruptly aware of how dry his throat was, how tight were the muscles across his chest. He wanted out of this place, but he dared not move.

Foolishly he had issued an unspoken challenge, and was just as foolishly determined to see it through.

The lights flickered then, so quickly he wasn't sure if it had actually happened, and he could feel a subtle change in the air pressure, sense the building shudder as if something had slammed against it.

The storm, he thought; it's back.

Valknir didn't seem to notice. He emptied his glass, smacked his lips loudly. "You don't know much about me, do you? My kind."

"More than you think."

The mahjra shook his head in a mild scolding. "I've been around too long to be bluffed by someone like you, Mr. Proctor. Don't insult me. It's . . . insulting." He rested his elbows on the table, steepled his fingers under his chin. "You are, as the saying goes, a babe in the woods, yes? No. A sheep among wolves. Worse; a lamb."

Proctor gave him an insolent, one-shoulder shrug.

Valknir's answering laugh stayed deep in his throat. "Amazing. I've heard some things about you, you know. You have a certain reputation. Here and there."

Proctor rotated his nearly empty glass with two fingers, slowly, feeling the melting ice cubes bump softly against the sides. "And this is supposed to be . . . what? A compliment? A threat?"

"Good heavens, no, Mr. Proctor, not a threat at all. A simple matter of survival, a man as well read as you should know that." A finger up—pay attention. "The man who better knows his enemy has the better ground. And I know a hell of a lot more about you than you know about me."

Again, Proctor couldn't help it; he laughed, a single explosive sound. "Sorry, Emile, but I think Pogo said it better, for this particular situation."

Valknir frowned. "I don't know what you mean. Who is that? What did he say?"

"It doesn't matter who he is," Proctor answered. "What he said was something like: I have met the enemy, and he is us."

"I don't get it."

"Of course not."

A draft circled the table, fluttering the napkins before moving on.

Suddenly Valknir grinned expansively and clapped his hands once, rubbing his palms together briskly. "I'm telling you the truth, Proctor, I really am having a wonderful time. And now it's even better, all because of you."

"I'm glad you're happy."

"I am. Really, I am."

Proctor spun the glass one more time before pulling his hand away. "You won't be."

Valknir's grin became a delighted smile, a hand pressed to his heart. "I can't get over just how amazing you are. Amazingly stupid. Amazingly arrogant." He popped another pretzel into his mouth. "I love it. I really love it." The grin stayed; the voice lowered. "For every step you take against me, Mr. Proctor, someone will die. Remember that, should you get the urge to play hero." He licked his lips as if anticipating a feast. "For every *thing* you think you know about me, there are a dozen you don't." He waggled a warning finger. "And that, my friend, is going to kill you." Another pretzel as he rose, not a tall man at all and slender. "I'll leave you to pay the check, if you don't mind."

"My pleasure."

"I suppose it would be too much to shake hands, one worthy opponent to another."

Proctor's smile was cold. "Absolutely."

"I thought so." He bent over, cocked his head, a faint splash of fire in his eyes, one hand firm on Proctor's shoulder. Pulled it quickly away, backed up a step, scowling. Whispering harshly: "It will be dark soon, Mr. Proctor. Fair warning—the night is mine."

He straightened, slipped a hand casually into a pocket, and walked away, waving a friendly farewell to the bartender. At the exit he sidestepped with outspread arms and exaggerated apologies to the two men about to enter, turned, and waved to Proctor before slipping out of sight.

Nothing left of him but the faint scent of cloves.

TWENTY-SIX

Proctor felt as if he were going to explode.

After a long moment drawn thin to its breaking point, he reached for his glass and stopped, startled at how violently his hand trembled. He slapped it flat on the table and pressed it hard against the glass top as Taz and Doc joined him. Without acknowledging them beyond a curt nod, he closed his eyes, willing his heart to beat, his lungs to work, and his temper not to go nova.

fair warning.

He could feel his neck muscles begin to quiver, so taut were they, and he concentrated on them, relaxed them as best he could; he corralled the obscenities that swirled through his mind; he licked dry lips.

"Boss?"

Keeping his eyes closed, his voice tight and deep: "In a minute."

There had been a time once when Valknir's constant smiling mockery would have sent him lunging across the table for his throat; there had been a time once when he had been too filled with his own sense of righteous purpose and retribution, and the affront he had just received would have exposed him for what he had been—too young, too hotheaded for a reasonable, much less rational, response; and there had been a time once, not so long ago, when he believed he had outgrown the dictates of his temper.

"Proctor."

Tight-lipped: "In a minute, Doc, in a minute."

He was angry for a number of reasons, not the least of which was because he had been, finally, afraid.

Afraid of how easily Valknir had manipulated him, and taunted him, and had gotten so close Proctor could almost feel the flesh of his throat parting.

He took a stuttering breath, eyes still closed. "That man. The one you bumped into. That was him."

"Who?" Taz said.

"Who do you think?"

A pause, then: "Son of a bitch."

Proctor heard Doc mutter something and leave, returning a minute later to place three glasses on the table. He smelled liquor, strong liquor, and he swallowed hard. Waiting until he could open his eyes and not scream his anger. When at last he did, and was able to focus, Taz was pale and Doc rigid; Taz's tumbler was already half empty, Doc's still untouched and on the table, cupped in his palms.

"You got a good look?" His voice was strained.

They nodded.

"You can describe him to Lieutenant MacEdan if you have to?"

They nodded again.

When Taz made to rise, however, Proctor said, "Wait," and after several deep breaths, he gave them as close to a word-by-word account as he could of his conversation with the mahjra.

every step you take against me

"We have to be careful."

"They're going to die anyway," said Doc bluntly. "He wants to freeze you. If you worry too much, you won't be able to do anything."

"I know."

"Then it stands to reason we should have as many people working with us as we can."

Proctor picked up his liquor and sipped it, grimaced, and put it down quickly. Whatever it was, it was too strong, but the taste and the reaction shocked him onto a ledge just above his still boiling rage. Fighting for control had seldom been so difficult.

"It's a big hotel, Doc. And think for a minute what we'd have to tell the lieutenant.

"Okay, Granna, here's the deal—your psycho killer is a young guy, looks about my age, blond and brown-eyed, ordinary build, boring brown suit. No horns, no tail, no fangs, no cloven hoofs. How do I know he's the one? He told me. We met over beer and pretzels just a little while ago, and he told me."

Doc nodded. "Yes. I see your point. I suppose that means we're pretty much on our own."

Proctor watched with grim amusement as Taz emptied his glass in a couple of swallows, and choked, tears instantly filling his eyes. A napkin took care of the tears, a weak smile suggested he was all right now, don't mind me, I'm a jerk.

"And when we find him?"

"Well, that's easy," Taz declared hoarsely. "We finish him."

"How?"

"I don't know. Guns, stakes, silver bullets, knives, hell, I don't know."

Proctor shook his head. "Neither do I. And if we are lucky enough to confront him, with whatever weapons we pick, and we're wrong . . ." He lifted his right hand; it was reasonably steady. "He said he knew me. Of me. How did he know I was here? How did he know what I looked like?"

Doc looked pensive; Taz bit down on his lower lip.

"Right," Proctor said to the younger man. "The three of us, Mr. Cobb . . . and Miss Acmarov. I seriously doubt the old man would tell a stranger all about me, do you?"

"Boss, I—"

"Where is she, Taz?"

"She wouldn't—"

Proctor stared him silent. "I didn't say she told him. In fact, I doubt she did. But she told somebody, and we have to find out who." He toyed with his glass, pushed it away. "Taz?"

The young man shrugged helplessly.

Doc cleared his throat. "She said something about an early performance today. A supper show, I believe. And a rehearsal beforehand."

Proctor stood. "Where do they rehearse?"

Taz pointed at the floor. "One floor down." A weak smile. "She told me before. They have a rehearsal thing down there. That's where her cousin works, too, sometimes. On the piano."

"The piano," Proctor said flatly.

Taz shrugged. "He writes song and stuff, I think."

"Get her."

"I can—"

"Now, Taz." Proctor frowned. "Get her. Bring her here. I don't care what she's doing, just bring her. Now."

Taz jumped at the vehemence in Proctor's voice, nearly tipped over his chair as he stood. A shaky nod, and he was gone.

And Doc said, "It wasn't his fault, you know." He lifted his chin. "I'll find that woman for you. If you insist."

Proctor didn't apologize, shook a finger when Doc made to rise. "Hang on a minute." He sagged back in his chair, lowered his head so that his chin nearly touched his chest. "Doc, we've got a problem here, and I don't know how to solve it."

Bruno Gladman couldn't go any higher unless he climbed out a window to get up to the roof. He wasn't sure what floor he was on, but he could tell this wasn't for the ordinary guests. Everything looked too rich, too classy.

And it was only a matter of time before the cops found him.

He was pretty sure he hadn't hit the lady lieutenant, but he hadn't stuck around to find out. As soon as he'd fired, he raced down the hall and slammed through a fire door into a stairwell. They would expect him to try to get out of the hotel as fast as he could, so he'd gone up instead and wandered the hallways at a trot until he realized he was trapped.

He had to go back down.

What he needed was a little luck, and stairs that dropped below the main floor. Even in his panic, he knew that the hotel was too large for them to cover every inch every second. Not for him. He was a nobody. He wasn't the Ripper.

His eyes filled with sudden tears, and he wiped them away angrily.

He used a different fire door, and looked over the railing,

into a darkness that pooled at the bottom. Not a sound beyond the slow muffled howl of a wind.

He gripped the metal railing with his left hand, held the gun in his right, and climbed down as quietly as he could. As fast as he could. Each step one fervent prayer closer to staying alive.

Proctor avoided Falcon's eyes, the disapproval he saw there. And the uncertainty. Instead he pulled something from his pocket, the red chip, and rubbed it between his thumb and fingers as if it were a worry bead.

A long silence before he finally said, "I'm sorry I snapped at him, okay? I'll make it up to him later."

Falcon nodded. "You're under pressure. It's understandable."

"No, Doc, it's not." He rapped the chip against the table. "Nothing's understandable around here. Least of all me."

Falcon picked up his drink, swirled it, took a sip. "You're saying you're not yourself, is that it? That this . . ." He gestured with the glass. "That this is unusual."

Proctor set the chip down and folded his hands on the table. "Doc, there's no time to explain how things usually go when I find out it's not a scam. You'll have to trust me when I say, this is not usual for me. I learn fast. I have to. But . . ." His expression twisted in frustration. "Damn." He pushed at the chip with his folded hands. "It's like I'm living in a cloud, Doc. Sometimes I see things clearly, but most of the time I can't see anything but shapes, and I don't know how to get rid of it."

Falcon sipped again. "Perhaps, if what you tell me is true, he's already used that mesmerizing ability."

Proctor managed a smile. "Clouded this man's mind, did he?"

"You can't discount it."

"But I only met him tonight. A few minutes ago. Unless he's so powerful he can—no, he's not. He's . . . no."

"Then count yourself lucky that you're still alive."

Proctor nudged the chip again, staring at it, not really seeing it. "That's the other point, Doc—he could have easily killed me, but he didn't. He threatened to, and I thought he was just playing with me, mocking me. But he could have done it so easily. He could have fixed the bartender so the guy wouldn't notice anything for a while, then killed me right here. Or he could have used those eyes on me and walked me out like we were old friends, and done it somewhere else. But he didn't."

"Why, Doc?"

Doc scratched the side of his nose. "Something you said?"

"I doubt it."

"Something you did?"

"I didn't do anything."

Doc leaned forward, just a little. "But you don't know that, do you?"

Proctor banged the table softly with his double fists. And again. "That's exactly the point. I haven't a clue what the hell to do. I tried a bluff of my own, but he knows damn well I don't know jack about him. He's . . ."

Falcon sat back. "In control. Just as he said. And that, as Paul might say, pisses you off."

"Doc, you have no idea how right that is."

The older man grunted. "I have a question."

"I don't have any answers."

"How did you know his name? How did you know he wasn't just a murderer?"

Proctor closed his eyes. Swallowed. Looked at Falcon and said, "I had a dream."

By the time Bruno reached the fourteenth floor, he had taken to descending two steps at a time.

The wind, and his footsteps, were too loud.

Between the twelfth and eleventh floors, his hand slipped off the railing, and he sprawled onto the landing, his head glancing off the concrete-block wall. He gasped at the pain, at the split second of darkness, and when he tried to stand, realized he'd done something awful to his right ankle. When he checked it, sucking in a harsh breath at the fierce tenderness around the ankle, he saw blood from a nasty scrape. Nothing to worry about there, if he could only still walk.

It took a few tries to get to his feet, and as he leaned against the railing, panting, he heard the clank and hiss of a door opening far above him.

He held his breath, sweat on his face and hands, running ice down his back; he listened and heard nothing; he hopped on one foot to the stairs, listened again, and heard someone call his name softly.

He hopped-fell into the landing corner, the gun aiming up the stairwell toward the ninth floor.

He knew that voice.

And a moment later, he recognized the laugh.

Doc pushed his glass away as Proctor finished telling the dream. "I see a couple of things, possibly."

Proctor waited.

"Either the dream was genuinely prophetic—something you might consider—or it wasn't a dream at all, in which case that entertains another unpleasant notion we need not go into right away. Or you somehow already knew the name and attached it to the dream."

"You're saying she's not human. Or has, I don't know, powers."

Falcon looked pained. "I'm saying that's not what should concern us now, Proctor, if indeed that's the case. What—"

Proctor lowered his head and thought for a moment, then raised it slowly, his eyes narrowed. "Find her, Doc. I don't care how. Spread money around, I don't care how much. Bribe the staff, bribe that Baron guy, I don't give a damn. Find her, Doc. Believe me, it is definitely something that concerns us now."

Bruno fired twice, and twice the mahjra grinned, waving at the air in front of him as if batting the bullets away. Then it leaned over him and grabbed his wrist, squeezing effortlessly until the tears came and the gun fell.

When Bruno could see again, his mouth opened to scream, and Valknir clamped a palm over it with a scolding shake of his head. The nail, the claw, on his other hand was less than an inch from the corner of Bruno's left eye.

"Are you a gambling man, Mr. Gladman? Don't answer, it's all right, I won't think you rude. Think instead. Think about how long I'm going to let you live. Think about how quickly you're going to want to die."

It happened so swiftly, Bruno didn't understand at first what the mahjra held so delicately between its teeth. When he did, and the pain in the empty socket arrived, he shrieked beneath the hand and began to struggle.

And Valknir grinned and bit down.

TWENTY-SEVEN

Proctor could only sit for a few minutes after Doc left. He thought he understood now why he'd been so indecisive and tentative since arriving, and the understanding had, like a strong wind, cleared his mind. At least for the moment.

Falcon probably thought he had been either hypnotized or bewitched, and for now that was all right. It wouldn't do for him to know that Proctor figured bewitched was indeed close enough, but not in the sense Doc would be thinking.

He laughed quickly, and quietly.

Lana, he thought, you are not going to believe this when I tell you.

He stood, tapped a finger on the table, swept the chip and a few pretzels into his pocket, and settled his tab with the bartender. With a ten-dollar bill he was assured the man would tell Taz and the woman to wait until Proctor returned. He couldn't stay, not now. He had to move.

His first stop was the lobby, which was nearly deserted, a disconsolate couple arguing feebly with a female clerk about a charge to their room, the woman casting apprehensive looks at the row of glass doors, each look making it seem as if she'd shrunk a little more.

"Great," Proctor muttered.

Despite the awning, the doors were touched with patches of ice. A coating of ice on the boards gave them a glossy shine.

The rain had turned to sleet.

The desk clerk's voice was unintentionally loud: "Sir, I'm

sorry, but the roads are getting worse. If you really do want to drive in this, you'll have to get your car yourself."

The man sputtered, ready to explode, until the woman put a hand on his shoulder.

Proctor passed a palm over the glass, shivering at the cold, and pushed the door open. The wind threatened to take it from him, and he could hear the sleet, crackling like soft lightning, husking over the boardwalk as if it were made of dry grass.

The casino was nearly deserted. Dealers and croupiers stood at empty tables, mannequins in white shirts and black vests embroidered with nautical trim. No one looked up as he passed; no one urged him to sit in on a hand, or have a turn at the wheel, or take a pair of dice. Unnaturally quiet; even the jazz trio had stopped playing. Now, the clatter of a slot machine was intrusive, not background noise.

The South Promenade was empty, the guard gone from the men's room, the two restaurants with only a handful of patrons each.

At the back the bell captain paced at the doors, shaking his head. There was no one under the lifeboat, no waiting cabs, no cars. The sleet bounced off the street like hail.

"Pretty bad?" Proctor said.

"Worse than snow," Delmonico answered sourly. "Can't drive in this shit. Man, I'm gonna be stuck here all night."

Proctor moved closer, and frowned when he saw three patrol cars parked on the road arc's far side. "Trouble?"

"How the hell should I know? Nobody tells me anything. They come running in like they was making a raid, no one tells me what the hell's going on."

The cold here was bad. It gathered in the small alcove and insinuated itself into his bones. He rubbed an arm briskly and nodded commiseration and thanks before he hurried to the corner, looked up the North Promenade, and saw a hotel guard at each of the elevator banks. As he watched, a young man left the casino floor and was pointed to the first elevator bank.

"Problem?" Proctor asked when he reached the first guard.

"Routine maintenance," the man answered with a straight face, hands cupped behind his back. "Taking advantage of the lull. If you wish to go to your room, please take the elevators closest to the lobby, sir. Use the escalators for the Gallery. Thank you."

Proctor did just that, and saw similar guards at the banks there, too. Another killing? Something with Bruno? He knew none of the men would tell him a thing, so he moved down to the shops, noting how few customers there were, how the clerks looked less bored than anxious. He wandered in and out, pausing once at a collection of ruby-like accessories in the jewelry store, from letter openers to corkscrews. He took out his chip; it looked to be the same, but couldn't be. From the prices he saw, the chip alone would be worth thousands.

The Davy Jones was empty. The theater's ticket booth was closed. Only the dealers and hostesses were in the high-roller rooms.

He'd had enough, seen enough.

It would take a blind man not to notice that the Lighthouse was under siege.

Half an hour earlier, Lieutenant MacEdan had looked at Sergeant Cox and said, "I don't care how many rooms there are. You will check every damn one of them until you find that idiot. Mr. Baron here will go with you, to let you in when there's no answer." She shook her head. "Forget it. Just go in, don't bother to knock."

Then she turned to a young uniformed cop, whose forehead was marred by a large welt, and whose holster was empty. "And you, Finn, will take two of Mr. Baron's people, and you will check every stairwell. And every step you take, you will pray your gratitude that the son of a bitch was a lousy shot."

Anger and nerves kept her rigid. "Tobias, remember—he's armed and scared shitless; that makes him dangerous. Do not take him down. When you find him, call me. Nothing more."

Now she stood in the twelfth-floor elevator alcove, listening to the crackle of the radio on her topcoat lapel. Part of her was glad they hadn't found Gladman yet; he was a nice guy, a little on the dense side, and didn't really deserve the vengeance she'd seen in her sergeant's face. She already knew about the weather, and tried not to let it bother her. After all, it could be worse, the Ripper could be back here as well. After she thought it, she turned and wrapped a knuckle three times against the wood paneling between the elevator doors.

Then the radio sputtered, and she heard, "Oh, Jesus, Lieutenant, we found him."

Mischa sat on the piano bench, his back to the keys, watching the dancers on the low stage. The director was on a house phone, presumably trying to get hold of Mr. Baron. When he finally hung up, he shook his head, closed his eyes in a frown, and pointed.

"Acmarov, you know the score?"

Mischa nodded.

"Good. You play tonight. Can you do it?"

"Yes, sir, sure."

"We'll see." He clapped his hands to line the girls up, then explained how the storm had left them with a minimal complement of musicians. "But just one person in the audience, we go on anyway, you understand?"

They nodded unhappily—a handful of them were missing as well.

Then the director snapped his fingers. "Logetta. Damn, I forgot her. Acmarov, you know her?"

"Yes."

"Get her. She can haul drinks later, I need her here."

Mischa didn't argue. He promised to be back in ten minutes and hurried for the service elevator. This was perfect: not only would he get a chance to play—an audition, really—but he'd be able to keep an eye on Dacey, make sure she was all right. If he worked it right, she'd think this was his idea, and he had a feeling he knew how she'd show her gratitude.

Granna breathed deeply through her mouth, but it didn't prevent the stench of fresh blood from churning at her stomach. She could even smell the end of her career. None of the top brass would admit agreeing to keep the poor guy here. It had been her call, and she'd lost him.

Sergeant Cox puffed up the stairs, a bedsheet in his hands. When he reached the landing, he tossed it over the body.

It didn't help.

This was bad, much worse than the others.

Not only was Gladman's face mutilated and his throat slashed, but four long gashes had been made in his chest from throat to stomach.

Like claws, she thought; just like claws.

There was something else, too, that made her say, "Tobias, I want Proctor."

Reno Baron came out of his office bathroom, a towel in one hand, his face still damp from a quick washing. He couldn't remember ever having thrown up so thoroughly and so violently; he couldn't remember ever feeling so cold. But he still had something to do for Lieutenant MacEdan, so he moved weak-legged to his desk, dropped into his chair, and pulled the telephone toward him as he took a business card from his jacket pocket. This was no ordinary 911 call; on the card was the chief's private number.

He picked up the receiver, tapped for an outside line, and waited. Frowned. Tried again. Was about to try a third time when Greta, without knocking, opened the door and said, "Mr. Baron, I'm sorry, but I thought you should know—Stu still isn't here yet, and the outside lines are all down. We can't dial out."

Dacey stood at the waitress station, tapping a foot, watching the others drift like ghosts around the mostly empty tables and slots. Behind her, she heard a man asking the bartender about a woman. A specific woman. Curious, she half turned to catch a glimpse, and recognized the speaker as the kid's bald friend.

"Are you sure?" the baldy asked.

The bartender nodded apologetically even as he slipped a bill into his trouser pocket.

Before she could turn away, the man looked right at her. "Miss?"

She knew from his expression that he remembered her, but she smiled anyway when he moved closer and pressed a fifty into her hand. "I'm looking for a woman, a Miss Haslic," he

said, and described her. He was a cool, very formal, but she
had a strong feeling he was also a little desperate.

She was about to say no, when suddenly she had an idea,
one that would more than square her with her partner. She
looked at him wearily. "What you want her for?"

"Business," he answered. "Mine Not yours." He held up
another bill. "Do you know where I might find her?"

Dacey frowned. "This is legit, right?"

"Absolutely."

She kept her gaze away from the bill he held. "I don't
know," she said doubtfully. "I mean, if you're jerking me
around, it could be my job, you know?"

"I promise you it won't come to that."

She looked away, at the tables, at the floor. "You sure?"

He added another bill, a twin to the first. "Positive."

She took them reluctantly, was tempted to tuck them into
her cleavage, and changed her mind. A little too much, she
thought; a little too much.

"Please tell me," he said.

Finally she smiled. "I can do better than that, mister. I'll
take you."

Proctor saw them at the table, Taz holding her wrist as if
preventing her from leaving, looking up with relief as Proctor hastened over.

"Boss," he said.

Proctor ignored him. He braced his hands against the table-
top and leaned over. "Miss Acmarov, after you left to go to
your rehearsal, did you tell anyone about our conversation?"

Suze scowled. "I don't think that's—"

"Did you?" It wasn't a shout, but it might as well have
been, from her reaction. "It's important," he added. "Very important."

She shrugged. "Yeah, I guess. I mean . . . yes."

"Who?"

"A friend, that's all. What's going on, Taz? What's—"

Proctor rapped the table with a knuckle, startling her into
looking back at him. "Who?"

"Like I said, a friend."

He waited, staring.

"It's okay," Taz said softly. "We have to know, Suze, we really have to know."

"This is too weird," she said, shaking her head. "You guys aren't cops, right? This is just too bizarre."

Proctor wanted to strangle her, or dangle her over the wall until she told him what he needed to know. Instead he bowed his head for a moment, then tried to ease some of the intensity in his voice. "You're right, we're not cops. But this is really very important. No one's in trouble, I promise you, but I wish you would tell me your friend's name."

"Go ahead," Taz urged with a smile. "I'll sit in the front row and throw money or something."

She grinned at that, more at the tone than the humor. "You do, I'll get fired." A second of debate before she pulled gently away from Taz's hand. "Look, I really do have to go. And I really will get fired if I'm not back like five minutes ago." A smile for Taz before she turned to Proctor and said, "Dacey. Her name's Dacey Logetta."

"Thank you," Proctor said, but she only nodded curtly and hurried away.

Once she was gone, Taz said. "Holy shit."

Proctor snapped his head around. "What? You know her?"

"Yeah," he answered. "And I think there might be a problem."

Proctor dropped into a chair. "Tell me."

TWENTY-EIGHT

Delmonico had to look at his watch twice before the time registered: five after five. He groaned silently. It felt like he'd been on duty since dawn. He yawned, not bothering to hide it. He took off his cap, scratched hard through his hair, squinted at his watch for the third time, and groaned again. Loudly.

Then, cap on, hands clasped behind his back, he stood at the center door and willed the goddamn sleet to turn into anything, he didn't care, as long as it wasn't goddamn sleet. It didn't work. Light glittered off the sheath of ice that covered everything except a narrow band of tarmac directly under the lifeboat. Only twice in the last hour had he seen a vehicle out there, and they had moved so slowly he figured he could sleepwalk faster. One had been a city sander, but he could tell it wasn't doing much good—the sleet was too heavy. Just like everyone else, he was stuck here.

He puffed his cheeks, blew out a disgusted breath, and turned just as a young cop reached him, looking none too happy himself. "Hey, Finn," he said, but received nothing but a curt nod for his effort. Oh, boy, he thought; that ain't good.

He watched as Finn, one hand holding his cap on against the wind, slid and skidded toward the patrol cars, once nearly dumping himself off the low curbing. Delmonico saw him lean into one of the cars and step back sharply.

Oh, boy, he thought; that ain't good, either.

The cop checked the other two cruisers, angrily slapped the roof of the last one, and tried to run back to the hotel. If

Delmonico hadn't seen the expression on the guy's face, he would have laughed.

The doors hissed open.

"Who's been out there?" Finn demanded.

Delmonico nearly stood at attention. "Nobody. I been here all day, nobody's been out there but the guests leaving. At least an hour anyway."

"You sure about that, Jack?"

"I ain't blind, Finn. Nobody here but me and the crappy weather."

The cop stomped away, muttering into his shoulder radio, slapping at his wet uniform, and Delmonico moved to the doors, trying to see into the cruisers.

"A problem?" Baron asked behind him.

The bell captain told him what had happened, knowing something was definitely wrong because the manager's perfect white hair wasn't so perfect anymore. Finn returned, taking a position by the doors. Delmonico didn't ask, and neither did Baron.

"Something I should know about, sir?" he asked Baron.

The manager only said, "The phone lines are down," and stared at the storm. "And the damn ice has screwed up the satellite dishes. We're lucky to get static."

Delmonico smiled. "Can I quit, then?"

Baron grinned. "No, Jack, you can't. You're stuck with me." A glance at the cop, and he tapped the bell captain's arm. "Just help the officer here keep everyone inside, all right?" He took a step toward the casino. "And, Jack?"

"Sir?"

"No heroics, okay? Anything happens, get the hell away."

And that, Baron thought, ignoring the man's startled, puzzled look as he headed into the casino, was a really stupid thing to say. Aside from being true, it was unnecessarily melodramatic. There was a small comfort, however—he suspected Jack would get all the details from the cop anyway.

He moved through the casino slowly, making sure the few customers saw him, answering a few concerned questions with good cheer, soothing fears, assuring those who asked that the storm wasn't about to spoil anyone's good time. He noticed the numbers had grown, and suspected his guests didn't want to stay in their rooms, alone with the storm. By the time he reached the lobby, he was ready to scream, and he was insanely relieved when he saw the old man sitting at the fountain. Cobb had a sandwich in his hand, a Styrofoam cup of coffee on the bench beside him. A breach of hotel rules, and Baron, at this point, didn't give a damn.

"How are you today?" he asked. A disgusted gesture at the storm. "Aside from that, that is."

Cobb shrugged. "I've seen better." He wiped a corner of his mouth with a napkin, raising an eyebrow as two uniformed policemen stationed themselves at either end of the entrance doors. "You, too, I see."

"You have no idea."

Cobb chewed thoughtfully. "Bet I do."

Baron laughed. "Thanks, but I won't take that bet, if you don't mind."

They listened to the wind.

They listened to a woman at Registration complain about the television.

They listened to a sharp hollow laugh in the casino.

I think, Baron thought, *I'm going to shoot myself.*

"You ever been to Florida, Mr. Baron?" Cobb asked.

"A couple of times, why?"

"I see on the TV some people, they get stuck in hotels and houses when a hurricane's on the way, they have parties, you know? Lots of candles and food, they got batteries for those boom box things." He shrugged. "I guess they're stupid being there in the first place, all the warnings they get down there, but they make the best of it, it looks like. Beats hiding in the cellar."

Baron turned his head slowly.

"Nice place this is," Cobb said. "Too damn big to be a tomb, though, you know what I mean?" He sighed. "No offense."

Baron walked over to the doors and watched the sleet, saw increasing numbers of white flakes shoot past the light. Then he turned, smiling. "You want a job, Mr. Cobb?"

"What, here?"

"Yes."

"Doing what?"

"Keeping me sane."

Cobb sniffed. "No offense again, but taking a job like you have in a place like this isn't exactly what I'd call sane in the first place."

Baron laughed silently, rubbed his hands together, and hurried over to the registration desk, long strides Cobb couldn't help noticing had a definite spring in them. He had a feeling there'd be a party in the casino before long, maybe some free food, big discounts in the restaurants, maybe a free show. He looked at what was left of his sandwich and shook his head—should've waited.

He ate; he drank; he considered trying to pry some information from the uniforms, but they didn't look at all in a mood to talk. Especially not to him. It was, he knew, the Ripper. Somewhere in the building, and the department unable to get here in force. He had already seen the streets from the back, and with the sleet changing over to snow, he doubted anyone else could get here shy of walking. If experience had taught him anything, that lady lieutenant was in a world of serious trouble.

He finished the sandwich, sipped at the cooling coffee, and for the first time in a long time wondered what the hell he was doing here. He was old. He was slow. He was unwelcome. What good would any of that do poor Fred?

He clasped his hands and lowered his head.

Maybe he should just go back to his room and sleep until all this was over, then go home and figure out what he would do with the rest of his life.

He snorted disgust at himself, turned his head without lifting it. On the other hand, the casino had already begun to sound a little more lively. Maybe a turn at one of the tables wouldn't do any harm. Couldn't hurt, that's for sure.

A groan as he stood, more from habit than actual discomfort. He gathered his lunch debris together, walked around the fountain, and stopped when he saw a young man leaving the casino. Without thinking, he raised his voice and said, "Excuse me?"

The young man stopped, frowning.

Cobb smiled apologetically as he walked over. "I couldn't help noticing." He gestured vaguely at the man's curly black hair and face. "You're a cousin to my friend? The young lady who fell through the door?"

Mischa's frown snapped off. "Hey, you're the cop, right? The one who helped her out?"

"I tried," Cobb answered modestly, stuffing the sandwich wrapping and empty cup into his pockets. He shook Mischa's hand. "She's all right, I'm guessing. I saw her this afternoon, she looked all right, but you never can tell."

"She's fine," Mischa assured him.

Cobb watched him scan the lobby. "Looking for her?"

"No. A friend." Mischa pulled at a lock of hair. "Maybe you've seen her, huh? A redhead? Kind of . . ." He grimaced, hands moving in an attempt to describe her. "Kind of . . ."

Cobb smiled. "I know, you don't have to tell me. And I'm sorry, no, I haven't seen her, I don't think."

"Damn." Mischa scowled, yanked on his hair again, and backed away. "Look, Mr. Cobb, I'm sorry but I've got to go. It was nice meeting you, okay? And you should get inside. It looks like they're getting ready to have a party or something?"

Cobb nodded his thanks, and Mischa ducked back into the casino, his frustration growing into anger. For no reason, he began to think that failure to bring her back to rehearsal would mean he wouldn't get his chance to play tonight. He took the escalator up to the Gallery and looked into the Briny, where he saw two men seated at a railing table. One of them looked up and suddenly pointed at him; the other turned and, after a moment, beckoned him over with a friendly wave.

Mischa's first instinct was to turn away, ignore them, get on with his search. His second was to give in to his curiosity and find out what they wanted. They didn't look threatening or anything, and he was pretty sure he hadn't seen them before, which probably meant they didn't work for the hotel. Besides, he was tired of trudging all over the place, and maybe, just maybe, they'd seen Dacey around.

Oh, what the hell, he thought.

The introductions were made by the younger of the two,

and the one called Proctor said something about talking with Suze earlier, about, of all things, those dopey mahjra stories Gram used to tell them when they were kids.

"That was a long time ago," he said. "I don't think I remember any more than my cousin does."

At that moment Proctor stood abruptly, and Mischa looked back at the entrance, just as two policemen entered and headed straight for them.

"Proctor?" one of them asked.

"That's me," Proctor said.

"Lieutenant MacEdan wants to see you. Now, sir, if you don't mind."

Proctor turned to his companion. "See what else you can find out, Taz. I'll be back as soon as I can." He looked at Mischa. "I'm sorry about this. If you have a couple of minutes, I'd appreciate—"

"The lieutenant's waiting, sir," one of the cops insisted.

Proctor smiled and followed them out, checking back to be sure Taz had managed to keep Acmarov there, nodding when the cousin, clearly hesitant, took a seat. He didn't bother to ask his escort what was going on; they were obviously under orders not to say a word.

At the elevators he saw Cox, who shook his head sharply before a single question was asked, and they rode up to the twelfth floor in uncomfortable silence. Once there, he automatically started for his room, but a hand to his elbow turned him toward the fire exit.

"You ever seen a dead body?" Cox asked as he pushed the fire door open.

"Yes."

"Not like this you haven't," and almost pushed him through to the landing.

He had to grab the railing to keep from falling, and turned quickly on the sergeant, would have said something, but heard his name and saw Granna sitting on a step second from the top, hunched into her topcoat, hands in her pockets. She patted the space beside her.

He saw the sheet-covered body, smelled the blood, and joined her. "Bruno?"

She nodded.

"The Ripper?"

She nodded again.

Sergeant Cox squeezed past him, deliberately slamming his heels against the stairs' metal tips.

"What's with him?" Proctor asked, not bothering to lower his voice.

Granna did. "You're not official, Proctor, and he resents it." A quick grin. "He's seen too many movies, I think."

Proctor didn't answer the grin. "So what's so different about this that I have to see it?"

She nodded, and the sergeant yanked off the sheet.

Proctor swallowed hard.

"That's not all," she said quietly. She touched her forehead, and Proctor squinted through the dim light. The blood was smeared across Gladman's face, soaked into his shirt and the top of his trousers. "Closer," she said.

"I don't think so."

She touched her forehead again. "Above his eyes."

He looked again, and shrugged. "I don't get it."

"Neither do I. He carved a *P* in there, Proctor. Right into the bone."

TWENTY-NINE

The bile was there, he could taste it, almost smell it, but kept it down by shifting away from Granna, half turning so his back was against the wall, just below the handrail. Without thinking, he pulled the red chip from his pocket and let his fingers worry it.

"That's you, isn't it," Granna said as Cox recovered the body.

A hesitation before Proctor nodded. "Probably."

"Why?"

He knew he was about to get in serious trouble, the possibility of facing charges not beyond consideration, but at the moment he was too angry to care. Valknir's arrogance had taken one step over the line.

"I talked to him."

Granna took a deep breath. "Today?"

"Yeah. A while ago."

"You sure it was him."

"Oh, yes."

"You talked to him, and you didn't tell me?"

"That's obstruction," Cox said angrily from the bottom of the steps. He pointed at the body. "Accessory. Shit, I don't know. But it means this is your fault, you stupid son of a bitch."

Proctor ignored him, kept his voice calm. "I told you this wasn't the same as before, Granna. I wasn't lying."

"Oh, gimme a break," the sergeant said.

Granna lifted her shoulders, raising her collar higher around her face. She stared at the body for several seconds, shaking

her head once. She told Cox to send one of the uniforms after
a camera, preferably a Polaroid, then find a place to put the
body after the scene had been recorded. She wasn't about to
leave Bruno here. Then Cox was to make sure all of them
had the suspect's description. He protested, close to yelling,
before stomping away; she said nothing until she heard the
fire door slam and they were alone in the stairwell.

"He's got a point, you know. A lawyer could make an accessory charge stick. Obstruction, at least."

Proctor admitted the possibility, then told her about his conversation with Valknir. When he finished, he told her what the
man was.

"Oh, right. I'm supposed to believe this?"

He lifted a shoulder. "Whether you do or not is your problem. I've got problems of my own."

She allowed herself a smile. "Déjà vu all over again, you
know?"

"Not quite."

She sobered. "No. I guess not." A shudder. "I can't. I just
can't let myself go with this, Proctor. You have any idea what
the captain will say?"

"Sure. But whether you do or not, by the time it's over,
you'll come up with something else anyway. A perfectly reasonable explanation that will make everyone happy. Especially
you." He stared at his hand. "It won't stop the dreams, Granna,
but you'll still have your job." He shifted again. "Eventually
you'll decide I was nuts from the start. Eventually you'll figure I snookered you somehow, and the odds are you won't
want to speak to me again."

She looked at him sideways. "You think?"

"Maybe."

"Just maybe?"

He didn't answer, and she looked away. He could see her
jaw working, her eyes close and open. He didn't think she
would arrest him, put him under guard; he didn't think she
was really all that angry at him. What she probably—

"It gets worse," she said, her lips pulling back into a smile.

"What? What does?"

"Baron told me someone, and I'm guessing it's this guy

you told me about, someone did a number on the backup electrical system. If the lights go out again, they aren't coming back on, and what the hell are you doing there, what is that thing? You're driving me nuts."

He looked at his hand. "This? I don't know. Some kind of chip we got—one of those welcome to the hotel package things."

She reached out, and he dropped the chip into her palm. She looked at it closely and said, "I don't think so, Proctor."

"What do you mean?"

"I mean, no hotel is ever going to give away this for free."

Doc followed the woman past the guarded elevator entrance, turning left into a narrow alcove just before they reached the lobby. Suspicion suggested it was a con, that she was out to see how much more he would give her, but after speaking to literally dozens of people, she was all he had for the moment.

"She's rich, you know?" Dacey said, fingering a small key from her jacket pocket. She slipped it into a slot beside a brushed steel door and turned it. "One of those I-want-to-be-alone types we get once in a while." A quick smile as the door slid open. "Trust me, they're a real pain."

He hesitated before joining her in the car, keeping well to the back as she used the key again. "Where are we going?"

"There's a couple of rooms above the eighteenth, ten times bigger than my apartment, for God's sake. You should see—" She laughed brightly. "Well, you will see, right?" She looked over her shoulder, her expression somewhat fearful. "I need a favor."

Here it comes, he thought, and looked down at her, expressionless, promising nothing.

"If she gets mad, I need you to tell her it's not my fault, okay? I need this job, Mr. Falcon. I really need this job."

"I will do my best not to involve you more than you already are, Miss Logetta. That's the best I can do."

A nod, and she faced the door again, her weight shifting from foot to foot.

Doc didn't move beyond folding his hands in front of him,

one over the other. He wasn't concerned about this mystery woman's wealth; he dealt with the wealthy all the time and knew how to talk to them without ruffling feathers. Well, most of the time, at any rate. And from her interest in Proctor, he suspected this would be a simple matter of persuasion.

He also had to admit he was fascinated by the fascination Proctor had for her. He knew Proctor was no celibate, but this one . . . this one seemed to have taken hold in a way he could not yet understand.

The redhead hummed softly over the soft rush of wind in the shaft. A hand fussed briefly with her hair. A move as if to face him, and she changed her mind.

"Don't suppose you're gong to tell me what's up, huh?"

"Correct."

"Lot of money you're throwing around."

"Yes."

She bounced a few times as if urging the elevator to hurry up. "She in trouble?"

He didn't answer.

"Almost there."

As soon as she said it, the elevator stopped and the door opened. She stood to one side and waved him through with a flourish and cheerful curtsy. "Welcome to the rich folks, Mr. Falcon."

The room was huge, circular, all its walls glass. He stepped away from the elevator, noting the city's glow west and south, noting it barely made a dent in the room's pervasive gloom. A handful of hurricane lamps, some electric, some with candles, sat on various pieces of shelving and furniture, casting shadows that made the dark areas much darker. Just off center was an arrangement of armchairs and a love seat with a low table in their midst.

The carpeting on the floor was utilitarian, not decorative.

The ceiling was low.

Every few seconds the room brightened and the shadows danced as the Lighthouse beacon swept overhead.

He turned and said, "I trust there's an explanation?"

She stood in the doorway, one hand keeping the door open. Her answer was a broad unpleasant smile.

He sensed movement before he heard it, started when something flew past his right arm and the redhead snatched it out of the air. Held it up, a vial of some sort, and pulled it to her chest.

"For real?" she asked breathlessly.

"For real," a voice said behind him. "You know what to do?"

She backed into the elevator, nodding. "God, yes."

Doc took a step toward her, but the door had already begun to close. The last he saw of her was a mocking wink and wave.

The last he saw of the room before something struck the back of his head was just after a hand gripped his shoulder and the voice said, "Welcome, Mr. Falcon. And relax. You're not going to die just yet."

Taz nearly leapt from his chair. "They what?"

Mischa didn't get it. "What's the big deal?"

"When?" Taz demanded. "When was this?"

"How should I know? The last I found out, she was talking to this bald guy, and I still haven't been able to find her. She's gonna be in major league trouble, the dope."

Taz saw it then, the look when Mischa spoke about Dacey, and he rolled his eyes. Son of a bitch, the guy's in love with her. That's just great.

He dropped a couple of bills on the table and pushed back his chair. "I gotta go."

"You mind telling me what's going on?"

Taz did, so he didn't. He rushed out of the lounge, thinking the only chance he had was to find Lieutenant MacEdan. If Proctor wasn't with her, then he'd have to figure a way to get into that private elevator on his own.

"Son of a bitch, Doc," he muttered. "What the hell are you up to?"

Proctor stood in the hall and held the chip close to his eyes. "You're kidding," he said, aware he had been saying it since they'd left the stairwell.

Granna made a face, bumped his shoulder with hers. "I'm not kidding, and that's the last time I'm going to tell you."

They turned at the sound of an elevator's chime, and two uniforms hurried toward them, one carrying a stretcher awkwardly under his arm. She directed them into the stairwell, held the door open and said, "Proctor, I'm smiling, but I'm still really pissed, you got it? If I could, I'd take you downtown for a friendly talk, but I can't." Her face hardened. "I'm going to take care of this business first, then I want you with me, you get it? You will not take a step without my say-so. No more screwing around. I'm getting sick of dead bodies."

He nodded, then pointed along the hall. "I'm going to my room. I'll be right back."

She stared, nodded, and he hurried away, turned into a hall that brought him to the hotel's south side and his room. Once inside, he went to the window and checked the storm—more snow now than sleet—before turning on a lamp by the couch. He sat and dropped the red chip onto the coffee table.

Except it wasn't a chip, wasn't plastic, wasn't stone. It was amber. Red amber. Rare enough in its pure form to cause a jeweler's heart to flutter. He poked it with a finger, frowned at it, poked it again. He leaned close and sat back, shook his head and rubbed his face.

He didn't have to work to know who had put it in his pocket; what he had to work at was how. And why.

A gift? He didn't think so.

A warning? He doubted it.

He folded his hand over his stomach, lowered his chin, and stared at the red amber as if, by simple intense examination, it would yield the answers he wanted. He grunted. He put a foot on the table's edge and grunted again. He figured he had a few more minutes before Granna came for him, or sent Cox after him, but he had a feeling he could have all night and it wouldn't be enough.

The lamp dimmed, and he held his breath. When it brightened again, he said, quietly, "Be damned."

It was an amulet of some kind.

Protection.

Valknir hadn't killed him in the lounge, or tried to take

control because of the red amber. Proctor remembered the moment the hand had touched his shoulder and had drawn away. Too quickly. As if he'd been burned.

A smile.

One that faded when he looked up and saw Petra sitting on the edge of the bed.

She wore a dark shirt and loose jeans, a dark silken scarf tied loosely around her neck. Window light took the color from her hair; lamplight made her lips appear darker than they were.

"Don't you ever knock?"

She smiled. "Only when I have to."

"Then, it wasn't a dream."

"No."

"I don't like surprises."

She lowered her head in apology, but he had a feeling she wasn't at all contrite. Which didn't make him angry, as it might have done; it made him grin and sit back, foot back on the table.

"He's turning this place into a slaughterhouse."

"Yes, I know."

"I'm going to stop him."

"How?"

"You tell me." He frowned. "You could have told me before. You could have told me from the beginning." The frown became a glare. "I might have been able to save Bruno Gladman's life. That really . . . really pisses me off."

Her head jerked up, and she studied him intently, as if she hadn't paid serious attention to him before. And she hadn't; he knew that. No matter what she claimed she already knew about him, she hadn't taken him seriously, and a man had died because of it. Maybe more than one—he also had a strong feeling Granna had not told him everything about the hotel search. There had been other bodies, other victims.

Sleet and snow ticked against the pane.

The lamp dimmed and brightened again.

Someone pounded on the door.

THIRTY

When Proctor opened the door, Taz and the lieutenant barged in, brushing him aside, arguing, Taz loudly, Granna's voice dangerously even. She gave Petra a curt nod; Taz gave her a quick puzzled grin. Neither paid attention to him until he slammed the door and demanded silence. And an explanation.

"It's Doc," Taz said quickly. "I think he's in trouble."

"What do you mean?"

"It's a damn chorus girl," Granna said disgustedly, moving to the window, standing with her back to it so she could see the whole room.

"The one I went upstairs with," Taz answered. "Almost."

Proctor held up a palm. "Upstairs where? What the hell are you talking about?"

"Before," Taz said. "You know, before."

"No, Taz, I do not know before. You went upstairs someplace? With a woman?"

Taz nodded.

"And now Doc is with her?"

He nodded again.

"Jesus Christ, why the hell doesn't anyone tell me anything?" A glare for Taz, a milder one for Petra. "I can't read minds, you know, damnit."

"Well, I'm trying to tell you," Taz said. He rubbed his hands against his shirt, against his pants. "He's gone up there with her, and I think—"

"Enough," Proctor snapped. He looked to Petra. "Do you know what he's talking about?"

Petra, one hand gripping the pendant, nodded. "I think so. His nest."

Proctor closed his eyes. "Jesus."

"What nest?" Granna said.

Proctor put a hand to his forehead, took several slow breaths, shook his head sharply. "Granna, I'm telling you right now, if you don't want to know about Valknir, about what I told you . . ." For a moment he thought she would leave. When finally she turned to look out at the city and, after a long moment, nodded, he wasn't sure if he was pleased or not. "Okay, then. Taz, how do we get up there?"

"She had a key. She said it was a private way to that old restaurant on top. They stopped using it years ago. You can only get into it from the lobby or the eighteenth floor, I think."

Proctor grabbed his jacket off the chair and swung into it. "We'll get Baron to give us one. Tell me on the way, Petra. I'm guessing we don't have much time."

She didn't move. "We may be too late."

"He's my friend," Proctor said grimly. "No such thing as too late."

In the hall he hurried toward the elevators, ignoring Sergeant Cox, who waited in the alcove. "Taz, you know where Baron is now?"

Petra reached around him and pressed the "up" button. "We don't need him. I think I can do this."

Cox leaned against the wall, arms folded across his chest. "That ain't gonna work, lady," he said smugly.

"He's right," Granna said. "We've been sealing the floors off one by one, moving everyone out. When we check a floor off, the maintenance guy does something with the control computer, so the elevators won't go higher than he tells them." She lifted a shoulder. "We're as high as it gets now."

"And as soon as you're outta here," Cox told him, "we'll check this one off, too." He smiled.

Proctor fought with the urgency that made his breathing short and shallow. "Down then," he said, voice deceptively calm, and pressed the button. The door opened immediately, and they all got aboard, Proctor pressed into a back corner.

He glared at the sergeant's back until they reached floor eleven, where Cox got off after a whispered instruction from Granna.

"He's a good man, Proctor," she said, facing the door. "He's probably saner than me right now."

Proctor said nothing.

He watched the red numerals tick their silent way down to ground level, aware of the anxiety that made it impossible for Taz to stand still, aware of Petra beside him, calm save for the fingers that refused to leave the red pendant. He took the amber from his pocket and opened his fingers so she could see it.

"Protection," he said quietly.

"Yes."

"Will it hurt him?"

"Oh, yes."

"Will it kill him?"

"If . . . if it is right." Her other hand fluttered in frustration, searching for the word. "Circumstances? If they are right."

"What does that mean?" Taz asked impatiently. "Full moon? Sacred day of the week? In the head? Next month? What?"

Granna stiffened but didn't turn.

"The ground," Petra answered evenly. "He must . . . his strength comes from ground connection."

"Jesus," Taz said. "You mean you can only kill him when he's flying?"

The car stopped with an unsettling jump. The door opened, but no one moved. Even Granna turned around.

"He doesn't fly," Petra said. "Not like wings. He . . . he soars? He uses the air. He—"

"Glides," Proctor suggested.

"Yes. Something like that. More, but something like that."

"Swell," said Taz as he followed the lieutenant out of the elevator. "So we have to wait for him to take off? Or maybe he's afraid of mice, huh? We throw one at him, he jumps back, and in the middle of the jump—oh, Jesus."

As they moved into the North Promenade, Proctor heard the noise from the casino—music, laughter, a few shouts, some applause. Through the nearest open doors he saw how crowded it had become, with roving waitresses carrying trays of champagne and liquor glasses. Son of a bitch, he thought; the guy's throwing a blizzard party.

"Taz, where's this private elevator?" When Taz pointed toward the front, he added, "Go in, see if Baron's there. Get him if he is, get right back if you can't find him right away."

Taz obeyed without protest, and Proctor thanked him silently as he swerved toward the lobby, spotting the narrow elevator entrance just as the front desk came into view. He also saw four cops at the doors, and guessed there was a like number at the back, and someone stationed wherever the supplies' delivery bay was. He had a feeling their orders did not contain instructions to detain and nothing more.

One look at Granna's face confirmed it.

What he didn't know was how far she'd let him take this.

As he stared in frustration at the keyhole beside the brushed steel door, Petra touched his wrist lightly. "What will you do?"

"I was kind of hoping you'd know."

"You cannot fight him. He will be too strong. He has fed too much." She held the amulet away from her chest. "This, and yours, they will only . . ." A frown. "Delay him."

"What if I shove it down his throat?"

"He will bite your hand off."

"Then, I'll cross that bridge when I come to it."

Her smile was sad. "You are a fool."

"I've been told."

Her fingers closed around his wrist. "Don't be a fool, Proctor."

Whatever answer he might have given was lost when Baron, practically shoved by Taz, came around the corner. He demanded to know what this was all about, that the Barnegat had been deserted for years, and didn't they realize he had more important things on his mind, like keeping a couple of hundred guests from panicking?

Although Proctor stepped forward, it was Granna who reminded the manager that panicking guests were better than more dead guests, so stop whining and hand over the goddamn key before she hauled him in for obstruction. He sputtered, looked doubtfully at the decidedly non-police presence, and yanked a small set of keys from his trouser pocket. A moment's fumbling, and he handed a small silver one to the lieutenant, who immediately passed it on to Proctor.

"I should go with you," Baron said, obviously not meaning a word of it. "Hotel property and all."

"Trust me," Granna told him as she maneuvered him away without actually touching him, "you don't want to. Your guests, Mr. Baron, need you far more than I do."

Another bout of posturing, mostly complaining that the guests were disturbed by all the cops, did they have to be so damn visible? and he marched away, head up, arms swinging.

"Idiot," Granna muttered. And, as Proctor fit the key, "I'm going up there, you know."

He didn't argue.

And once they were all inside the small car, he inserted the key again, and turned it.

Hang on, Doc, he thought as the elevator shuddered upward; for God's sake, hang on.

Murray watched them crowd into the elevator, sniffed, and shifted along the padded bench until he faced the casino. The uniforms behind him had done nothing but snap and growl when he tried to question them, and the desk clerks, especially the busty blonde, ignored him as if he weren't there.

So, he'd watch. Maybe learn something, maybe not.

His left hand slipped into his topcoat pocket. Too old to be John Wayne, but he could still shoot straight.

Dacey, her face glowing with sweat from the running climb up the fire stairs, practically kicked in the door to the room where she had her things. Her lungs felt as if they were working at five miles above sea level, her heart refused to stop its thumping at her sternum, and her hands shook so hard she had to grip the edge of the bathroom sink before they flew off her wrists.

Forty years from now, he'd told her, you'll look five years older, no more. You must be sure.

How much more sure could she be, for God's sake?

The vial waited for her on the shelf.

He had grinned. Just add water, drink, and wait. It'll hurt a little, maybe more, it's been so long, I barely remember, then you'll be ready for the last step. Be sure, my dear. Be absolutely sure.

He hadn't told her what that last step was, but she didn't care. Drink blood? Kill someone? Dismember a child? Disect an animal and eat the entrails? Forty years from now look only five years older?

She grabbed a plastic glass, tore off the protective cover, and filled it with cold water. Then she unstoppered the vial and poured the grey powder into the glass.

We don't always eat the eyes, you know, or the tongue. They can be dried, powdered, saved. For emergencies . . . or for turning. Be sure, Dacey. Be very, very sure.

She stirred the mixture with her finger and held the glass up. Looked at her reflection and ordered calm.

"You heard the man," she said to it. "Be sure."

And suddenly she wasn't.

Maybe it was poison, this stuff. Maybe it was punishment for her screwing up so many times. Maybe it was some kind of curse, some kind of potion that would turn her into a monster. Maybe it was nothing at all but a practical joke.

She licked her lips nervously.

Then she put the glass down and took off her jacket, the room's cool air shivering across her bare shoulders, the tops of her breasts. She kicked off her shoes. She opened the medicine chest door so she wouldn't have to look at her reflection.

"Stalling," she whispered.

What if it was a trick?

"Come on, girl, pour it out or drink it."

Look twenty-nine at sixty-two.

She picked up the glass and wondered if Charleen was in there, those little dark bits swirling around in the water.

"Oh, God!" she yelled, and drank it down without stopping. Threw the glass away, heard it shatter in the tub. Stumbled back into the doorway, clutching her stomach with both hands, fighting the urge to vomit.

She slumped against the frame, sucking air, blowing it out, a tentative smile, a tremulous laugh.

Nothing.

She felt nothing.

Not until she leaned over to pick up her admiral's jacket, and felt as if something had exploded inside her. Her eyes widened, and she gasped as she dropped to her hands and knees; her mouth opened as the explosion tore at her like a legion of claws digging from groin to throat.

It wasn't pain.

It was agony.

And she had no breath left to scream.

The elevator stopped, and Proctor heard a rustling behind him, knew it was Lieutenant MacEdan drawing her weapon. He held the red amber chip tightly in his left hand, gestured to Taz to stay on that side of him as the door opened, and he stepped into the room, the others fanning out behind.

The wind screamed at them as he moved cautiously toward the center, snow skidding across the glass walls, sticking here and there, melting into serpentine trails whose shadows crawled across the ceiling and floor. A quick count of a dozen lanterns. A quick survey—he could be behind that wet bar on the left, those chairs in the middle, the three-shelf bookcase on the right. Splinters of shattered furniture. Twinkling shards of shattered glass.

The utter cold.

The stench of blood.

The stench of death.

Petra said, "He's not here."

Taz yelled, "Doc! Doc, where are you?" Running across the room, turning as he did, his breath smoke and his voice pitched high. "Doc!"

Proctor grabbed Petra's arms. "Where?"

She shook her head. "I don't know."

"Damnit, Petra."

Then Taz wailed, and Proctor ran, skidding around the side of the couch, grabbing the back with both hands to keep himself from falling.

Oh, Jesus, he thought; Jesus, no, please, no.

There was just enough light to see the ragged *P* drawn in blood across Doc's forehead, blood that came from the space where his left eye used to be.

THIRTY-ONE

Proctor stood so rigidly he began to tremble, watching as Taz knelt by Doc, gagging as his hands moved helplessly above the fallen man's face. Granna leaned over the couch and cursed; Petra inhaled sharply and pushed around Proctor to join Taz, gently easing him to one side. Proctor watched her fingers touch Doc's wrist, the side of his neck.

Calmly: "He's alive."

Proctor nodded stiffly. "Taz, find something we can carry him with. We have to take him—"

Petra looked up at him. "No." She jerked her head toward the elevator. "He's down there now. Hunting. These are his grounds now, and he's hunting. Playing his own game." Something glinted in her eyes; the light, or a tear. "Stop him, Proctor. He's mad. It will be a bloodbath."

"We can't leave him," Taz protested, his eyes dry, the tears in his voice. "Jesus, Proctor, we can't leave him here; he'll bleed to death."

With one hand pressed lightly against Doc's chest, Petra reached up blindly until Proctor took her hand, felt the warmth, felt the strength. "I will take care of him. I can do this." She nodded. "Please, there's no time. I promise you he will not die."

"Boss!" Taz protested.

The warmth, the strength, the way the pendant caught the lanterns' light.

"I swear to you," she whispered, squeezed his hand and released it. Another look, and she slipped the pendant from around her neck, forced it into his hand and closed his fingers around it. "Hurry. You must hurry."

He looked at the others, saw and felt their skepticism, felt and heard the raging storm, heard himself say, "All right."

"Proctor!" Taz said, on his feet in a hurry. "Are you nuts? Are you—"

Proctor started around the couch. "We're going after the man who did this to Doc. You can either stay here and cry, or you can help me." He looked at Granna, saw the gun in her hand and the doubt on her face. Waited for her to protest, not caring if she did. Then he snapped a thumb toward Petra. "She's wrong." He tapped a finger against his chest. "These are my grounds now, and I'm the son of a bitch doing the hunting."

In the elevator:

"Boss, that thing on Doc's head. He wants you to come get him."

"I know."

"He'll be waiting."

"Yeah, I guess he will."

"So . . . you know how to kill him?"

"Nope, not yet."

"Then how—"

"This. It has something to do with this."

"That's just a piece of red stone, Boss. You gonna pull a David or something?"

"If I have to, Taz. If I have to."

On the fourth floor:

Dacey finally screamed, rolling on the floor, slamming her spine against the doorjamb, her head against the tiles. She could taste blood, her blood, as her teeth gnawed through her lips.

She screamed hoarsely, and wept.

And abruptly the pain was gone, and *he* was there, standing over her, smiling.

"Bastard," she whispered; she could speak no louder.

"You lived. I told you there would be pain."

She had torn her blouse open; her stockings were shredded.

"What now?"

His smile widened. "You will stay here. I have things to
do." A quick laugh. "I'm having fun, aren't you?"

She couldn't move, could barely breathe. "Then what?"

He leaned over, and his fingers drifted over her eyes, her
lips. "Guess what the second course is."

He started for the door, and she managed to sit up, using
the door's frame for support. "No."

He looked back. "Too late, my dear. Either you do, or you
die." He opened the door, looked back again. "Don't worry.
In a few days you'll heal. No one will ever know the difference."

"Powder again?"

He laughed and pulled the door closed behind him.

She heard the laughter all the way down the hall, and when
it stopped, all she heard was the wind.

In the rehearsal hall:

Mischa slammed into the room, flapping his arms, shaking his head, stopping abruptly when he realized neither the
directors nor the dancers were here. Only Suze, sitting on the
edge of the low stage, a sweater pulled over her tights.

"What?" he demanded.

"Baron's got everyone upstairs. No show. We're waitresses.
I'm supposed to tell you."

"Well, that's just great." He spun around and slapped the
wall. "Great. Damnit, this is . . ." He slapped the wall again.
"Jesus, this sucks." He stomped over to the piano and kicked
at the bench, sat, and shook his head, bowed it, and stared at
his feet. "My big chance. Shit, my big chance."

He heard his cousin cross the floor, felt her fingers comb
swiftly through his hair. "Mike, come on. He asked you once,
he'll ask you again."

"Yeah. Sure."

A playful slap to the side of his head. "You find Dacey?"

"Nope. Just some guys looking for her, that's all."

When she didn't respond right away, he looked up, and frowned at the concern in her eyes.

"A young guy, maybe our age? Lots of hair?"

He nodded. "One of them, yeah. You know them?"

"They asked me about her. Mike, they asked about the *mahjrachin.*"

"They asked me, too." Suddenly he grinned. "Hey, maybe they're . . ." He put a finger to the side of his nose and pushed it out of shape. "You know." Then he hummed a few bars of *The Godfather* theme. "Maybe she sleeps with the snowmen."

"Not funny, Mike, not funny."

He laughed, and pulled on her arm to get him to his feet. "Okay, okay, I'm sorry." He looked around the room. "So now what?"

"So now we're supposed to go upstairs and keep the customers happy." She made a sour face. "I get to haul free drinks around. You get to play the piano in the Tides."

He blinked. "I what?"

"You heard me."

"But no one will hear me there, for God's sake. Except maybe the drunks."

She pushed him toward the door. "Mike, stop bitching and let's go. It's spooky down here." Another shove, not quite so gentle. "Maybe Dacey's showed up."

He didn't argue. She was right about it being spooky, their voices and footsteps echoing against the wood. The room was suddenly too large, and he grabbed her hand, pulled her after him.

"I hope she's all right," he said as they waited for the service elevator.

"Dacey? Hell, Mike, she's always all right."

In the elevator:

"Boss, that Pogo thing you told me about. You know, what you said to him?"

"What about it?"

"You meant he's his own enemy, right?"

Proctor nodded. "He knows too much, and he doesn't know enough."

Granna grunted. "So what doesn't he know?"
"Me."

In the lobby:

Murray yawned so loudly, so widely, he felt his jaw pop.
A wince, a mildly embarrassed check to be sure no one heard
it, and he scratched vigorously at his ear. Thinking maybe it
was still early but felt like midnight, maybe it wouldn't be
such a bad idea to go up to his room for a little while, take
a short nap. Revitalize. Reinvigorate. Clean out the cobwebs.

It couldn't hurt, and besides, all that noise was giving him
a headache.

A smart thing that manager was doing there, all his girls
walking around with free drinks and little sandwiches, himself patting backs and shaking hands, helping the old people
with their chairs, making sure the younger ones didn't forget
the bars up on the Gallery.

A smart thing.

But it was giving him a headache.

On the other hand, if he left, he might miss the right moment. The Ripper, or whatever he was, Murray was sure he
was here. Those cops, they weren't hanging around, holster
flaps unsnapped, just to keep people from going out into the
storm.

That son of a bitch was here, and all he needed was one
clean shot.

At the registration desk:

"I'm telling you, Greta, that guy's got a gun."

"Patrick, gimme a break, okay? Don't you have something
to do? Carry a suitcase or something?"

"Do? What's to do? They're having a goddamn party. I'm
supposed to help you back here, and I don't know shit about
how any of this crap works, there isn't a single person in the
world dumb enough to try to make it here through all that out
there, what the hell is there for me to do?"

"You could shut up, for one thing."

"And you could stop looking in that stupid little mirror and see if I'm right, that the old guy's got a gun. It's in his coat pocket."

"So what do you want me to do, go over there and ask him to hand it over, we have a policy against guns in this hotel?"

"You could tell one of the cops. They're not doing anything."

"You tell them. I'm not moving."

"Jesus, you're a bitch. No wonder Stu's hiding out."

"Patrick. Go to hell."

"You know, Greta, I hope the Ripper tears your goddamn throat out."

The theater was closed, the ticket window dark. The accordian gate that blocked entrance to the lobby had not been locked properly, and in the darkness behind, Emile Valknir stood with his eyes closed.

Listening to the storm.

Listening to the people.

His hands clenched and unclenched; his breathing was slow and regular; every few seconds he would lean forward, his nostrils flaring, as he caught a scent and savored it, remembered it; every few seconds he isolated a voice out of the throng and promised himself he would silence it.

There were, of course, far too many to take.

But there were enough.

Enough that, in the morning when the storm passed, those who came through the doors would find the dead easily; and the living, the survivors, would be little more than the cowering insane.

By then, he and the woman would be long gone. And by tomorrow night, she would be one of his.

Assuming, of course, she hadn't killed herself already.

His hands unclenched.

His eyes opened.

The plan was simple: Proctor would be the first.

In the elevator:

Proctor grinned and snapped his fingers. "Damn."

Taz jumped. "What?"

Proctor looked at Granna. "I need your help, Granna."

She refused to look at him. "It's going to be illegal, right?"

"Of course."

"And I'm supposed to look the other way?"

"Whatever it takes."

"He's going to kill us, Proctor. You know that. We go after him, and he's going to kill us."

"Not if you're careful."

"You guarantee it?"

The elevator stopped.

Proctor shook his head. "You know I can't do that. You know what he's done, and you can pretty well figure out what he's going to do. I can't promise a thing."

The door opened, and the car flooded with noise.

She was the first to leave, and he watched in admiration as her shoulders squared and her chin rose and she scanned the lobby, a careful nod to the guards who stood by the board-walk entrance.

"I'm going to stay with my men," she said when Proctor and Taz came up beside her. "You do what the hell you want, but I'm staying with my men."

"Thank you, Granna."

She scowled at him. "Go to hell, Proctor. Leave me alone and go to hell."

Immediately, he grabbed Taz's arm and guided him down the promenade. "One chance," he said, nearly breaking into a run.

"I don't get it."

Proctor grinned mirthlessly. "You will. How do you feel about a little smash-and-grab?"

They were halfway up to the Gallery, when the lights dimmed and the escalator faltered, stop-and-go, and threw them off balance. They grabbed the rails before they fell, and Proctor said, "Shit. I should have known it was too easy." He took the remaining stairs two at a time, Taz directly behind him, muttering, swearing. At the top, Proctor veered left and began to run; Taz swung right, pushed through a group of men at the entrance to the Briny, spotted an empty bar stool and took it, grunting because it was heavier than he'd thought. The bartender yelled as he ran out of the lounge, but no one actually moved to stop him.

He saw Proctor already making the turn at the Promenade's far end, prayed this would work, and ran as fast and best he could.

He hadn't gone ten feet before the lights went out.

THIRTY-TWO

Proctor froze and closed his eyes. Held his breath. For several long seconds the hotel was completely silent, and he counted slowly. At ten he heard timid voices begin to rise in complaint; at twelve he heard Baron's baritone assuring everyone everything would soon be back to normal; at fifteen the black beneath his eyelids lightened; at sixteen he heard weak cheering, a smattering of applause.

He opened his eyes carefully, keeping his head turned away from the casino, waiting for his vision to adjust. The halogen lights had snapped on, their glow rising above the Gallery's inner wall, softening but not banishing the dark around the edges. With a snap of his fingers, he found the jewelry store; with a defeated sigh he put a hand to his head just as Taz rounded the corner, puffing, the bar stool dragging behind him.

"Forget it," Proctor told him. "Damn. I was wrong." He explained that he remembered seeing a few pieces of what might have been red amber displayed inside, one of them usable as a knife; but a gesture showed Taz that the shop was closed, all its displays gone, undoubtedly locked away in a safe someplace. A dim, battery-powered antitheft light barely lit up the back wall. "Hell." When he saw the puzzlement on the younger man's face, he told him what Petra had said about the rare amber. "Now all we have is this," and he held out the chip and the pendant.

Taz stared at them for a few seconds, then took the chip and bounced it on a palm. "So we make do, right? That's what you and Doc always tell me. Make do." A sardonic grin. "Come on, Boss, this is Doc we're talking about here. That fancy suit of his is ruined. He'll kill us if we don't do something about it."

You're scared to death, Proctor thought amid a rush of affection; you're scared to death, and you're lecturing me.

"Okay."

"So how do we find him?"

Proctor headed for the inner wall. "I have a bad feeling that isn't going to be too hard."

Being careful not to look directly at the brightest areas of the halogens' reach, they looked down to the casino floor. The high-intensity lamps leeched color from even the brightest clothes, making it seem as if they were looking through a cloud. The wheels still turned, the dice still rolled, all the exposed skin looked uncomfortably deathly pale. Reno Baron glided swiftly through it all, his laughter loud, his enthusiasm an attempt to turn disaster into an adventure.

From what they could make out, power was gone all over the city.

Proctor moved slowly along the wall, keeping a good three feet away to stay out of the light, directing Taz to keep an eye on below while he checked as best he could the Gallery level. The glow was strong enough to illuminate parts of the Briny and the Tides; he could see pale faces, the frequent glimmer of faceted tumblers, shadowed movement as guests shifted from one table to another or leaned over the wall into the light, one or two calling down to a friend or a stranger.

The noise level rose slightly, voices slightly less brittle, the music from the wandering jazz trio turned Mardi Gras band less frantic. A familiar show tune prompted rounds of increasingly lusty singing. An apparent stroke of luck at a craps table promoted a stadium-like cheer.

"This," Taz said, "is just too damn bizarre."

Proctor didn't disagree.

The casino-side wall of the Tides was fretwork, just like the Briny, breaking the glow into twisting flat bands of hazy white. They faded before they reached the back, but they were still strong enough to let him see someone standing at the entrance.

For a heartbeat he froze, squinting to bring the face into

focus, relaxing when he realized the man had dark hair, not light.

"Boss," said Taz quietly, "he could be anywhere."

Proctor signaled him to keep looking; it was all they could do.

An angry shout made him take a hasty step toward the wall; a woman's forced laugh stopped him.

The trio played on.

Hopeless, Proctor thought; this is hopeless.

Then Taz said, "Boss," and pointed.

The man at the Tides' entrance was still there, but he was jerking, struggling, his face oddly blurred, and it took awhile before Proctor understood that someone had come up behind him and had clamped a hand over his mouth and nose.

He ran.

There was virtually no light at all when he reached the corner; he misjudged the width of the corridor and slammed a shoulder into the wall. Ricocheted as he grunted the brief pain away. Saw up ahead two figures struggling, before one was thrown to the floor and the other walked away.

It was Valknir.

Proctor didn't know what made him cry out, but he did, and the mahjra kept moving, not looking back, not giving a sign that it had heard. So intent was the chase that Proctor nearly stumbled over the fallen man. He glanced down as he sidestepped, and skid-stumbled to a halt. Dropped to one knee just as Taz reached him.

At this low level the halogen glow was almost too dim, but it was sufficient to let them see what was left of Mischa Acmarov's face, what was left of his shredded chest.

"Aw, Christ," Taz moaned, backing away so quickly he nearly tripped over the stool. He braced himself against the wall, then looked into the lounge. His voice was tight: "Proctor."

Proctor rose and turned. "How bad?"

"Four or five. The bartender, too. Aw, shit, Proctor, Jesus Christ."

It was the change in Taz's voice that warned Proctor, but Taz was too quick. He snatched the stool up by the legs and took off. Shouting. Demanding. Proctor lunged for him, missed, went back to one knee when his shoe slid through a spreading pool of black blood. By the time he was up and running, Taz was already halfway to the escalators, slowing, the stool up and behind him like a clumsy baseball bat.

Valknir waited, head cocked slightly to one side.

Proctor called after Taz, a hand fumbling in his pocket for the pendant Petra had given him.

Valknir smiled pleasantly, and crooked a long-nailed finger: *come on, boy, I'm waiting.*

Despite the music, despite the gamblers, there was sudden silence on the Gallery. Everything moved too slowly.

Taz feinted a swing with his unwieldy weapon, and the mahjra flinched and took a step sideways as Taz veered out of reach of the wild-swinging hand, spun around and slammed the stool into the mahjra's spine. Valknir arched his back and went down, rolled over and tried to stand, but Taz swung again, catching him in the side.

Proctor gripped the pendant hard in his left hand, trying to think what to do, what Petra had wanted him to do, while Taz swung a third time.

One time too many.

Valknir grabbed one of the legs and yanked, using the momentum to pull himself to his feet while wrenching the stool from Taz's hands. He tossed the stool aside contemptuously, took a single step, and backhanded Taz across the chest, lifting him off his feet and into the theater lobby gate. The gate rattled like gunshots, and Taz crumpled, and didn't move.

Proctor slowed, breathing hard.

The mahjra looked over his shoulder. And smiled.

Not a word.

Valknir spread his arms, widened his eyes. An invitation to play.

Proctor stopped, not looking down as his fingers searched the pendant and chain.

Below, someone shouted, "Happy New Year," and the trio broke into a ragged "Auld Lang Syne."

His thumb passed over the catch twice before he realized

what it was, and when he pressed it, the pendant slipped from his hand; a second before he realized he held a sheath of some kind.

Valknir's expression changed: *I'm waiting, fool, I'm waiting.*

Taz moaned.

Without taking his gaze from the mahjra's face, Proctor crouched, his fingers cautious now as they slipped around the red stone. He felt a bite, dared a look, saw blood on one finger—the scalloped silver setting was the edge of a sharpened knife.

Taz moaned, and stirred.

Valknir turned, hand out, nails growing, gleaming.

"I don't think so," Proctor said, picking the pendant up by its chain.

Valknir laughed as he straightened, and shrugged, and said, "It makes no difference to me which one of you dies first."

Proctor walked toward him, the pendant spinning slowly in his hand. "It better."

Puzzled, the mahjra sighed as if accepting an unpleasant obligation, held out his hands, and flexed his fingers to be sure Proctor saw the claws. "Do you know what it's like to scream without a tongue?"

Proctor moved closer.

"Do you know," Valknir said, "what it's like to see without your eyes?"

Proctor's face felt like stone.

Taz shifted, and the gate rattled softly.

Valknir's eyes widened slightly when he saw what was in Proctor's hand. A smile that didn't last. "You've been studying, Mr. Proctor. Good for you." But still, he took a step back.

Proctor didn't speak.

From the corner of his vision he could see a trickle of blood slip from Taz's hairline down his temple toward his jaw. He could see the mahjra finally begin to weigh his chances, judge his opponent, take another step back.

And stop.

"That will hurt," Valknir admitted with a nod to the spinning chain. "But it won't kill me. You have no idea how strong

I am. And you have no idea how mad I'll be if you touch me with that disgusting little bauble."

Proctor lunged, and laughed without a sound when Valknir backpedaled so quickly he nearly tripped. He lunged again, the spinning chain blurring, the pendant cutting the air with a faint whistling sound.

"Taz," he said.

Taz blinked and opened his eyes.

"Taz, get up."

"Two against one," Valknir said. "I think I'm going to be afraid."

"Get up, Taz."

The gate rattled.

Proctor backed off a step, angling toward the inside wall. When Valknir advanced, after a sneering glance at Taz, Proctor leaned over the wall quickly, looked, then put his back to it. He let the chain slow until the pendant dangled in his hand—rocking like a pendulum.

And waited.

"Enough." Valknir lifted his head. "I smell blood yet to be spilled."

"Like I said," Proctor told him. "A cheap horror movie."

Valknir growled and charged, and Proctor spun away at the right moment, bringing a fist into the mahjra's kidney as it slammed against the wall. It grunted and turned stiffly, and Proctor punched it again, in the stomach, then the throat, dropping it to one knee, one hand gripping the wall's top so it wouldn't fall all the way.

Proctor waited.

"I suppose," Valknir said, "that was for the bald one."

Proctor shook his head. "Nope."

"Too bad," and he sprang from the floor before Proctor could react, swinging his arm to catch Proctor across the chest. He fell against the back wall, lost his breath, gasped when the mahjra grabbed his shirt, spun him around, and flung him several feet toward the theater. When he landed, he rolled and regained his feet, ducked under a swinging arm, and landed a solid punch to the point of Valknir's chin.

Valknir grunted but didn't buckle; he only shook his head quickly and rubbed a hand over his face.

In a half crouch Proctor moved to his right, keeping the casino at his back. His chest felt as if a truck had run over it, and his spine protested each time it had to move. He wouldn't have been surprised to learn he'd broken a knuckle on his left hand.

Moving slowly. Moving sideways. Knowing from the mahjra's expression that Valknir couldn't understand why he didn't use the pendant, didn't bring it out. Its effect was evident—Valknir hadn't killed or seriously injured him yet, and hadn't been able to use his hypnotic control—but keeping it hidden was clearly not how it should be used.

Keep wondering, Proctor thought; figure it out, you're so goddamn smart.

Taz was on his feet, swaying weakly.

"I wonder," Valknir whispered, "if we're having fun yet."

The voice and face were human, but nothing Proctor had ever seen could have been more monstrous. He rubbed his chest gingerly. He tried to straighten, but couldn't.

"I think I am," the mahjra said.

Proctor said, "Smash-and-grab, Taz."

"He's useless, little man."

Proctor smiled for the first time. "You're not doing so well yourself."

Valknir slumped against the wall, shook his head sadly, and charged.

There was no time to think, no time to pray.

Proctor braced himself, yanked the pendant from his pocket and held it in his right hand at his side. Listening to Taz's yell, listening to the mahjra's laughter, listening to the sound of good cheer down below.

No time to think:

Valknir grabbed him with one arm around his waist, the other raised to slash those claws across his face; Proctor clamped his left arm around him, pinning the mahjra's arm between them, and brought the pendant up between them and arched his back; Taz slammed the stool into Valknir with a scream, and Proctor felt the wall's edge scrape down along his back as he pushed off his feet.

No time to pray:

They fell.

Into the white light, into the singing and applause and the strolling good-time music.

Spinning slowly as Valknir tried to slow their descent, but with one arm pinned, he could do nothing but fall, and try to gouge Proctor's eyes out.

"Now this," Proctor said just before they hit the craps table, "is for Doc," and rammed the amber pendant into Valknir's chest.

Valknir hit first, Proctor atop him, and the table shuddered and groaned and finally collapsed.

Proctor couldn't breathe for the long seconds afterward, could only hear startled screams and alarmed shouts, some of which he was pretty sure were his. Hands clutched at him frantically, pulling him off the mahjra, easing him to the floor, then suddenly leaving him alone.

He stared at the lights that blinded him, every part of him aching so badly he couldn't tell if he'd broken anything or not. He had to know, though; he had to know.

He turned his head and saw the table, dice and chips scattered everywhere, two, maybe three people lying beside it.

But Valknir wasn't there.

He tried to move, yelled at a pain that was everywhere at once, and sat up. Swallowed blood and something else. Reached out blindly until someone took his hand and he used it to help him stand, ignoring the frightened admonitions, the terrified questions, holding his left arm across his stomach, unable to raise his head.

He saw him.

Staggering toward the lobby, bent over, right hand sweeping a path clear ahead of him while the left grabbed whatever it could to propel him forward.

Stop him, Proctor said, lips moving without sound; stop him, please someone stop him.

They gave him wide berth as he stumbled forward; they gave the mahjra the same after Baron tired to stop him and there was a flash of a hand and a scream and a arc of blood.

Taz, Proctor thought; for God's sake, where are you?

He fell. He got up. He followed, careening off chairs and slot machines, not caring about the pain because there was too much to feel.

Dark wet stains on the carpeting.

Closer, but not close enough, and somewhere within the pain was the realization that the red amber was still embedded in Valknir's chest. The mahjra was dying and didn't know it; or knew it and still aimed to escape.

At the step before the beautiful etched-glass doors, Valknir stumbled, almost fell, then straightened and looked over his shoulder.

Connection to the ground.

Despite the pendant, he was healing.

Proctor couldn't stand straight at all, but he didn't stop moving, didn't say a word when Valknir turned away . . . and stopped.

Proctor heard the shots. Two of them. Thunder. Saw the back of the mahjra's head explode. Saw the creature fall backward, and saw the old man in the doorway adjust his Russian hat, step forward, look down, and calmly fire another bullet into Emile Valknir's face.

Proctor gave up the chase then and dropped to his knees, holding onto the lip of a slot machine to keep him off the floor. Panting. Looking up and grinning when Murray said, "Sometimes, you know, you don't have to be a good shot. All you gotta be is damn close."

THIRTY-THREE

Too many hours passed before Proctor was left alone.

It was Taz, grimacing and limping slightly, who with Baron's unquestioning assistance, assured the guests with grand gestures and laughter, that they had just witnessed not a murder but an amazing new kind of theater. Live and unconfined to anything so prosaic as an ordinary auditorium. Drama and magic combined; some derring-do and stunts, and no, he could not, under penalty of death, explain how the dead man's body had vanished, or where the bitter cold mist had come from, and had gone.

It was Granna who culled several willing doctors from the stunned gamblers and sent two up with Cox to the Barnaget, kept two more to take care of the "stuntmen," who'd been injured in the fall, and one with Proctor.

"You will not die until you explain," she'd ordered.

"Whatever you say, Lieutenant."

"And why," she'd said grumpily, "does that sound like a curse, coming from you?"

It was Officer Finn and three others who made sure, under specific orders from their lieutenant, that no one saw the bodies in the Tides.

It was Zach Berls and Patrick who found a way to get one of the generators running so one of the elevators and some of the lights would work.

It was Murray Cobb who took charge of Proctor when the doctor was done, assuring him between coughs and sneezes that nothing was so wrong that a few weeks strapped in a bed wouldn't cure.

"You remind me of your father, you know. He did stupid things, too, trying to make things right."

A strong arm around Proctor's waist in the elevator and down the hall of the twelfth floor.

"So tell me, was it worth it? All these bruises and cuts and flying around like Superman, was it worth it?"

"He's dead," Proctor answered.

"You were lucky," Cobb said.

Murray made sure there was water and plenty of aspirin by the bed, that the temperature was cool enough to allow a good sleep, that there was an array of tiny liquor bottles from the cabinet under the television just in case the aspirin didn't work, and stood by as Proctor, refusing help, washed himself at the bathroom sink, undressed, and went to bed.

"You want me to stay?"

Proctor smiled. "No. I already owe you too much."

Cobb shrugged. "You owe me nothing. You did a little, I did a little, we make the world safe for democracy, right?"

Proctor laughed, and groaned. He'd been given a shot, he didn't know what it was, but it hadn't taken all the pain away. Some busted ribs, a severely wrenched shoulder—he had a feeling he wouldn't feel better for another ten years.

Cobb stroked his mustache, lifted a hand, turned to leave. "One thing," he said.

"Sure."

"This fella you chased tonight, is this the kind of investigations you do?"

"Sometimes, yes."

"Interesting."

"Sometimes. Yes."

"I'm too old for that," Cobb said, and left. Poked his head around the corner and smiled. "Actually, I'm only sixty, you know. This morning I thought it was old, now I'm not too sure." He saluted Proctor with one finger touched to his brow. "You stay alive."

Proctor listened to the old man's footsteps, heard the door

open, and called, "Murray, wait!" For a second he thought Cobb hadn't heard him, then heard the footsteps again.

"You need something?"

Proctor told himself it was probably the painkillers, the retreat of all that adrenaline, the background throbbing that made it difficult to think.

Nevertheless he said, "You want a job?"

Cobb leaned back, surprised. "Me?"

Proctor nodded.

"Doing stuff like . . ." He pantomimed flying and fighting.

"Not always, no."

Murray sniffed, stroked his mustache. "You don't smoke, I notice. I smoke. That a problem?"

"Nope."

"I'm old."

"No, you're sixty. You said so yourself."

Murray scratched one short sideburn, then the other. "Maybe I'll think about it."

"Good. Talk to Taz, he'll give you my address and number. Call me when you make up your mind."

Murray nodded, left, returned again, face in a deep frown. "This is a serious offer? You're not drugged up stupid? This isn't gratitude for saving your young life from the forces of evil, something like that?"

"It's serious," Proctor said, trying to match his expression with the sentiment.

"I'll think. I'll talk to the kid. Maybe I'll call." Another salute. "Good night, Proctor."

"Good night, Murray. And thanks."

Less than an hour later, Taz, who had talked an extra key from the manager, came in and found Proctor sitting up, pillows bunched behind him, staring at the window.

"You're supposed to be sleeping."

"I can't." He inhaled slowly. "Okay, tell me."

Taz sat sideways at the foot of the bed. "You want the long or the short?"

"Short."

"He's . . . he'll be okay. It was . . ." He looked away, took a breath. "The doc I talked to said it was a clean cut, like surgery. Petra stopped the worst of the bleeding somehow."

"Didn't they ask her?"

Taz still wouldn't look at him. "She was there when we got there. Next thing I knew, she was gone."

"Where?"

"I don't know, Boss. I haven't seen her since."

Silence, and the storm outside.

"Who is she, Proctor?"

Proctor closed his eyes. "The truth is, I don't know."

"But—"

"Taz, no offense, but I'm really tired."

He felt the bed shift as Taz stood. Said, "Leave them open," when he heard him move to close the drapes. A moment later he opened his eyes; Taz still stood there, hands in his pockets.

"It's all right," Proctor told him. "I'm okay, mostly, and Doc will be, too. You did an amazing thing tonight, Taz. I owe you my life." A finger raised for silence when Taz opened his mouth. "No. I'm tired. I hurt like hell. As soon as the storm lets us, we'll go home, work it all out then."

"Work what out?"

"How to fix that damn Jeep."

Taz sighed, grinned, promised to see him first thing in the morning, and left.

Silence again, and the storm.

He closed his eyes and pulled the blankets to his neck. Listening. Waiting.

Hoping.

She didn't come.

He didn't dream of the plain, didn't have nightmares of the mahjra or Doc Falcon's mutilation or falling forever while the mahjra tried to fly.

He dreamt instead of a dark green dress with silver threads that caught the stormlight.

EPILOGUE

She had hidden in a closet, no one searched, and now she was alone. Standing in the bathroom, a scalpel in her hand. Blood in the basin, blood on her chin.

It had been easy, actually, getting what she needed. A little vamping of the hotel doctor, a rifling of his bag, plus a bottle of liquor that lay mostly empty now on the floor.

Do it or die, he had said; you'll heal after a while.

The tongue, all in all, had been easy, and as she stared at her reflection, breathing hard, gathering strength, she knew why he'd been crazy.

It was from cannibalizing himself.

It was the pain.

Sweet Jesus, it was the pain.

Hushed voices in a large room. A handful of candles in soot-black twisted candelabra throw more shadows than light, and in the background the sound of a slow steady wind.

In the darkness above, where candlelight cannot reach, the muted flutter of wings.

"He lives."

"Yes, I know."

"He killed a mahjra, for God's sake. How the hell did he know? It wasn't our doing, that foolish Valknir, he deserved to die, but how the hell did Proctor know?"

"He had help."

The scents of death; the scent of dying.

"We can't wait any longer. I think we've underestimated him."

"Patience. It will happen. We can't lose patience."

"You say that all the time, but still he manages to live. and learn, damnit. He's learning."

"Patience."

Chairs scrape; the wind sighs.

"All right. But only for a little while longer. Do you understand? You can have all the patience you want, but ours has just about run out."

"I understand."

"We hope so. Because if you don't, we're all going to die."